SMALL TOWN
Girl

Linda Cunningham

OMNIFIC PUBLISHING
DALLAS

Omnific Publishing
P.O. Box 793871, Dallas, TX 75379
www.omnificpublishing.com

First Omnific eBook edition, October 2011
First Omnific trade paperback edition, October 2011

The characters and events in this book are fictitious.
Any similarity to real persons, living or dead,
is coincidental and not intended by the author.

Library of Congress Cataloguing-in-Publication Data

Cunningham, Linda.
    Small Town Girl / Linda Cunningham — 1st ed.
    ISBN 978-1-936305-92-6
    1. Cintemporary Romance — Fiction. 2. Small Town — Fiction.
    3. New England — Fiction. 4. Firefighter — Fiction.
    I. Title

10 9 8 7 6 5 4 3 2 1

Cover Design by Micha Stone and Amy Brokaw
Interior Book Design by Coreen Montagna

Printed in the United States of America

This book is dedicated to the most fantastic group of Small Town Girls on the planet, The Ladies of '69! They are Martha, Kathy, Jane, Joanne, Nancy, Elaine, Pat, Sharon, Marie, and Joni, each of them a romance in progress and a true inspiration.

Chapter One

Lauren Smith looked up from her desk when she heard the knock on her office door. "Come in," she said absentmindedly.

The door opened. It was Kelly, Lauren's colleague at the museum. Lauren, as curator of the distinguished Thompson Museum for the Arts in the heart of Manhattan, was technically Kelly's boss. However, as they had been best friends since they met in college ten years ago, this ranking was a formality generally ignored.

Kelly entered Lauren's large and rather posh Curator's Office, holding out a business-sized envelope to her across the desk. "The doyenne just handed this to me," she explained. "It's a registered letter. To you. It has the dreaded 'Personal and Confidential' stamp on it. They signed for it on your behalf."

Lauren wrinkled her brow quizzically. "Hmm," she said, accepting the envelope and turning it over in her hand, "I'm not expecting anything." Smiling, she looked up at Kelly. "Maybe *The New York Times Magazine* wants to do a piece on the Thompson!"

Kelly made a sarcastic sound. "Bah! I looked at the sender. It's some law firm from Vermont." She paused, furrowing her brow in thought. "Vermont. We're not affiliated with anyone in Vermont, are we?"

Suddenly, Lauren was not listening. At the word "Vermont," her stomach gave a little nervous jump. She stared at the envelope. The law firm's name was not familiar to her, but the name of the town was. Clarks Corner. Founded in 1790 by the Clark brothers, who emigrated from Scotland and became wealthy stonemasons in the New World. Lauren's mother had grown up there. Her grandmother had lived there, too, but she had been dead for three years now. Lauren's mother had inherited the house, but she and Lauren's father had long since moved away. She couldn't remember whether her parents had ended up selling the house, whether they had rented it, or whether it was just sitting there empty.

"What are you staring at it for?" urged Kelly. "Just open it!"

Lauren looked at her friend, twisting her mouth into a skeptical line. She picked up her silver letter opener, slipped the gleaming blade under the flap, and made one smooth motion. She reached in and gingerly withdrew the folded letter inside.

"Why are you acting so weird?" persisted her friend. "What does it say?"

Lauren swallowed and unfolded the letter.

"Well?" prompted Kelly.

Lauren scanned the document, took a deep breath, and began to read it aloud.

Dear Ms. Smith,

Upon probating your grandmother's estate, we discovered a last will and testament in her name, stating her wishes regarding the distribution of the estate held by her at the time of her death. All assets, real and liquid, were forwarded to her next of kin, your mother, Mary Hamilton Smith, as per her wishes. However, we recently received a request from Mrs. Smith to transfer ownership of the real estate (parcel 4326–Town Tax Map 2008) to you. Enclosed is a copy of the transferred deed. Please feel free to call with any questions or comments you have on this matter. A key to the front door is enclosed for your convenience.

Sincerely,

Christopher Page, Esquire
Sweeney, Dillard, and Page
Attorneys-At-Law

"Well!" repeated Kelly, although this time as an exclamation. "They sent a key through the mail. Imagine that!"

"Leave it to my mother to do something like this and not even tell me about it," muttered Lauren, staring down at the letter in her hands.

Kelly, always practical, said, "What does that mean? Why didn't your mother tell you? Do your parents still live in San Francisco? Didn't your mother ever say anything to you about changing the deed?"

Lauren stayed quiet for a moment, trying to ignore Kelly's rapid fire questions and get her mind around this unexpected news. "My mother never said anything to me about it."

"So exactly what did your grandmother have for real estate?"

"Just the house, I think. She died in the same house she'd always lived in. I spent a lot of my summers there with my grandmother when I was a child. I just took it for granted that my mother and father inherited everything." Suddenly Lauren became agitated. "What do I want a house in Vermont for, anyway? That's why I didn't pay any attention to what became of my grandmother's estate. I don't care. I have everything I want here. This is where my life is. Not in Vermont."

Kelly shrugged. "Well, it's bound to be worth something. You can sell it. What kind of house is it? I never went there with you."

Lauren suddenly felt somewhat guilty. Since she had gone away to college, her visits to her grandmother had become fewer and farther between. Lauren had been to Kelly's family's country house in Connecticut many times. It was a gracious brick Georgian home in Greenwich, close to New York. Kelly's family was just what Lauren would have liked her family to be. Kelly's father was a doctor, her mother a decorous homemaker with a perfect pageboy. Lauren couldn't imagine what Kelly's family might think of her own mother and father. They were hippies. They had spent their youth protesting for the cause du jour, leaving their only daughter with the gentle grandmother in Vermont. Now that they were older, they had moved to California where Lauren's mother had become a potter. She wore her gray hair long, and her fingernails were often caked with clay. Lauren's father was a musician—a fiddler, to be exact. He traveled around the country to different music festivals and gigs, and he gave lessons on the side. Whenever asked, Lauren would say that her mother was an artist or sculptor and her father was a teacher. She sighed. Thank goodness they lived on the West Coast!

"Hey!" said Kelly, breaking her colleague's reverie. "Is the house worth anything?"

"Well, I assume so," Lauren replied. "I better call these lawyers and find out what to do about it." She stared at the letter and sighed. "I guess I'll just have them put it on the market and sell it."

"Don't go turning over something like this to total strangers," admonished her friend wisely. "You've got to go up there, Lauren. You've got to go there yourself and see to this personally. When was the last time you were there?"

Lauren thought, pausing before she spoke. "I went up for the day for my grandmother's memorial service. So, I guess a little over three years ago."

"And the house has been empty ever since?"

"Well, I guess so. I don't know."

"You'll have to call your mother and find out what's going on. I mean, property is property. You'll have to see to it. Lauren, why are you so odd about your family?"

"How am I going to get away?" Lauren said absently, completely ignoring Kelly's question. "What about Charles?"

Kelly's voice became instantly cynical. "You can take a couple of days. I'm perfectly capable of seeing to things here at the museum. As for Charles, you could take a week's vacation in Hawaii, come back, and he probably wouldn't know you'd been gone! He leaves you all the time to do business all over the world—London, Singapore, Tokyo. You can certainly take a couple of days to go to Vermont. An engaged couple shouldn't have that kind of double standard."

"Kelly!" Lauren exclaimed angrily. "Don't start on Charles!" Lauren's choice of fiancé was the one bone of contention between the friends.

Kelly blew through her nose in exasperation but let the subject drop. "It's only noon. Why don't you run home, pack some stuff for a couple of days, and drive up to Vermont. I'll keep an eye on things. Call Charles and let him know what's going on. Is he even in the city?"

"Yes, he's home," answered Lauren. It was one of the reasons she didn't particularly want to leave New York. Charles wasn't home very often, and their time together was important to her. She glanced down at the large diamond on her left hand. After all, they had a wedding to plan.

"Really, Lauren, it's the responsible thing to do."

Lauren gave a resigned sigh. "I suppose you're right. I guess it won't take long. I'll just list it with a Realtor and let them handle it. I don't really care."

"You should get going. Go home. Stuff some things in an overnight bag. Don't forget your toothbrush. You should get out of the city before the commuter traffic starts. It should only take you four hours or so to get there. You can get there before dark."

Lauren hugged her bright-eyed friend. "You always look after me!"

An hour and a half later, with her friend's assurances and encouragement, Lauren found herself crossing the New York-Connecticut border, traveling north on Interstate 95 in the smart little Mercedes Charles had bought her last Christmas. Once on the interstate, Lauren reluctantly activated her Bluetooth and called her parents in California. Her mother answered.

"Mom?"

"Lauren! What a nice surprise!"

"Mom, why didn't you tell me you deeded Gramma's house to me?"

Her mother's hearty laugh nearly split Lauren's eardrum. "Surprise! Your father and I had no idea what to give you for a wedding present. You seem to have everything imaginable. So we gave you Gramma's house. Perhaps you and Charles would like it as a summer place. Either that or you can do whatever you like with it."

"Oh, Mom," said Lauren, chagrined. "You didn't have to do that. Can't you and Dad use the money? You could sell it."

"Oh, we don't need anything, honey," said her mother. "And Gramma loved you so much. She would want you to have it."

"Well, ah, thank you so much, Mom. Actually, I'm on my way up there now to look the place over. Thanks, Mom, and thank Dad for me, too."

"I will, honey, I will. You drive carefully now. I love you. See you soon."

"I love you, too, Mom," Lauren replied. "See you soon."

The wide highway stretched before her. The early summer day was warm and clear, and the traffic was relatively light. Lauren had always enjoyed driving. It gave her a chance to be alone with her thoughts. She steered the car easily into the middle lane, accelerated to seventy-five miles an hour, and adjusted herself for the long trip.

Just outside New Haven, Lauren saw the large green sign. White lettering proclaimed: SPRINGFIELD MA, I-91, LEFT LANE. Lauren switched to the exit lane. Once on Interstate 91, the traffic subsided to almost nothing. She knew she could stay on this road all the way to Vermont, following the Connecticut River north. As she settled in for the drive, Lauren remembered that her grandmother had called it "the road that led people home." An odd little flutter rose up, unbidden, inside her. To dispel this sudden onslaught of feeling, Lauren consciously began to think of her wedding, meticulously going over the details in her head.

It was to be one of the most amazing weddings New York society had seen in a very long time. Celebrities would be attending. Business people from all over the world would be there. Vera Wang was designing the dress already!

Lauren smiled happily to herself as she gave her mind free rein. *I've done all right,* she thought, mentally patting herself on the back. *I broke out of the hippy mode. I got myself a terrific job, and I worked my way up the social and economic ladder. And now I'm marrying Charles Hobart.*

Lauren thought back to the first time she and Charles had met. It had been at a fundraiser for the museum. Charles was contributing a great deal of money, and he was the guest of honor. His donation would put the museum's endowment well in excess of the Board of Trustees' goal. The board members had been delirious with the fact that they had scored such a coup! A huge donation from Charles Hobart. Lauren had had to suffer through two weeks of lugubrious meetings while the Board had decided everything from the menu to the speakers to which works of art should be showcased in the function room on that night.

Lauren remembered the night in minute detail. As curator, she'd had to sit at the head table next to Charles Hobart, introduce him, and stroke his ego with scintillating conversation. She was to be professional and friendly without being obsequious. She had dressed carefully in a white knit dress with a high neck. It had flattered her trim figure, hugging her bust, nipping in her neat waist with a black leather belt, and outlining her athletic hips while still appearing modest. The only jewelry she had worn was a pair of drop diamond earrings, a present she had given herself upon her appointment as head curator. She had pulled her thick, golden blond hair back into a soft classic French twist, more sophisticated than the slightly haphazard up-do or ponytail she wore daily.

Lauren had sat beside Charles Hobart and had chatted politely and intelligently all through the speeches, the dinner, and finally, the award to Charles himself. She had found him cosmopolitan and urbane, with a wry sense of humor. He was a mature man, perhaps twenty to twenty-five years older than Lauren, with smooth gray, almost white, hair and steel blue eyes. He was tall and physically fit, and his expensive suit fit him to perfection. His even features and deep chuckle made him attractive, although Lauren had the feeling he held himself in check, held something back, that his laughter never boomed forth in hearty peels. He was a man who was adept at controlling and manipulating whatever situation developed around him.

She had been utterly unprepared when he'd called her at her office the following Friday evening.

"This is Charles Hobart," he had said in his deep, smooth voice. "I was wondering if you might come with me to the theater and dinner afterward at Nobu?"

Lauren was so taken off guard, she'd stuttered, "T-T-Tonight?"

Charles had chuckled softly. "Yes. I know it's short notice, but I took the liberty of asking Debbie Johnston if you were in a relationship. She said no, so I took my chances. Yes, tonight."

Debbie Johnston was chair of the Board of Trustees. Lauren's initial indignation at the unpermitted sharing of her personal information had been almost immediately overcome by her capitulation to flattery. "Well, I — " she'd stammered. "Yes, I'll go."

"Wonderful!" said Charles Hobart, as a man to whom the possibility of rejection had never occurred. "I'll pick you up at the museum in an hour."

They'd had a lovely evening. They had seen *Jersey Boys* at the August Wilson Theater on West 52nd Street, not far from her little apartment in Murray Hill. Afterward, the dinner at Nobu had been beyond delicious. Then they had taken a romantic trip around the city, winding slowly through Central Park in Charles's chauffeur-driven Bentley, talking about incidentals, getting to know one another. It had been the wee hours of the morning when he'd dropped her at the door of the modest, post-war building common to the neighborhood. He'd given her a chaste kiss on the cheek as she turned to go inside, but he hadn't left without securing a date for the following weekend — in Paris…

Adjusting her position in the driver's seat, Lauren lifted her left hand to the top of the steering wheel. The large gem caught the late afternoon sun and split the light into a million sparkles, dazzling Lauren's eyes. Yes, she thought, she'd done well for herself, managing to hold the interest of one of the most powerful businessmen in the country until he had proposed marriage. A simple signing of a prenup later, and they were planning the wedding.

Lauren's thoughts darkened a little at the thought of the prenuptial agreement. It was rather a sordid detail to what should be a mutually happy occasion. *However,* she sighed to herself, *that's how things are done now.* It was only prudent. It was only professional. It was for everyone's protection.

Lauren was beginning to get tired. She shifted her legs and glanced at her watch. *Not too bad,* she thought, looking up to find the nearest highway sign. There it was, ahead of her. Exit 6, one mile. Finally! She would be glad to get there. No more than half an hour left to her drive. She slowed the car and took the exit off Interstate 91 to Route 103 North. It was amazing how she remembered the way, as though she had traveled it yesterday and not three years ago. She drove the ten miles to town at the posted fifty mile an hour speed limit, looking around at the fields and trees. She turned off the air conditioning in the car and opened the window. The breeze swirled in, rustling her hair almost affectionately and bringing with it the scents of fresh-turned earth, green leaves, and the first flowers of summer.

As she drove, she was shocked to feel her eyes well up with tears. She couldn't imagine why that would happen. She brushed them away with the back of her hand. It must be some strange nostalgic reaction, she thought ironically. She slowed the car as she drove into the little village. Yes, it was all familiar. It hadn't changed a bit, she thought, somewhat derisively. *These people must be stuck in a time warp!*

There was the little mom-and-pop grocery store on the corner. The main street was lined with prettily painted houses in the Victorian style and the rambling Traveler's Inn. On the small green in the middle of town was the war memorial. A bronze soldier stood guard over the names of the fallen in a circle of tenderly-cared-for geraniums, lobelia, and sweet alyssum.

Lauren drove slowly past the big brick church with its old cemetery, surrounded by the high moss-covered stone wall. She couldn't help but admit to herself that it was really quite beautiful. A right-hand turn at the end of the green took her up over a quiet street, studded here and there with more recently built homes, mostly white clapboarded Capes in the traditional New England style. They were neat houses, set back from the road, encircled by manicured lawns that spread out from them like the dresses of ladies of a bygone era.

Following the dogleg at the end of the street, Lauren made another right-hand turn. Now she was on the dirt road that climbed up the hill to her grandmother's house. There were very few houses on this road, and the smell of pine-scented woods flooded in the open window of her car. The road was narrow and not very steep, but it climbed steadily until the woods fell away and the old hay fields that bordered her grandmother's property opened up before her. A short distance more and she could see the house, sitting serenely on top of the hill, its picket fence a little askew from neglect, but still graceful and shaded by the giant old maples standing like sentinels along the road. The house was large, two full stories under a peaked roof. It was white clapboarded with dark green shutters and a wraparound porch that faced south and west to catch the most sun in this land of long, harsh winters.

Lauren pulled into the driveway, parked her car, and got out. She yawned and stretched her arms into the air, twisting her body from side to side, limbering herself after the long drive. Then she walked into the front yard.

It was late afternoon, and the sunlight was coming from the west, softly filtered through the maple, beech, ash, and oak trees that grew along the stone wall around the perimeter of the property. Through the hedge of lilacs at the far end of the lawn, Lauren looked out across the graceful and lushly foliated hills that gave Vermont its title as the Green Mountain State. She was in the heart of ski country, and although most of her time here had been spent during the summers, she could pick out the ski areas, rising around her in the distance. There was Stratton to the south, and Bromley Mountain. To the north, Okemo, and if she turned and looked back over her shoulder, she could see Ascutney, the closest and wildest one, rising protectively up over the Connecticut River Valley.

A flood of memories deluged her mind, and Lauren struggled to sort them out. She saw herself as a little girl with braided hair, climbing trees, oblivious to skinned knees and knuckles, just to peek in a bird's nest and see the baby fledglings huddled together awaiting their next meal. She could hear the frantic squawks of the mother and father robins and her grandmother's call, admonishing her, "Lauren, don't be bothering those birds. They need some privacy!"

And she remembered the rainy days, too, when she was forced to stay inside. She and Gramma would make chocolate-chip cookies, which Gramma called by the old fashioned name, Tollhouse cookies. She remembered the little room upstairs where she used to sleep, always lulled by the purring of a warm cat nestled cozily under her chin.

"Well," she said out loud to herself, "I might as well go inside and assess the situation." She crossed the lawn to the porch, the long, uncut grass tickling her bare legs.

Inside the house smelled musty, but there was no evidence of burst pipes or a leaky roof. Someone had at least kept the heat on in the winter. Lauren wandered slowly from room to room. She was surprised by her feeling of nostalgia. The house was almost exactly as she'd remembered it. The old white enameled kitchen table and caned-seated chairs still sat in front of the large kitchen window. Lauren could remember sitting there, patiently waiting for her grandmother to come in from the garden with fresh mint for their afternoon iced tea and homemade chocolate chip cookies. In the dining room, the built-in china cupboard still protected the china and crystal. Lauren opened the glass door carefully and took out a delicate stemmed goblet. *This must be almost a hundred years old*, she thought, *how odd my mother just left all this stuff here with no regard as to what it had meant to the woman who treasured it. Well, that was Mom.*

She returned the goblet to its place on the shelf and continued on into the living room. The old sofa slouched in front of the fireplace. Lauren recalled the pleasant evenings when she would curl up on the sofa while her grandmother sat in the overstuffed chair and read her bedtime stories. The old floor reading lamp still stood at attention behind the chair. On the wall, Lauren saw the shadow box that displayed the ribbons her grandmother had won for her daylilies. Those flowers had garnered the top prize year after year at the county fair. Lauren sighed and returned to the kitchen.

The refrigerator was running, so she knew the electricity was on. Her parents had likely arranged for a neighbor to keep a check on such things. Lauren was thankful for the refrigerator. It was empty, but at least it was cold. She went back out the screen door to her car and carried in the few supplies she'd brought up from the city. She had bottled water, a small carton of half-and-half, a coffee maker, and some freshly ground coffee. She put the liquids and the coffee in the refrigerator and set the coffee maker on the soapstone countertop.

Then she turned to the kitchen sink and turned the faucet. There was a hiss and a spit, and water began to flow. *That's a good sign*, Lauren thought. She felt grubby from the drive and ran her hands under the cold water. She picked up a bar of soap that still lay in the soap dish and lathered her hands. Then she twisted the quaint porcelain knob marked "H" and waited for the water to warm up. It did not. There was no hot water. No hot water! Lauren blew through her nose with exasperation. Hot water was something she would absolutely have to have if she was going to stay here for a couple of nights. She couldn't see herself filling a bathtub with water she had heated on the stove in the old tea kettle. She would just call a plumber.

She reached for the old phone book that lay covered with dust on the kitchen table. It was five years old, but she would take her chances. Flipping through the yellow pages at the back, she found Cochran Plumbing and Heating. She noticed with satisfaction that they were located in town. Now if she could only get them to come out here this late in the afternoon. She reached in her pocket for her iPhone and punched in the number.

Chapter Two

"Anybody home?" a deep voice called out as the screen door slammed behind her.

Lauren nearly jumped out of her skin. "Oh! You scared me!" She whirled around to face the intruder.

He stood just inside the kitchen door, not the least bit apologetic. "I thought you called with a furnace problem."

"I did," she responded.

"Well, here I am. What's the problem?"

He couldn't have been in the house for more than a minute and already he was irritating her. It was annoying enough to discover the problem in the first place. She didn't need some smart-ass plumber to compound the situation.

Lauren scowled at him, trying to decide on the best way to handle him. He stood there, easy and relaxed. She had to admit he wasn't exactly what she had been expecting when she called the Cochran Plumbing and Heating Company.

Automatically, she assessed him. He wasn't that much older than herself, probably between thirty-five and forty. About six feet tall, he was dressed in scuffed work boots and jeans, belted low around trim hips. Lauren couldn't help noticing the jeans were tight enough to betray muscular thighs underneath. A snug fitting black T-shirt with the obligatory company logo printed on it sheathed well-developed biceps, strong shoulders, and a broad, hard, muscled chest. His dark brown hair was cut short, but not so short Lauren didn't notice it would be thick and quite wavy if allowed to grow out. And only his obviously overt masculinity kept his full lips from seeming almost too soft.

He waited, watching her. He blinked twice. His eyes brought Lauren up short. They were hazel with flecks of green in them, set off by bristly black lashes and accentuated by dark, slightly arched brows. There was a visible sparkle to them almost as if those flecks of green were small dancing lights. *Not unpleasant*, thought Lauren. *Not at all.*

"Well?" he said again.

Lauren realized she had been staring, and she blushed. "I can't get the hot water to run," she said, turning around hastily to the sink. "It's cold." She was suddenly aware that perhaps the old white cotton shirt she had thrown on before leaving the city was opened one button too many.

"Shut the water off, and we'll see what the problem is," the plumber said, picking up a red tool chest. With his free right hand, he reached out to her. "I'm Caleb Cochran," he said.

Hesitantly, Lauren shook his hand. It was a strong hand with a firm but gentle grip. Her heart beat a little faster. *I must be overtired,* she thought, annoyed at her inexplicable attraction to this stranger. *It's the plumber, for crying out loud!*

"I'm Lauren Smith," she replied. He stepped past her in two graceful strides and shut the water off himself.

"Hi, Lauren. I'm going to have to get into the cellar. That all right with you?"

"Of course. It's this way," she said, but Caleb Cochran seemed to know just where the cellar door was. "Have you been here before?" Lauren asked.

"Oh yeah, a long time ago. When Old Lady Hamilton lived here. It's been vacant for a while now. What'd you do, buy it?" The cellar door made a god-awful creak when he opened it.

"No," Lauren said, suddenly irritated again. "Old Lady Hamilton, as you put it, was my grandmother. I'm here to get it ready to sell. My parents live on the West Coast, and I live in New York. I'm an only child; when my grandmother died, she left me the house. *Hence,*" and here Lauren accentuated her words snottily, "*Hence,* the responsibility falls to me. I have no use for it, so I'm selling it. Is that enough information for you?"

He didn't turn to look at her, but as he started down the stairs, he said simply, "No disrespect meant." He flipped the light switch, and she followed him into the dimly lit basement, unable to keep from noticing how his muscles rippled under the cotton of his T-shirt. "Shouldn't have trouble selling this place. It's a nice old house with plenty of land. I always liked it. All it needs is a little fixing up."

Nice? Lauren looked around. *Maybe after a crew spent a year here.* She thought of Charles's apartment on Central Park West. The four-thousand-square-foot penthouse apartment with its long, regal windows overlooking the vista of the brilliant city. The apartment that would become her home in just a few short weeks.

"It was nice when my grandmother was alive. I actually stayed here quite a bit during the summers with her. It's neglected now. I'm just going to sell it as is," Lauren found herself babbling. Caleb made no reply as he descended the stairs.

The cellar was typical of the old houses in the area. It was damp with a stone foundation. The floor was dirt except for the poured cement slab where the furnace, water pump, and water heater sat. Caleb went over to the furnace, seemingly unaware of her presence behind him.

"What is it?" she asked. He didn't answer her, but flipped a switch on the wall instead. The furnace kicked on, in spite of the warm temperature outside. It rattled for about thirty seconds and then shut down. Caleb repeated the motion with the same results.

"Well?" she prodded.

"Well, what?" He didn't look at her, engrossed as he was in the workings of the furnace.

"What the hell is wrong with it?" she protested impatiently. "Why can't I get any hot water?"

This time he turned to her. "Keep your shirt on," he said with a friendly smile, and as he said it, his gaze dropped to her breasts. Lauren was once again uncomfortably aware of the undone buttons. And maybe her khaki shorts were too short. "The water's heated off the furnace," he explained. "There seems to be enough fuel in the tank. For some reason, these pipes here are hot, but the water in the tank is cold."

"These pipes here?" Lauren reached up to touch the copper pipes attached to the low ceiling of the cellar. Instantly, Caleb had his hand over hers.

"Careful!" he commanded sharply. "This is oil-fired forced hot water heat. Those pipes are red hot. You'll burn yourself!"

She did not pull back from his hand. Instead, she was aware of a moment, a moment of pure physical contact in which something passed between them. Something warm, something pleasant. Something *intimate*. Lauren was sure Caleb was aware of it, too. It was as if she was suddenly off balance, and now she was slightly confused. Why did this man, this plumber, have such an effect on her? She looked at him. His eyes searched her own for just a second, then Caleb slowly opened his hand and released her. He looked away quickly. "Sorry," he said. "Didn't mean to scare you."

"I'm not scared of you," she said, bristling, making an effort to ban her confusion. "Hey, maybe it's this valve here." She reached up toward an overhead valve.

"Please, just stand out of the way," he reiterated, leaning forward in a gesture to move her back a safe distance. His eyes were on her so he didn't see the pipe wrench until he stepped on it. He was thrown off balance, stumbling backward. In an instinctive effort to right himself, Caleb threw up his hand. His forearm smacked loudly against the red hot copper pipe. "Arggh!" he cried, clapping his scalded arm to his side.

Caleb doubled over, clutching the burn. Lauren rushed to him, mortified. It had been her fault! "I'm sorry, I'm sorry," she cried. "I didn't mean to get in your way! Are you all right? Caleb, are you okay?" She was suddenly aware she had used his first name.

He held up his forearm. A red blotch was forming where the pipe had burned him.

Lauren took over. "You're burned," she said, reaching out and taking his wrist in her small hand. "Come upstairs. We have to look at that." She led him by the hand, and he obediently followed. Her heart was beating hard in her chest. She was embarrassed. Embarrassed that her inexplicable attraction to this man had caused him to be hurt.

Embarrassed at how much of a fool she must seem to him now. And yet, she was aware of his immediate capitulation. He was following her up the stairs, like some powerful animal struggling to keep his innate wildness under control for her sake. She shook the thoughts from her mind to tend to the business at hand.

Once they were back in the kitchen, she pulled one of the old chairs away from the table. "Sit down," she ordered. He seemed rather amused, but he sat and watched her as she went to the sink and ran a clean dishtowel under the cold water. She rung it out, then crossed the room back to the table. She pulled out another chair and placed it facing him. She sat down and gently took his arm. Suddenly, she was all business. She pressed the cold compress to the burn. He flinched.

"I'm so sorry if I'm hurting you, but we have to get cold water on that burn." She leaned forward, forgetting about the buttons on her shirt. She was intent on her task until she looked up instinctively to judge his pain threshold, and saw his gaze. Caleb's eyes had traveled to the round swell of her breasts, tipped toward him, encased in a snowy white lace bra. Lauren could feel the heat of a blush pushing its way up her neck, flushing her cheeks. "Here," she said hurriedly, straightening in the chair. "Hold this on it for a while. I'll wet another cloth. There might be some ice left in the freezer. I'll look." She stood quickly and opened the freezer compartment of the old refrigerator. Thank goodness there was ice in the blue plastic trays.

Lauren was agitated, blaming herself for the mishap. She popped the ice cubes out of one of the trays and wrapped them in the damp dishcloth, holding it out to him. "Thanks," he said with a smile.

"Does it feel better?" she asked. Suddenly, reality set in, and she thought of the possibility of getting sued. You never knew about these locals, be they attractive or not. Her Mercedes was parked in the yard. If they thought they could get something out of a wealthy New Yorker, anything might happen. She decided to make an effort to tone down the attitude. At least try to be nice.

"I'm fine, thanks." He gingerly held the cold towel to his burn. Lauren found herself watching the muscles in his arms ripple as he applied the compress, ministering to himself. Under the t-shirt, she could see his chest knit with muscle. Again, he reminded her of some kind of wild animal struggling with the pain. Lauren had an unbidden impulse to reach out, to stroke him, to comfort him.

She fought the feeling by turning back toward the refrigerator and nervously opening the door. There was no denying it. He had a magnetism that pulled her in.

"I don't have much in here. I'm only here for a couple of days. I just brought the basics with me. Would you like some iced tea or water?"

"No, thanks," he said. He looked around. "Are you here alone? Is your husband with you?"

"I'm not married."

"Then what's that rock on your finger?" He pointed to the two carat diamond solitaire nestled in its platinum setting, surrounded by more baguette cut diamonds.

"I'm engaged," explained Lauren.

"What's he do for a living? Bet he's not a plumber!" Caleb flashed white teeth in a broad smile.

Lauren smiled in spite of herself. "No, he's not a plumber. He's a businessman in New York. He has a tech company, does international tech trade."

"Like iPhones and stuff like that?"

"Yeah, something like that. To tell you the truth, I'm not exactly sure. It's a lot of different things. Very complicated."

"And very lucrative," Caleb replied with a snort.

Lauren's ire was aroused again. She had been babbling with too much information. "And what's wrong with that? Jealous?"

"Hell, no. I don't begrudge anybody the right to do the best they can for themselves. I do just fine. I've got my own company. I provide jobs for eleven people. I got my own home. You couldn't pay me enough to live in New York City. I'm where I want to be. Hope he is, too." Caleb paused and looked at her. His eyes wandered over her face, as if searching for something. "And you?"

"I am most definitely where I want to be," she said, indignant at the question. "And anyway, it's none of your business." She forgot her fear of being sued. This man was annoying, with his muscles and white teeth and palpable virility.

"No need to get so prickly. What do you do? Or are you one of those kept women?" he said. Instantly, his regret showed in his face.

It was obvious to Lauren that he hadn't meant it to come out the way it did, but her temper flared anyway.

"That was rude! That was very, very rude!"

He put the compress down on the old enamel-topped table and held up both hands in a placating gesture. "I'm really sorry. I didn't mean it." His voice softened. "Please. I didn't mean it. I misspoke. Really, what do you do?"

Lauren paused before she answered, looking into his eyes, but he seemed sincere. She regained her composure and answered him. "I'm a curator at the Thompson Museum for the Arts in New York City," she said. "I majored in Antiquities in college."

Caleb Cochran didn't seem impressed. "It's weird you don't know what your fiancé does."

"I know what he does."

"Apparently not really."

"It's complicated business."

"And when you get married, you'll be part of it. Don't married couples share everything? I know when I—" and then he stopped, his lips closed in a thin line. Lauren thought she saw his eyes grow dark. He stood up abruptly. "You need a new valve," he continued. "It's an old system so I'm going to have to order the part. How long you here for?"

"Well, I wanted to leave day after tomorrow. After I get things set up with a Realtor."

"It'll cost you extra, but I can probably get it overnighted and put it in tomorrow."

"I don't care how much it costs. Just get it done!" Lauren couldn't hide her impatience. She didn't need to deal with a stranger's bizarre criticisms.

He blinked at her, his face expressionless. Then he walked across the room and stood by the old screen door. "You're used to being in charge, and you're kind of rude yourself. How about 'Thanks, Caleb. That would be nice.' Something for the effort."

She stared at him, his hips set forward in a self-confident way, his arms folded across his chest. His body language was blocking her out. He had put up defenses.

"Whether or not I *like* being in charge is insignificant. I *am* in charge," she said defiantly. "And I like where I am."

"And where are you?"

"Not stuck in some East Podunk town smelling of fuel oil and soot!"

She knew it was a vicious thing to say, but right now she didn't care. How dare he come in here, flexing his muscles, preying on her sympathies with his burn and his sparkling eyes, drawing her into personal conversation! Lauren waited for his comeback, but Caleb cocked his eyebrows at her, and gave the slightest wry smile. Then he turned on his heel and left. The screen door slammed behind him.

"And don't let it hit you in the ass on the way out!" she muttered. Although, she had to admit, it was a pretty nice-looking ass.

Lauren watched his white pick-up truck as it disappeared down the dirt road toward town. She was alone in the old house.

Before she could think further about Caleb, her iPhone rang. She glanced at the screen. Charles!

"Darling," he said. His voice was deep. "How's everything going up there in the wilderness?"

"Oh, Charles! I just got here, and it's frustrating already. I got up to the house. It's a mess, and on top of it all, there's no hot water."

"No hot water? Well, call a plumber."

Lauren made an exasperated sound. If only he knew! "I did call a plumber, Charles," she said somewhat sarcastically. "He came and burned himself on the furnace. It was a fiasco! And I still have no hot water. He won't have the part until tomorrow."

"Burned? I hope he's not the litigious kind. We don't need a lawsuit."

"I can handle it. I don't think he's the type, anyway. And I still have to go into town, find a Realtor, and do all the paperwork." *Leave it to Charles*, she thought, *to think of litigation first.* Suddenly, she felt very alone. Although she was not the cloying kind, she heard herself saying, "Charles, do you miss me?"

He laughed. "You've only been gone a day!" he exclaimed. "However, I do miss you, darling. The place is positively desolate without you."

"I miss you, too," she said. "I just want to get this place fixed and listed and get back to the city."

"Will you have to stay another night?"

"Probably one more night. There's more paperwork to fill out tomorrow."

"You said the place was a mess. Do you think it will interfere with the sale?"

She looked around her. "Well, it just looks like it's been vacant for a long time. You know, just kind of grimy. Things need cleaning and tightening. The lawn needs mowing. I'll hire someone to come and at least get that done. That's probably what my parents would suggest. It's hard to get a straight answer out of them. If I call them to ask their opinion, they'll just laugh and say, 'Do what you think is right, honey.'"

"Just get it taken care of. Don't bother your parents with it. They'll take two weeks to make up their minds. And it's your house, legally. You can just let them know when the house sells."

"You're right, Charles. They're such…such *hippies!*" It was true. It seemed to Lauren that her parents had never progressed beyond the mid-1970s. They had been nomads most of her childhood, moving to different parts of the country as the whim or the weather suited them with what seemed to Lauren very little consideration for her sense of security or comfort. Once, they had actually lived in a tepee. She recalled them always running off to different protests, leaving her behind to stay with her grandmother. They lived outside San Francisco now, in a tiny house powered by a windmill and solar panels. Maybe that's why she loved the city. The stability of the huge buildings. Her steady, prestigious job. The orderly grandeur of Charles's penthouse. And Charles himself, ambitious and powerful.

"Listen, Lauren," Charles was speaking again, "I'm not sure I'll be home when you get here. I may have to go to Singapore tomorrow."

Lauren's heart sank. "Oh, Charles, no! You just got back from London the day before I left for here. You'll forget what I look like! When are we going to get some time together?"

She heard his patronizing laughter through the phone. "How could I forget what you look like? Those big blue eyes! That glorious hair! That tight little body! I'm an old man, Lauren, and just looking at you makes me feel young!"

"Nonsense, Charles," she scoffed. "You're not old at all."

"There's twenty-five years between us. And two previous marriages of mine."

"Yes, yes, you tell me that all the time. And you know what? I don't care!" It was true. The age difference between them had never bothered Lauren. To Lauren, he represented security like she had never known, growing up as she had with her shabbily dressed, unkempt hippy parents. She loved nothing better than to be seen on Charles's arm at various events around the city. She had worked for this. She had attained her goals.

"Go buy yourself some new shoes," he continued. "Some Jimmy Choos. Whatever you like. And when I get home, we'll go to Nassau for a break together."

"I'd rather just stay home with you, alone together," Lauren said quietly.

"Then that's what we'll do," he answered indulgently. "Just think, soon you will be Mrs. Charles Reynolds Hobart III. And I will be a lucky man. I love you, darling. Sleep well. I've got some phone calls to make. I'll call you tomorrow to let you know the flight numbers and where I'll be staying in Singapore."

"I love you, too," Lauren said, dejectedly. "I'll talk to you tomorrow. Bye."

She clicked off the phone and wandered back into the kitchen. She reached in the refrigerator for a bottle of water. It wasn't quite dark yet, but there was no TV and nothing to do. She took her bottle of water and slowly climbed the back stairs to the little bedroom under the eaves. The door was open. She went in, turned on the quaint little lamp on the bedside table and opened the window.

This was the room where Lauren had slept as a child, years ago, every time she and her parents visited her grandmother. It was a small room, but it was decorated sweetly with flowery wallpaper and white painted furniture, with an eastern facing window that allowed the sun to pour in every morning.

The bed was unmade. Lauren had brought pillows, sheets, and a duvet with her. Cautiously, she drew back the old bedspread, hoping she wouldn't uncover a nest of mice, but the mattress was dry and clean. The room was airing out nicely. As she worked making up the bed with the clean linens, the fresh country smells came through the open window, aromas that Lauren had nearly forgotten, like grass and the seductive smell of the riotous rose bushes that bordered the old neglected flower garden. She leaned out the window. It was a pretty view, down the valley. She could see the lights from the center of the small town, blinking on, one by one, as the dusk deepened and the evening fell. The world was washed in the most romantic shades of blue. The quiet of the night enveloped her as she stood watching the first stars begin to prick pinholes in the night sky. Lauren sighed. It had been so long since she had been somewhere where she could see the stars. Almost reluctantly, she drew herself back inside and stepped back from the window. She undressed, slipped into her pajamas, and climbed into bed.

Lying there in the deepening twilight, Lauren was restless. She felt vaguely upset, unsettled, even a little irritated. She felt like something had happened, or was about to happen, and she didn't know what it was. She tried to read the paperback mystery she had brought with her, but it didn't hold her interest. She stared at the ceiling, listening to the frogs in the pond at the bottom of the meadow, until she finally fell into a fitful sleep.

She was walking through a long tunnel. It was very dark. She knew she was looking for the light at the end, but it kept elusively evading her. The path was narrow, and she felt as though the sides of the tunnel were closing in on her. She walked on, her heart pounding. Finally, she could make out a light in the distance. She started to run for it, but it grew dark again, and the tunnel more narrow. She called out but could not understand her own words.

Suddenly, a man appeared before her. She could see the strong shape of his body. He held out his hand. "Take it!" he commanded.

"I can't," she said, recoiling from him, back, back into the tunnel.

"Take it!" he said again. He frightened her, but the tunnel frightened her more. This time, she took the hand. It was warm and drew her in close.

Now she could see. The man was naked. He leaned forward, kissing her. She could feel the pressure of his lips. Her head swam with a sensation, a thrill, as the kissing continued. She reached out to reciprocate his touch. She could see him, all of him. He was erect and beckoning to her with a smile.

Lauren sat up in bed in a cold sweat, her heart rattling her ribcage. She ran her hands through her damp hair. Her dream had shocked her. "This is ridiculous!" she said out loud. She turned on the light and glanced at her iPhone on the bedside table. It was three in the morning. Totally agitated, she leaped out of the bed and paced a couple of times around the room. "It's just a dream," she said, still talking audibly. "Just a dream. Forget about it!" She leaned out the open window and took a deep breath. Slowly, her heart rate returned to normal. Just forget about it, she had told herself, but she couldn't forget about it. The man in the dream had been Caleb Cochran.

Chapter Three

Lauren was awake the rest of the night. When the dawn finally broke, shrouded in the morning mists of summer, she climbed out of bed. The fog hugged the old house. Lauren could feel the mist on her face through the open window. She slipped out of her pajamas and started to pull on jeans and Charles's old white shirt she had worn the day before. She hoped Cochran Plumbing and Heating showed up early. She couldn't face a cold shower. And then she changed her mind. She'd be damned if she would face Caleb Cochran with flat hair and dirty clothes. That was probably why he had tried to get the better of her the day before. Today she would show him just who she was—a taste of sophistication would set him straight!

The water seemed especially cold, but Lauren steeled herself, letting that cold water clear her head and slough away the memory of last night's dream. She soaped and rinsed quickly, then washed her hair. By the time she stepped out of the shower, her skin was prickling with goose bumps. Standing in front of the mirror, she dried herself carefully with a towel she had brought. The mirror showed a healthy young woman, prettier than average, with a long graceful neck and shapely legs. Although she was not tall, her figure was proportionate and feminine, round in the right places.

When Lauren dressed for a night on the town with Charles, it often took her all afternoon to get ready. She would check and re-check her hair, make-up, and clothing to make sure she measured up to the standard she felt was necessary as Charles's fiancée. Now, as she passed the mirror, she hardly noticed her reflection. Instead, she found herself slipping in and out of a daydream, replaying her conversation of the day before with Caleb. She was remembering those arresting eyes with their subtle green lights.

In the small bedroom upstairs, she readied herself to face the day, and primarily, Caleb Cochran. She dried her hair, fluffing it with the blow-dryer until it was full and luxuriant. She chose her clothing carefully. She put on her bra and panties, lacy white, decorated with lavender ribbon. Then she pulled on her Dolce & Gabbana skinny leg jeans and pawed through her travel bag for a shirt. It had to be sexy, but properly cool, too. She found it, bringing it triumphantly out and holding it up before her. It was her Nanette Lepore corset-designed sleeveless top. It fit her like a glove, flaring out just slightly over her hips. There was a ruffle around the neckline that dipped just enough to show a bit of cleavage and still appear innocent. The perfect summer weekend top.

"Ha!" she sniggered as she slipped it on. She looked sweet and more than a little sexy, yet still somehow prim and unapproachable. It was just the look she wanted. Next, she applied her make-up carefully, balancing her mirror on the windowsill where the morning light flooded into the room. She put on small, gold hoop earrings. Lastly, she swept her hair up in a sexily messy twist and secured it with a tortoise shell barrette. She slipped on her gold London Sole ballet flats and skipped downstairs to make some coffee.

Coffee would have been a challenge, but Lauren was prepared. She had packed a French press and some gourmet ground coffee from Dean & DeLuca. She boiled water in an old pot and poured it into the press, then, coffee mug in hand, she wandered out into the back yard.

It really was beautiful and soothing. The morning mists were evaporating, and the sun was shining through the maple trees, illuminating the old garden and the white picket fence. Lauren wandered through the plants, forgetting herself. Her grandmother had taught her the names of all the plants when she'd been a child, and she'd been surprised at how easily they came back to her now after all these years. There were blooming daylilies, and iris that had gone by. There were white Shastas and bright fuchsia phlox. Yellow coreopsis and black-eyed Susans, Queen Anne's Lace, and foxglove. Then there were the herbs. Mint and oregano, wild onion, and thyme. Lauren plucked a mint leaf with her thumb and forefinger, squeezed it, and held it to her nose. The fragrance was heavenly. Aromatherapy wherever you looked.

"You Miss Smith?" a voice called to her.

Lauren turned around. A tall, thin older man with equally thinning hair was leaning over the gate.

"I'm Lauren Smith," she said, both hands around her coffee mug. "Can I help you?" People just seemed to pop out of nowhere around here!

"I'm Bob Cochran, Caleb's dad. I help him out with the little jobs from time to time." The man chuckled. "I'm supposed to be retired, but he asked me to install a valve here in the furnace line. No rest for the wicked, as they say." He chuckled again at his own joke.

The disappointment hit her like a heavyweight champ's right hook. "Oh. Oh-ah—" Lauren stammered. "Um, come on in. I'll show you the way."

"I'll get my tools." Bob went to the white van that was parked in the driveway, opened the big back doors, and stepped inside. Lauren heard him rummaging around, then he came through the gate, carrying a work tote. She couldn't stand it any longer.

"I—I thought Caleb was coming," she said, trying hard to keep her voice light.

The old man didn't look up, but continued in the direction of the front door. "Nah. It's his day at the firehouse, and the other guys are busy on the big jobs. He doesn't usually do the small jobs, anyway. He came out here yesterday 'cause he was in the area. I get these jobs." There was that chuckle again. "Can I go in?"

"Oh, oh, I'm sorry. Just go in and through the kitchen to the left. Do you need help?"

Bob Cochran looked at her quizzically. "No, I don't need help. I know the house well. Thanks anyway." He smiled politely and disappeared into the house.

Lauren stood, stunned, in the garden. Slowly, she lifted her coffee mug to her lips and took a sip of the hot liquid, but she didn't taste it. Had she been a fool to think he might be back? To see her? The engagement ring Charles had given her suddenly flashed in the morning light. She looked at it blankly. *What's the matter with me?*

she thought, suddenly annoyed. And did everyone in town know the inside of her house?

Still, she was feeling frantic. She had to find out more about this man who had elicited such a reaction from her. Just to put her mind at ease. She had given up trying to deny to herself that she was attracted to Caleb Cochran; as was her personality, she just wanted to face it and put the feeling to rest. Once and for all. His father would be just the man to ask.

Lauren hurried into the house and went down into the cellar. Bob was kneeling down on the damp, dirt floor, searching through his tool box for some elusive tool.

"Will this take long?" she asked nonchalantly.

"Oh, no," Bob said, not looking up. "This is a simple job. I'll be out of here in half an hour."

"Good," replied Lauren, with affected authority. "I need to go into town and find a Realtor." She paused for a moment. "What did you mean, 'Caleb's day at the firehouse'?"

"He's a volunteer there one day and two nights a week. In this town, we've got only two full-time firemen, so us volunteers fill in."

"He's a busy guy," remarked Lauren.

Bob set to work removing the old valve. As he did so, he said, "You're listing this place? Gonna sell it?"

"Yes," Lauren answered somewhat belligerently. "I live in New York City. Why would I want this place?"

"It's a nice place, that's all. You don't find nice houses with this much good land so easily anymore. Especially here in Vermont."

Lauren hardly heard him. She walked in a small circle behind him, trying to figure out how to phrase her next question correctly. Finally, she said, "Um, about Caleb. Yesterday he burned his arm here. How is it?"

"Okay, I guess," replied Bob, struggling with a wrench on the pipe.

"Is he wearing a bandage or anything?"

"Oh, no. Nothing like that. He didn't even mention it."

"Kind of a tough guy, huh?"

"No, not particularly." Then Bob turned around, eying her somewhat suspiciously. "What are you getting at?"

"Nothing," Lauren said, chagrined. "Just trying to make sure he's okay." She was glad the cellar light was dim and he couldn't see her color rising. "I — I feel kind of responsible. It was because of me that — that he was hurt."

Lauren blinked as Bob Cochran looked at her, hard. Then he said, "Well, Caleb is fine. I know my son. He's okay."

Lauren gave up. "Tell him I asked about him, please?"

"I'll do that," said the man. Suddenly, he straightened up and faced her. He hesitated for a second before speaking. "Look, you seem awfully interested in Caleb's aches and pains. I wasn't born yesterday, and I'm his dad. Caleb is a good looking, really nice guy, probably this town's most eligible bachelor, I guess you'd say, but I can see you're married or engaged or something. There's a diamond the size of Gibraltar on your finger, so let me tell you something. Don't toy with him. He's been through enough!"

Lauren was silent for two seconds. Then she flared defensively, trying to cover her own embarrassment. "I don't care what he's been through! I was just concerned because he hurt himself here yesterday." She paused and then added for extra emphasis, "I don't want a lawsuit on my hands."

Caleb's father turned back to his work. "Is that the kind of people you think we are? No need to be afraid of that, miss. We're not interested in your money." Then he chuckled and continued with the repair. Lauren wandered upstairs and back out into the garden.

It wasn't long before Bob appeared. "Okay," he said. "The job's done. You should have more hot water than you can use."

"Thanks," said Lauren, subdued by the conversation in the cellar. "What do I owe you?"

"I have no idea. I just turn in parts and labor costs, and you get the bill."

"Oh, well, do they have the address to send it to?"

"Just call the office." The older man turned to go. His voice was gentler as he added, "I'll tell Caleb you asked about his burn. And, if you want a good Realtor, just go to Town and Country Realty. They're right in town. Ask for Joan. You have a good day, now."

"Yes, you too," said Lauren automatically. "Thanks again."

Lauren watched the van drive down the road. Suddenly, she felt she must get in touch with someone in the city. She had to ground herself somehow. She pulled her iPhone out and punched the number key to summon that paragon of practicality, Kelly.

"Hey, how's everything up in the wilderness?" said her jovial friend.

Ah, thought Lauren, *a sane voice.* She could picture her friend, round of cheek and figure, curly black hair cascading down her back. Bright black eyes snapping with common sense and intelligence.

"Well, it's crazy up here!" answered Lauren, exasperated. "There was something wrong with the hot water, so I had to call a plumber. Then he couldn't fix it until this morning. And he was rude! And then, I was awake most of the night, and when I did go to sleep, I dreamed about this plumber!"

"You dreamed about the plumber? What, did he have an ax or something? Maybe you shouldn't be alone with him."

"No, no, Kelly, it's nothing like that. It wasn't a bad dream. It was a, well, an intimate dream, if you get my drift."

"Really! Well, he couldn't have been too rude, or else he was cute. Was he cute?"

"I don't know! It was the plumber, for God's sake!"

"Yes, you do. He was cute, wasn't he?"

Lauren blew through her nose. "Well, yes, okay. He was cute, but he was annoying."

"Hmm." Lauren could hear the mocking tone in Kelly's voice. "He made a favorable impression of some kind, or you wouldn't be having erotic dreams about him."

"I think I just miss Charles."

"Oh, yeah, that must be it, for sure." Kelly's voice was dry and flat.

"Don't be sarcastic, Kell."

Kelly, her best friend and maid of honor, had always found it difficult to hide her instinctive dislike of Charles. Lauren knew she covered it up for the sake of their friendship, but Kelly had said once to her, when Lauren had first begun dating Charles, "There's just something that's a bit too smooth. Not quite trustworthy, I say."

Lauren had scoffed. "That's ridiculous."

Kelly had never brought it up again, but Lauren knew her feelings had not changed. Kelly, after all, did not have the frame of reference from which to judge Charles. Kelly's own boyfriend was a chubby history professor at NYU with the personality of a golden retriever. There was no way she could possibly relate to a person of Charles's stature. Still, Lauren loved her. Their friendship had grown steadily since college, and they had come to rely on each other through all the convolutions of their daily lives.

"What are you doing today?" Kelly asked, changing the subject.

"I still have to sign papers at the Realtor's. Why couldn't my parents have taken care of this?"

"You're way too hard on your parents. They live in San Francisco, for heaven's sake. And it's your house, after all. Your grandmother left it to you. It's much easier for you to do it. You're very prickly this morning."

"I'm sorry. I guess I'm just tired."

"Yeah, too much dream sex."

They both laughed at that. Kelly could always make her laugh. Lauren could count on her to put things in the proper perspective, and she hoped she did the same for Kelly. They talked a little longer about what was going on at the museum, then Lauren looked at her watch—a Cartier with a platinum face rimmed with diamonds. Charles had given it to her for her birthday. "Oh, Kelly, I've got to go. I've got to get into town and find a Realtor to list this place."

"Okay, get your work done and get back here," said her friend. "Careful, or you'll be going native on me!"

Lauren laughed. "No chance of that! Talk to you soon."

She hung up, shaking her head and smiling to herself.

Then she gathered up some of the papers she had received from the law firm, stuffed them into a manila envelope, and set out for the Realtor's office in town.

Town & Country Real Estate was located in the front rooms of one of the storybook-like Victorian houses on the green. Lauren noticed the gingerbread trim on the wide porch as she went up the steps to the front door. It made her feel almost as though she had stepped back into another era. Putting these thoughts aside, she walked into the office and approached the receptionist. "I'd like to talk to Joan."

Immediately, there was a rustling in the back of the room behind a cubicle divider, followed by the scraping of a chair on the hardwood floor.

"I'm Joan," said a woman who came out from behind the partition with a perky smile. "Joan Halloran. What can I do for you?" The agent was small, with large, popping eyes behind even larger glasses. She was middle-aged with short cropped graying hair and an annoyingly energetic manner. She took Lauren's hand and nearly wrung it off in a hearty handshake.

"I inherited my grandmother's house up on Highland Road," explained Lauren as she gingerly withdrew her hand. "I'd like to list it for sale."

"Really?" Joan the Realtor took her by the arm, luring her back to the cubicle. She pushed Lauren backward toward a small office chair and took her own seat behind her desk. "Have a seat here, dear, and tell me about it. Which house on Highland is it? I've lived here all my life. I'll know the house."

"My grandmother was Katherine Hamilton," Lauren explained, and before she could utter another word, Joan clapped her hands together.

"You're Katherine's granddaughter! Mary's daughter! The little girl who used to be there in the summers! I remember you! Yes, I do. Oh, everyone loved your grandmother. That place is a gem, although it could use some work. How did you hear about me?"

"I had to call a plumber when I got there," Lauren answered flatly. "Bob Cochran told me to see you about listing the house."

"Ah, Bob!" she said fondly. "Such a good person. I'll have to remember to thank him for the referral."

Lauren felt the need to return to the reason she had come to the real estate office. "How do I go about listing my house?" she asked, not wanting to encourage the woman by seeming too friendly.

"Well, let's fill out this form. This gives me permission to advertise. Then we have to do a checklist attesting to no lead paint, leaks, radon. Stuff like that. I'll do a walk-through and let you know where it needs help."

Lauren cut her off. "I don't want to do anything to it. Just sell it as fast as you can. Sell it as is."

Joan made a funny face. Lauren wasn't sure how to interpret it. "Well, we want to get the best price for it, don't we?"

"I really don't care what I get for it," said Lauren adamantly. "I just want it off my hands."

Joan pursed her lips as if trying to find another direction to come from, but her enthusiasm would not be repressed. "Well, we'll get a good price anyway. I know the house. I didn't get to be Realtor of the Year because I don't sell houses! Now let's get down to business." Lauren placed the manila folder of legal papers she had brought in front of Joan, who, in turn shoved a pile of forms across her desk to Lauren. Lauren began to methodically pore over them, signing here and there, checking this box and that.

Joan went over each document in Lauren's folder. Finally, she seemed satisfied. "I'll have to run all this past my boss. He should be back later this afternoon. And I have to go to the Town Office and dig up the tax maps. Oh, and I'll get one of the lawyers I work with to go over this too. Don't worry about a thing. I'll tend to the details. You'll have to sign some more forms and releases tomorrow after my boss approves everything, but you'll be in town for a bit, yet, won't you?" Without waiting for Lauren to answer, she stood up, and slapping her thighs with her hands, said, "Let me take you to lunch! We'll celebrate the upcoming sale of the house."

"Oh, no," said Lauren, smiling politely. "Thank you anyway."

"Now I won't take no for an answer. I didn't get New England Realtor of the Year by taking no for an answer!"

I bet you didn't, thought Lauren, and then, suddenly, she acquiesced. She might as well go for lunch. There wasn't anything to do until "the boss" got back. "Okay, you talked me into it," she said, trying to sound pleasant. "I'll go."

"Wonderful! Come with me. We'll walk down the street to the pub. It's really very nice. A decent bar and grill with a pool table. It's the local watering hole for everybody after work, but they serve the best lunch in town, too."

Lauren followed the Realtor of the Year, as she privately thought of her, out the office door and into the hot sunny July day. She looked around her. The town was actually very pretty in a bucolic way. She was remembering certain things about it, like the old Victorian houses clustered around a town common. All the buildings seemed to have window boxes full of scarlet geraniums. It was very picturesque.

Joan Halloran led the way up the front steps of one of the Victorian houses. "This is the pub," she said, indicating the big sign over the porch. "The proprietors live upstairs. It's the way a lot of us do things here. The pharmacist lives above the drug store. The owners of the bookstore live on the second floor of that building. It saves commuting in the winter and helps pay the heating bills!" Joan laughed at her own wit.

Inside was a surprisingly attractive room. Small tables were arranged comfortably about, making the best use of the space. Against the inside wall was a fireplace and opposite was a great bow window with two tables in front of it. In another life, thought Lauren, with her eye for old things, this would have been part of one of the reception rooms. On another wall was a bar that was a deep red chestnut color, so highly polished that it positively glowed. There was a huge gold-framed mirror behind it, flanked on either side by shelves upon which sat bottles of gin, scotch, whiskey, and vodka with colorful labels. A girl dressed in a logoed "McTavish's Pub" T-shirt was pulling one of the several beer taps at the far end of the bar. The place exuded a friendly, sociable atmosphere.

Lauren's eyes adjusted to the light, and it was then that she saw him. His back was to her. He was sitting at the bar with two other men, and although she had only seen him once, Lauren knew the way Caleb Cochran's shoulders knit together into the strong muscles of his back. She recognized instinctively the powerful arms and the way his muscles lengthened down from his rugged torso to his slim waist and hips. She felt her mouth go dry. Automatically she followed Joan, trying to concentrate on what the Realtor was saying.

Joan was babbling. "Come this way, dear. We'll sit in the bow window and look out on the street." They took their seats on either side of a small bistro style table. Lauren forced herself to look out onto the pretty little green with its white gazebo and plantings of vermillion geraniums, but her eyes kept wandering back to the bar, coming to rest on that particular place between Caleb shoulder blades. She assumed he was there eating lunch.

Suddenly, Lauren didn't feel hungry. Instead, she felt like running. Running away from the blithering real estate agent. Running away from the quiet and slow moving little town. And above all, running away from this stranger who had such an effect on her that she had erotic dreams about him.

"What can I getcha?" The girl who had been pulling the draft beer was now standing beside the table, holding a pad and pencil. Lauren looked up, surprised. She hadn't realized that a menu had been set before her.

"Oh, um," she stammered, "do you have BLTs?"

"Of course," said the waitress, somewhat impatiently.

"Then I'll have one of those."

"Anything to drink?"

Lauren wished it was five o'clock so she could have a gin and tonic, but it was noon. "Iced tea," she said. "With lemon." She was wondering if his father had told Caleb about their conversation. She wished she had just kept quiet! She was not good at keeping her mouth shut sometimes.

Joan the Realtor said, "I'll have my usual tuna on rye, Vanessa. With a black coffee." The waitress turned abruptly and disappeared into the kitchen. Lauren stole another look at the bar. Caleb's back was still to her. His elbows were on the bar, and she could hear him laugh as he carried on a conversation with the men to his right and left.

Suddenly, he caught her eye in the mirror. Busted! Lauren could feel embarrassment flooding over her like a smothering blanket. Damn! He had caught her staring at him.

Caleb flashed her a smile. Then, before she could react, he slipped off his stool and walked over to the table.

"Hi," he said.

"Oh, hi, Caleb," bubbled Joan Halloran. "How are you today?"

"I'm fine, and yourself?"

"Oh, busy, busy. You know summer is our busiest time and we — "

Caleb cut her off smoothly, turning to Lauren. "How's the hot water situation?"

She felt electrified by his presence, standing over her in such close proximity. She could feel the physical power of him. She could have reached out and touched him. Right there, at his waist, about his belt. She felt her fingers twitch, and she consciously composed herself.

"Oh, fine now, thank you."

"I might stop up later this afternoon and check on it."

Why did her stomach leap so at his words? "Oh," she said. "That's fine. I should be there."

"Well, then, I'll see you later." He smiled and turned toward his two cohorts who were waiting by the door. With a wave at the waitress, he exited the restaurant.

"Caleb's a good boy," said Joan, sitting back as the waitress returned with their order. "Comes from a good old family from right here in town. He was good friends with my son when they were growing up." She took a bite of her sandwich and shook her head slowly. "Poor guy."

Lauren looked at her curiously. "What do you mean? He doesn't seem like a poor guy to me."

"Well, business-wise, he's doing fine. Took over his father's fuel oil business and became a master plumber to boot. He's got a good reputation around here. I was talking about emotionally. His wife died, let's see, must be about five years ago. They had only been married a year. A vicious cancer. She only made it about nine months. It hit him real hard. They were so young. I think she was only twenty-six or twenty-seven. They had just bought a little house, right here, up that side street. I sold it to them. You can drive right by it on the way up to your grandmother's house. Let's see, my son's thirty-eight, so Caleb must be about the same age. A lot of women have been after him." Joan leaned forward, arching her eyebrows salaciously. "And you can see why!" Then she sighed. "Ah, well, he hasn't gone for anybody. He's locked his heart. Filled it with work, volunteering as a fireman, stuff like that. Too bad."

Lauren finished her BLT sandwich automatically, not tasting a bite of it. So that was what Bob Cochran meant when he had said Caleb had been through enough. It must have been horrible, and people were still protective of him. It said a lot for his character, but Lauren didn't know how to process the energy she felt emanating from Caleb. She was attracted to him, that was for certain, and she was sure it was reciprocated. She was ready to write it off as a mild flirtation, but this bit of information changed all that.

Lauren followed Joan back to the real estate office, where they discovered that "the boss" had not returned yet. Lauren waited an obligatory half-hour, and when he still hadn't shown, she said politely to Joan, "You know, I'm not leaving until the morning, so I could stop by early and get the papers taken care of. There are some things that I have to do at the house, and I've hired a high school kid to mow the lawn. I better go check on it. Also, you could call me if he does come back and I'll skip down. It's not that far."

"Okay, dear," said Joan with a kind smile. "I may give you a call later, then. You take care, and I'll see you tomorrow at the latest."

Lauren hurried out to her car. She was curious to drive up the side street Joan had pointed out to see whether she could pinpoint Caleb's house. She backed out of the parking place onto the main street and slowly turned up the road in question. It was quiet and tree-lined, the quintessential New England village street.

Then, as she proceeded up a small rise, she saw the house. The name "Cochran" was on the mailbox. It was a small, white clap-boarded house in the Cape style, with a good-sized garage attached. The garage was painted red and had obviously been an old barn. The property was pristine, with a split rail fence and a border of well-tended perennials along the road. Suddenly, Lauren felt both foolish and sad. She tipped her foot to the gas pedal and continued on up the hill to her grandmother's old house.

Lauren mused on the way. While she was sorry for Caleb about the loss of his wife, it was nothing that would affect her. She smiled a little. She had been lonely for Charles. Caleb was an attractive man; Joan had said as much, as had his own father. It was all very superficial and natural. He was just another good looking guy, tucked away in a small town, hammering out his life on a day-to-day basis. He would most likely never be any more than average and would probably develop a beer gut by the time he was fifty.

She, on the other hand, was looking forward to life at the top of the social ladder with Charles, free from financial worries, living in the penthouse overlooking Central Park, chairing committees for different charities around the city. The reality was that this was a material world, and she liked the finer things in life. She had worked hard from the time she had moved away from her parents' home, to leave their nomadic, idealistic, granola lifestyle behind, and she had succeeded.

Lauren's picture had already been in *Town & Country Magazine*, as well as in *New York Magazine*. The articles featured her position as curator of the prestigious Thompson Museum for the Arts. *The New York Times* hadn't missed the opportunity to publish an announcement of her engagement to Charles. Lauren sighed contentedly. Soon this business up here in the back woods of New England would be behind her, and she would never see these people again. *There*, she thought with satisfaction, pulling into the driveway, *I've taken care of that problem. I just reasoned it through.* She smiled confidently, congratulating herself on making the important choices that would pave her path in life with security, opportunity, and more than a little bit of glamour.

Chapter Four

When Lauren drove into the driveway of the old house, the boy was already there, mowing the lawn. He gave a wave from the small tractor-mower he drove, and Lauren waved back. The place looked better already. The yard started to show a shape, and the flower beds seemed more colorful. There was still a lot of weeding and edging to do, but the bright orange of the daylilies' faces illuminated the whole area under the big, shady maple. The freshly cut grass smelled divine. Lauren took a deep breath as she walked into the house. She felt uncharacteristically serene as she went inside.

In the city, Lauren still kept her own small apartment in Murray Hill, but she spent most of her time with Charles in the penthouse. Most evenings when she left her job at the museum, she walked the six blocks to the apartment building on West 67th, greeted the doorman, and took the elevator up to the private penthouse entrance. There was no need to unlock the door. The doorman would have already alerted Dennis, Charles's house manager. Dennis would be waiting for her, welcoming her with a smile. He would take her coat, and she would walk through the front foyer, decorated with Charles's Chinese porcelain collection, into the wood-paneled den.

Dennis would say, "Would you care for a drink this evening, ma'am?"

Lauren usually answered, "Yes, Dennis, thank you. I'll have a gin and tonic. With lime, please." While she gazed out the window, Dennis would disappear only to return five minutes later with a cool gin and tonic and a plate of hors d'oeuvres prepared by Tina, the cook. Lauren would say, "Thank you so much, Dennis." He would smile and retreat once again, leaving Lauren to sit and wait for Charles, relaxing by the crackling fire in the fireplace in the winter, or out in the balcony garden when the weather was warm. It was the one time in the day when she was not fielding calls on her iPhone, planning fund raising, directing this exhibition to be set up and this one to be taken down and this one moved to the front of the Windermere room, or tending to the petty complaints of whiny staff members.

Now she stood in the kitchen of the old farmhouse. The windows were open, and the smell of the freshly mowed grass wafted in on the late afternoon breeze. Lauren looked around her. Dennis and Tina were not there. Charles would not be joining her this evening. She was alone, surprised that she was rather enjoying it. Impulsively, she rolled up her sleeves and walked over to the kitchen sink. Everything was pretty much the way it was left when her grandmother had died, but the grime of neglect had settled over it. Lauren opened the cabinet under the sink and found cleaning supplies. She dragged them out, pulled on a pair of rubber gloves she found there, and began to clean.

As she worked, Lauren found herself daydreaming. The noise from the lawnmower floated in the background, but it was otherwise quiet. As she washed, swept, and dusted, thoughts of Caleb stole into her imagination. She wondered whether he would show up this evening or whether he was just being polite. She thought about her attraction to him. How could it be so instantly strong when she was in love with Charles? Lauren had spent most of her young life struggling to reach the top. She'd had few relationships, none of them serious until she met Charles. And Charles had fit into her plan so perfectly. To her, he epitomized success. She thought of what Caleb had said about her not quite understanding what Charles's company did. *A fair observation*, she thought. *I'll ask him when I get back to the city.* On that note, Caleb was right. It was necessary for a wife to understand fully her husband's business life, and he, hers. It was important to the core of the partnership which was, in her eyes, marriage.

The lawnmower stopped. Lauren looked up at the old clock on the wall. It was five fifteen. She smiled to herself. Dennis would not be bringing her a cocktail this evening, but she felt oddly content nonetheless. She looked around the kitchen, now neat and clean, the surfaces of the counters shiny, and the old linoleum floor three times brighter. She was pleased with herself. It felt cozy.

There was a knock at the door. Lauren opened the screen door. The boy was there, smiling at her.

"Lawn's done, miss," he said.

"How much do I owe you?" she asked.

"Thirty-five will do it."

She paid him with cash and watched as he loaded the lawn-mower into the back of his pick-up truck and disappeared down the road. Lauren was alone. She heaved a sigh and decided Caleb was not going to "check on things." She would have liked to have seen him, just to assure herself she could carry on a platonic conversation with this man and get through the night without any more erotic dreams featuring his erection.

Lauren went outside, wandering around the garden, inspecting the lawnmower's work. The lawn looked very good. The boy had weed-whacked along the fence, and the garden looked crisp and cared for. She was satisfied with the job.

As she stood there, Lauren's stomach suddenly gave a little growl. She realized she was beginning to feel hungry. There was no real supper food in the house. She had only bought coffee and juice, and some bottled water and iced tea, but she felt like having a cold beer. Too much country air, she thought wryly. Well, perhaps she would go down to MacTavish's Pub and get a hamburger and fries for dinner. It would be entertaining to observe the locals on a Friday night, anyway.

She skipped up the stairs and changed into a simple cotton sundress with a fitted bodice and full skirt. It was white with a pale blue embroidered pattern, very summery. And although she had no one to impress in this small hamlet, she was pleased with the way it showed off her small waist and rounded breasts.

It took her about five minutes to drive down into the village. She went alone into the small pub. All heads turned and looked at her, then turned back to their conversations and their drinks. Lauren noted immediately Caleb was not among them. One of the tables in the bow window was empty, so she sat there. The same waitress walked up, pad and pencil in hand as usual.

"What can I getcha?" she said.

They must have patterned the stereotypic waitress after you, Lauren mused before speaking. "Oh, I guess I'll just have a burger and fries."

"You want cheese with that?"

"Yes, provolone, please."

"We don't have provolone. We have American and cheddar."

"American, then," said Lauren. She consciously chose to ignore the waitress's irritating manner.

"Drink?"

"Yes, a Sam Adams on tap, please."

"Summer Ale?"

"Sure."

The waitress turned abruptly and disappeared into the crowd that was clustered around the bar, watching a baseball game on television. The crowd seemed to be split about fifty-fifty male and female. They laughed and cheered or booed at the game. It was a friendly place, even though she was alone.

When the waitress returned with her order, Lauren enjoyed her simple supper, but every time the door swung open, she caught herself looking to see if it was Caleb. Probably, like herself, his circumstances precluded their mutual attraction progressing any further than friendly professionalism. *I can live with that*, she thought. *Hopefully, he can.* She laughed softly to herself rather smugly.

When the front door opened again, this time Caleb Cochran walked into the pub. All the smugness that Lauren had harbored two seconds ago evaporated. Her stomach did a flip, and she struggled to conceal her pleasure at the sight of him. She quickly dropped her eyes to her plate and then peered out from beneath her thick lashes.

Caleb walked over to the bar. She saw the crabby waitress smile at him, heard him say something, and saw the waitress pull a beer from one of the taps, setting it in front of him. Lauren watched him, unconsciously mesmerized, as he turned around to face into the room, lifting the glass to his lips. He saw her instantly and gave a friendly wave before he made his way to her table.

"Hi," he said.

"Hi," said Lauren.

"Are you eating alone?"

"Yes, I am."

"Mind if I sit down?"

Lauren managed a weak smile and motioned to the empty chair at the table. "Be my guest."

"What are you drinking?" he asked, looking at her nearly empty beer glass. "Can I get you another?"

"Sam Adams," replied Lauren, beginning to relax a little. "Sure, why not."

Caleb caught the eye of the waitress. "Vanessa, can we have another Sam Adams over here, please?"

Vanessa nodded, pulled the beer, and sulkily set it in front of Lauren.

"Thank you," Lauren said, but there was no response from Vanessa. "What an attitude," added Lauren under her breath as the waitress made her way back to the bar.

Caleb laughed. "Aw, she's just shy."

"Oh, for heaven's sake. She's rude!"

Caleb lifted his glass and clinked the rim of her own. "Welcome to town," he said.

"Well, thank you," said Lauren. "Thank you for the beer, too."

"That's okay. Every once in a while I get a night where I can enjoy a couple of brews. See, I'm always on call for something. Either the business or the fire department. Tonight, I'm really off. My time's my own. That doesn't happen very often."

"You sound pretty busy," said Lauren, looking at him over her glass. His eyes were snapping green lights.

"I guess I am. I like to keep busy. I don't handle lying around too well. Never have."

"What else do you do? What do you like to do when you do have time off? Nobody can work all the time."

"My father thinks I do." Caleb laughed again. "But no, I do have other interests. I like to snowboard or ski in the winter, and in the summer I have my garden and I like to work on my house. I like woodworking. I've got a woodworking shop at home."

"Oh, that sounds nice. What sort of things do you do?"

"I'm no expert, but I'm trying to learn more things. I used to just do rough construction. Then I got into cabinetry. I made all the cabinets in my kitchen. Now I'm trying furniture."

"Really! What are you making now?"

"A bed," said Caleb. "A four poster, king sized bed."

There was an awkward pause, just enough for each of them to notice it. Then Caleb said, "And you? What do you do when you're not working?"

"Oh, I like to read. And I chair a lot of committees for fund raising in the city."

"That doesn't count. What do you do for *you?*"

Lauren stopped and thought. "Well, I'm a pretty good artist when I take the time to get out my paints. And I love interior design. I designed a lot of Charles's apartment."

"Ah, Charles, the elusive boyfriend."

Lauren felt suddenly annoyed. "What do you mean by that?" she asked, trying to control her temper.

"Nothing. Just, well, why isn't he up here with you? You'd think he'd be interested in seeing where your family came from."

Lauren gave a nasty little laugh. "There's nothing that would interest Charles less. He's got bigger fish to fry than getting to know where my family crawled out from."

Caleb's forehead furrowed with disapproval. "Sounds like you're ashamed of them. I always thought Mrs. Hamilton was a nice woman. I didn't know her very well, but my father did. Everybody in town liked her. My father went to high school with your mother, I think."

Lauren took a sip of her beer. "Don't get me wrong. I loved my grandmother. I spent a lot of summers here. It's just that...that I set higher standards for myself."

"Hmm," said Caleb softly. Lauren felt him looking at her. She looked up from her glass and saw him scrutinizing her carefully. "You don't seem to be that shallow."

"I'm not shallow!" Lauren was indignant.

Caleb gave a little laugh. "I don't mean to judge. I guess it's an individual thing, you know, what a person considers success."

Lauren squirmed a little in her chair, suddenly uncomfortable. Caleb said, "Look, your relationship and life are none of my business. I only meant to make you feel welcome in town while you're here, that's all. Guess I've put my foot in it again, like I did when I came to fix your hot water. Sorry about that."

Lauren relaxed. "Oh, that's okay," she replied. "I just want to get this house business over with and get back to the city. I've still got a lot to do to plan my wedding."

"Oh, yeah? What, for instance?"

"Well, I'm meeting with the wedding planner to discuss the venue. It has to be big enough. We're inviting a lot of people. Also, there's the menu, and Charles and I still have a couple of meetings yet with the lawyers."

"Lawyers?" Caleb blinked his green sparked eyes at her. "Why do you need lawyers for a wedding?"

"Just hammering out the last details of the prenup," Lauren responded nonchalantly.

Caleb laughed out loud. "Prenup? You've got a prenup?"

"Of course," said Lauren, somewhat uncomfortably.

"Whose idea was that?"

"What do you mean? Everybody has a prenup now."

"Ha! No, they don't."

"Well, I do. It's for Charles's protection as well as my own."

"It's planning for a divorce. When you love someone, you don't need a prenup. You don't even think about a prenup."

Lauren felt her hackles rise. What kind of provincial idiot was this man? "I'm not planning for a divorce. It's just a precaution."

"It's a plan," said Caleb, looking her straight in the eyes. "It's a plan for divorce."

Lauren raised her voice defensively. "I don't like your insinuation."

"What do you think I'm insinuating?"

"You're insinuating that Charles doesn't love me. And you don't even know him."

"Not at all. All I'm saying is that I don't believe in prenups. I think it's a plan for divorce, and people who enter a marriage under the shadow of a document drawn up by self-serving lawyers don't trust each other. And that doesn't make for a successful marriage."

"Prenups are nothing new, you know!" Lauren felt as though she was defending herself. "They've been done for years. Whenever there are enough assets at risk or historically to see that families form powerful unions."

"I know that," said Caleb slowly. He stared thoughtfully into his beer. "I wasn't the most enthusiastic student, but I've sat through enough history classes to know that marriages between powerful families had nothing to do with love." He looked up at her again. "And that's what I'm talking about. Two people in love. True love. True love doesn't require a prenup under any conditions."

Now Lauren was angry, and she spoke before thinking. "Who are you, anyway? Some kind of backwoods philosopher?"

The sarcasm of Caleb's hard laugh was not lost on Lauren. He pushed his chair back and stood up. "I'm not trying to burst your bubble. Sorry if I offended you—again. I'm just talking about my own beliefs. You're entitled to your own. And, Lauren Smith, I'll pick up the tab. It's how I do things. Have a good evening. In fact, have a nice wedding. I really wish you happiness."

He walked away before she could utter a word. She sat, momentarily stunned, and watched him walk to the bar, leave money with Vanessa, and walk out the door. He smiled at her and gave her a little wave before the door closed behind him.

Caleb had indeed paid for her dinner, but Lauren left a healthy tip for the waitress anyway. Maybe it would inspire her to smile more, she thought sarcastically. Then she gathered her purse, sighed, and stood up. Well, this evening didn't exactly go the way she'd planned. She couldn't seem to have a conversation with this man. He was so contrary. So obstinate. She shrugged to herself. That took care of the problem of this unwarranted attraction between them, she thought ruefully. She couldn't be attracted to a person with such different views about things from herself. Determinedly, she pulled the strap of her purse up over her shoulder and went out to her car to begin the drive back up the hill for her last night in the old house.

The night was clear and balmy. The air was fresh, and the first star was shining in the deep blue of the darkening sky. As she accelerated to climb the small rise in the road that ran past Caleb's house, her car gave a little cough. Lauren pushed the accelerator harder, but the car did not respond. She pushed the pedal to the floor; the car sputtered again and stalled. As it lost momentum, she turned the wheel and coasted to the side of the road. She tried to start the car one more time, but the engine only whined weakly and wouldn't turn over.

"Damn!" she said aloud, smacking her hands on the steering wheel. Darkness was closing in. It was about a mile back to the village. She had no intention of walking alone on a deserted country road back to a village where she was a stranger. She had no idea who to call locally in such a predicament. Then she looked down the road. Just where the road had begun to rise sat Caleb's house. She could see a light on inside. Someone might be home. Did she dare knock at the door? After their rather uncomfortable exchange at MacTavish's Pub, she really didn't want to confront him again from such a vulnerable position. And she could not be more vulnerable than right now, right here, in a strange place, in the dark, with a dead car.

"Damn!" she muttered again out loud, then thought more realistically, *what am I going to do now?* She really needed help. And what did it matter? She was leaving town tomorrow anyway and would never see him again. She was not going to stoop to playing games. It was not a matter of daring to knock and ask for help or not daring. It was not a matter of daring at all. It was just the intelligent thing to do. Her only option.

Of course she dared! What was stopping her? After all, other than Joan the Realtor, he was the only person she knew in town. "Come on," she convinced herself as she climbed out of the car. "It's nothing. He's nothing to you." However, she could not seem to still her thudding heart.

Lauren made her way tenuously up the front walk. Through the illuminated window, she could see the kitchen, so she made for the side door. Hesitantly, she raised her hand, then boldly knocked at the door. She could hear movement in the room and the door opened. Caleb stood in the doorway. He was naked from the waist up and his feet were bare. His jeans, obviously hastily thrown on, were zipped, but he held the button closed with his hand. His face registered surprise, then he looked worried.

"Lauren! What are you doing here? Are you okay?"

Of course, Lauren had never seen Caleb without his shirt, or so late at night. She stared. She was awed by how strikingly masculine he was. His muscles were knit together, sculpted, but relaxed, too, as though they were resting yet capable of springing into any kind of action at any time. She could see the lines at his hips that defined his loins. Lauren felt the blood rise up the sides of her neck and flush her cheeks till they burned. Caleb seemed to notice her blush and appeared suddenly aware of his state of undress.

"Ah, sorry," he said self-consciously. "I just stepped out of the shower and threw on my jeans." He gave a funny little smile. "Long time, no see."

"I need your help, Caleb," Lauren blurted out, ignoring his sarcasm. "Your house was right here, and you're the only person I know in town anyway. I was driving home from the pub, and my car just died. See?" Her situation suddenly sounded so juvenile and lame.

She pointed up the darkening road. Her stalled car was just visible at the top of the rise. Caleb's gaze followed the direction of her pointing finger. "You didn't run out of gas, did you?" he asked with his wry little smile.

"No!" she said, instantly furious. "I didn't run out of gas. I'm not stupid!"

"Whoa! Is your name Smith or Smith-and-Wesson? Take it easy." He laughed a little. "I wasn't suggesting you were. Well, then, I guess the famous German engineering isn't all it's cracked up to be. Should drive American."

Oh, for crying out loud! thought Lauren, exasperated. "Will you help me or not?" She couldn't control the edge to her voice.

Caleb opened the door wider. "Of course, I'll help you. Come on in while I get dressed, and I'll give you a ride home." She stepped just inside the door, obviously ill at ease. "I don't bite," he said sarcastically. He turned and left the room.

"You don't need to give me a ride home," she called after him a little nervously. "Can't you just look at it? Maybe you can fix it?" Weren't these country boys supposed to be able to fix things?

He called back from another room, "I'm not going to try to diagnose some foreign car problem this late. I'll just run you up the hill, and we'll see to it in the morning."

"I—I hate to inconvenience you. Isn't there a cab I could call?"

She could hear him moving around in what she presumed to be the bedroom. She looked around. It was a pretty kitchen. The cabinets were whitewashed with wrought iron hinges and pulls, in quiet contrast to the pale yellow walls. There was a window with a deep sill over the kitchen sink. Open shelves were on either side. Lauren noticed there was antique crockery displayed, a vase, a small trophy of some kind, and a silver frame with a picture of a girl in a white dress. Lauren leaned forward, peering for a better look at the picture. The girl was caught in the middle of laughing, her head back, her dark hair swinging out behind her, her hands clasped in front of her. She was looking straight at the camera and her beauty was undeniable.

Caleb came back into the kitchen, pulling a black T-shirt over his head with one hand and carrying his work boots in the other. He pulled out one of the chairs around the kitchen table and sat down to put his boots on. He answered her question as he laced them up. "In this town? Ha! No, you'll just have to put up with some small town chivalry." He straightened up and gave her a searching look. "Unless, of course, you want to stay here for the night."

"What are you suggesting! Never mind, I'll walk home!" She whirled around to the door. *Chivalry, my ass!* she thought. She should have known better.

He was on his feet and beside her. He touched her arm, and she turned around to face him. She was acutely aware of his physical proximity, the heat of him. Before she could protest, he said, "I wasn't suggesting anything. If you're afraid to stay there alone especially without your car, I'd certainly pull out the couch and you could sleep here. And what are *you* suggesting? What kind of person do you think *I* am? I don't make a habit of propositioning strange women." He paused, then added with a slow smile, "Even if they're as pretty as you."

He had turned the tables on her. Lauren had to return the smile. "Thank you. A girl can't get too many compliments."

"I was sincere."

They looked at each other for a long moment, each recognizing the mutual attraction, each confused as to what to do. They were standing so close together, Lauren was aware of the clean smell of him, fresh from his shower. He made a movement with his hand, just brushing her upper arm, as if to draw her in. Automatically, she tilted her head up and back, her lips slightly parted. Suddenly he let go of her, dropping his hand to his side. "Sorry," he said. "I didn't mean to overstep my bounds. I just didn't want you running out the door. Come on, I'll give you a ride home."

She went meekly outside. He closed the door behind them. "Aren't you going to lock it?"

Caleb laughed out loud. "You can tell you're not from around here! Nobody locks their doors. Here, climb in." He opened the passenger door of the white Dodge pick-up truck parked in the driveway. "Give me your hand. It's a long way up."

"I'm okay, thank you," replied Lauren primly. No matter how good his touch felt, there was no need to encourage anything, but he ignored her, and placing his hands around her waist just above her hips, he boosted her into the big truck. Her heart leaped at the thrill; even after he let go, shut the truck door, and walked around to the driver's side, Lauren could feel the pressure of his hands where they had held her. He had hoisted her as easily as if she had been a small child.

She felt unexpectedly safe as she settled into the seat and pulled the seat belt around her. The driver's side door opened, and Caleb stepped up into the truck.

"Sorry about the messy vehicle," he said, hastily gathering up some papers and putting them into the back seat of the extended cab. "This truck gets to be sort of an office sometimes, when I'm running from job to job."

"Oh, that's fine," said Lauren politely. "I understand."

Caleb backed the truck out of the driveway. They were silent most of the way. Lauren felt the awkwardness of the situation and said, "What time is it, anyway?"

Caleb answered, "Oh, it's not too late. A little after ten, I think. I'm usually sleeping by now."

"Really? At ten at night?"

"Well, I'm at the shop by six-thirty in the morning, so, yeah, I go to bed early."

"Sometimes we don't go out until ten!" Lauren laughed.

They were quiet again, and then Caleb asked, "You live with your boyfriend?"

"Well," said Lauren, "I guess not really."

"That's a weird answer. Either you do or you don't."

"I stay overnight a lot. Actually, most of the time. It's better than sleeping alone."

Caleb snorted. "Is that like saying it's better than a poke in the eye?"

"Hey, what are you saying?" She didn't particularly relish getting into the same type of discussion again that they'd had at the pub.

"Nothing. Just teasing you." He laughed quietly, looking at the road. She looked at his profile. It was an honest, almost noble face, strong of chin with a straight, large nose that flared slightly as he laughed. She decided he meant no harm and laughed with him.

"So, you got a big wedding planned?"

"Oh, yes," said Lauren, relaxing. "It's going to be the biggest New York has seen in a long time! Lots of famous people coming."

"Oh, yeah? Like who? Impress me with who's coming. I won't tell anyone."

Lauren laughed. "Well, both New York senators, for one thing. And Michael Douglas and Catherine Zeta Jones. And Michael Jordan. Derek Jeter and Alex Rodriguez. Others, too, but I forget. I know some of them, but most of the people coming are Charles's friends."

"I see. Your father going to give you away?"

"Oh, no, *please*, no. I'm not being given away by or to anybody. My mother and father will be there. They're not like me, though, so I'm not sure they'll enjoy themselves."

"What do you mean?" He looked at her then, puzzled.

Lauren struggled to explain. "Well, they're…they're hippies. Like naturalists and stuff. Tree huggers."

"What's wrong with that?"

"Nothing, I guess. It's just that I want more out of life."

"What's more to one person is less to another," Caleb said quietly. "Weddings are family affairs. I hope your mother and father enjoy themselves after all."

They were approaching the house. Caleb slowed the truck and swung into the driveway.

"Here you are," he said.

Lauren turned toward him, truly grateful. "Thank you so much," she said honestly.

"It was nice to run into you at the pub tonight. Sorry if I took liberties with the conversation. Tomorrow, you call Rick at Rick's Garage. They're pretty clever. They work on my vehicles all the time. They'll have you up and running in no time."

"That's good because I've got to get headed back to the city."

"Hey," said Caleb, suddenly. "Look what I've got!" He reached his long arm over the back of the seat and brought up a paper grocery bag. He sat it on his lap, reached in, and brought out a six-pack of Long Trail Ale. "How about a beer?"

Lauren laughed in spite of herself and put up her hands in mock protestation. "No, no, really, I can't. I already had two at the pub. Besides, I've got to—"

"Got to what? You said it's sometimes ten o'clock before you go out. Well, it's after ten now. You're late." He smiled at her. "Come on, have a beer with me. We'll sit right out here on the front steps of the porch. It's a beautiful night. You should enjoy it before you go back to that dirty city and breathe in all those exhaust fumes."

Smiling back, Lauren looked down at her hands. "Okay," she said somewhat shyly. "You talked me into it."

"Great!" exclaimed Caleb with almost boyish enthusiasm. They climbed out of the truck, Caleb carrying the six-pack of beer. They strolled across the lawn and sat on the top stair of the porch steps. Lauren could smell the spicy scent of the phlox. She watched while Caleb opened two bottles of the beer. Silently, he handed it to her. "Cheers!" he said, holding it up to toast her. "To a lovely lady who I've been privileged to meet."

"Why, thank you," Lauren said as she tinked her bottle against his. "I haven't done this since high school. And to a very chivalrous man I'm happy was home tonight." She felt her mood lightening. They sat for a few minutes, not talking, sipping their beers, listening to the night sounds.

The spring peepers, those shrill little tree frogs, had taken their summer sabbatical. The bullfrogs in the pond at the bottom of the meadow had taken over, sounding like a whole percussion section in a symphony orchestra. Nameless little insects tweeted and buzzed and chirped.

"Oh, look! Oh, look!" cried Lauren, pointing excitedly into the darkness. "Fireflies! I haven't seen them since I was a child!"

"You won't see many of those on Sixty-seventh Street," remarked Caleb.

"You know Sixty-seventh Street?"

"Small town doesn't mean small minds," said Caleb quietly. "I get around."

Lauren reflected on this, then chose the safer topic of fireflies. "They're so pretty," she said.

"You know, those signals they send are to attract a mate."

"Really? I'm not surprised. It's such a beautiful evening." Lauren turned to look at him. She wondered at how natural and at ease she felt, drinking beer here on the old porch with a man she hardly knew. "Thank you for suggesting this."

Caleb looked at her in a way that suddenly made her want to melt into his arms. The green lights sparkled in his eyes in spite of the darkness. "Ready for another beer?" he offered jovially.

"Set 'er up," replied Lauren playfully. Instinctively, she moved closer to him. She could feel the warm energy of him. He took her empty bottle and replaced it with full one.

"Are you chilly?"

"Oh, no," she said, taking a sip. "I'm quite warm, thank you."

Their arms were brushing. Caleb leaned forward, resting his elbows on his knees. She felt his thigh pressing against her own, but she could not move away from it. She felt so safe. So protected. She was female to his male, and her heart thumped a little harder.

Almost before she realized what was happening, they had turned toward each other, looking each other in the eye, finding no fault, no resistance. Caleb set his bottle down on the lower step and brought his hand up to cup her chin. Lauren trembled, but made no move to stop him.

He spoke quietly, almost in a whisper. "It's been so long since I kissed a girl," he said. "I want to kiss you now. I want it to be you." He leaned forward. Lauren closed her eyes as his full lips pressed lightly against her own. Her lips parted, surrendering to him, inviting him in.

"*So* long," he whispered again, hoarsely. Then he bent his mouth to hers again, this time more intensely, his tongue probing between her soft, lightly sugary lips, seeking, searching, exploring. Lauren opened her mouth, flicking her tongue against his, savoring the taste of him, smelling the musky male scent of him. His day's growth of beard prickled her gently, sending thrilling sensations through her body like she had never felt before.

His left hand slipped down her throat, softly encircling her graceful neck. His right arm reached around her waist, pulling her firmly to him, pressing her against his chest. He held her there as his kisses traveled down to the fragrant hollow of her throat, to that silken valley between her breasts. Through her dress, he traced her erect nipples with a finger. She moaned softly, unconsciously. His lips were on hers again, more aggressively as his fingers drew a path across the top of her bodice. She could feel her skin burn with desire wherever he touched her. Almost timidly, she lifted her own arms around his shoulders. The animal strength of him overwhelmed her.

Caleb moved his hand to her leg in a motion that was as confident as it was gentle. Easing her skirt higher and higher, he stroked the soft skin of her thigh. She made no move, but only clung to him more tightly. His fingers traced the outline of her panties.

"Ah." A gasp escaped her, and yielding, her thighs parted ever so slightly. Through her panties, he touched her. Lauren thought at that instant she could die of passion, of want, of animal need.

Caleb whispered in her ear, "Do you want me?" Lauren could not speak, but her body spoke for her, arching up against him. She bent her head to the hollow of his shoulder and nodded. His fingers pressed harder, and she moved to let him have his way. Their breathing became audible.

Suddenly, in one swift movement, she was in his arms. He carried her down two steps, and then knelt in the fragrant grass, laying her gently down. She was powerless to stop him, or herself, nor did she wish to. Her hair clip had fallen out, and her hair spread over the cool grass. She lay there watching him. He was pulling his shirt off, unbuckling his jeans. She laughed and held up her arms to him as he stood over her with all his masculine energy exposed, for just a moment, before she felt his weight on her, his hands pushing her clothing out of the way, his maleness pushing against the soft warm female place that lay between her legs, begging him to enter. Her body was aching for him to fill her with his hardness, but instead he whispered, "Take your dress off. Please. Please."

She rose up slightly and he helped her pull it over her head. He removed her panties with the smooth motion of one hand, and a single snap of her fingers released her bra which she tossed carelessly over her head. She lay back. Caleb knelt over her.

"You're beautiful," he said reverently. "You're the most beautiful woman I've ever seen." Lauren knew she was pretty. She knew her body was fit and firm, curvy where it was supposed to be, but this adulation, this admiration that she heard from the man who had set her to tingling the first time she saw him, made her revel in herself. Lauren was proud he found her beautiful, and glad to offer herself to him, without reservation. There was nothing else to do. At least for this time, this evening, they were one. She would figure it all out later.

Before her thoughts could go further, Caleb was flicking her nipples with his tongue. Then his mouth paid tribute to her, slowly, almost serenely. He was not in a hurry. He tickled her navel with his tongue. His lips caressed the rose petal soft skin of her belly, making her shudder with the purest pleasure. Then, he paused and laid his head upon her, on her warm lower regions from whence her passions flowed. She felt a deep sigh rack his body. She reached down and ran her fingers through his hair. Caleb looked up at her and smiled, then playfully buried his lips in that most sensitive part of her. She moaned in ecstasy and opened herself to his kisses.

As his soft, warm mouth explored her most private self, Lauren was overcome by something primal, something atavistic, a fulfillment so basic, a need so deep there were no words to define it. She felt she might die then and there unless he filled that aching void. He must have heard her thoughts, felt it through their mutual touch, for he raised himself up on his knees, his hands on her hips.

Lauren opened her eyes and reached up to him, placing her open palms on his muscular chest. She ran her hands down his body, until she held the proof of his passion in her hands, tenderly caressing the hard shaft. She felt a quiver in him. She looked up at him and their eyes locked.

"Do you really want this?" Caleb whispered. "Do you want me?"

"Please…" Lauren could barely speak. Her body throbbed for him. "Yes, yes. Please. I want you, Caleb. Please!"

He came into her then, slipping into her wet, secret place. He gasped at her heat. It aroused him even more. He began powerful thrusting with his hips, trying, trying to get even deeper in her, closer to her. Lauren moaned with the inexplicable, piercing relief of it. It made no difference that they had only known each other the better part of thirty-six hours, that they were here, naked on the grass, primitive in their passion, each for the other. Somewhere, on some plane, they were meant to be here, meant to be together, to be entangled like this in body and spirit.

Lauren was caught in a vortex of physical bliss, as though the whole world had slipped away and it was just Lauren and Caleb filling the emptiness with their passion. She felt the beginning of his climax, heard him moan with anticipation. She clutched her arms around him, struggling to hold him closer, closer. Suddenly she felt her pulse race, her breath caught in her throat as the involuntary sweetness of her own ecstasy washed over her like frothy waves on a crystalline, tropical shore, and she met him, heartbeat to heartbeat.

At last they lay still, breathing in unison. Lauren felt her vision return, and she opened her eyes. All the stars seemed to be brighter in the velvet sky. The glowing crescent of the new moon hung in the heavens like the most romantic chandelier. Caleb's face was buried in the hollow of her neck. She could feel his lips pressed against her skin. She felt as though the two of them were encased in a fragile glass ball that kept every care, every worry, every responsibility at bay. She sighed contentedly and softly kissed his ear.

Caleb raised his head and smiled at her before softly kissing her expectant lips. "You're so beautiful," he whispered, then his hands were on her upper arms. He said, "You feel cold. Your teeth are chattering. Come on, let's go inside. I don't want you to get chilled."

Lauren laughed. "I'm fine." They stood up, now a little shy of each other. Lauren didn't know whether her teeth were chattering because of the night chill or because of what had just transpired between them. She gathered her clothes up and holding them to her, she led the way into the house.

"Come with me," she said. "Upstairs."

"To the bedroom?"

"Yes. Unless you don't want to."

His spontaneous hearty laughter as he followed her up the stairs filled her with a deep happiness.

Caleb climbed into the bed first, holding back the covers. Lauren slipped between the sheets and snuggled up close, laying her head on the curve of his shoulder. She could hear the gentle thumping of his heart. He curled both arms around her and kissed the top of her head.

"Oh, Caleb," she whispered into his shoulder. "I'm afraid to talk. I'm afraid to wake up from this dream."

"Shh. Shh," he soothed her, kissing her fragrant hair again. "We won't talk now. It's not time to talk. It's time to be together. This is our time. These moments right now. Don't be afraid. Come as close to me as you can and don't be afraid."

Lauren had never felt so safe, so loved. Then, it wasn't just physical, she thought dreamily, feeling the rhythm of his breathing. The soft sounds of the night lulled them, and they drifted off to sleep as though they had been two birds in a nest of down, gently rocking in the night breeze.

Later, they awoke. It was not dawn yet, but the sliver of new moon had set and it was very dark. They explored each other all over again, each worshiping the other's body, reveling in the breathlessness of every moment. Lauren opened herself to him, and Caleb filled her every physical desire. Then it was her turn. With her hands and her lips, she caressed him, thrilling at the power of his muscles, wondering how he could be so hard and yet so gentle at the same time. Wondering how he could raise her to such heights with a simple touch.

At five o'clock, the dawn crept in. Lauren peered over Caleb's shoulder to look out the window. She watched as the brilliant rays of the first sunlight pierced the gently swirling morning mists, illuminating the tiny water droplets so that the very air seemed washed in gold. Caleb moved, and she felt his arm around her.

"Are you awake?" he whispered.

"Yes. Just watching the sun come up. It's beautiful. I'm rarely up this early."

Caleb chuckled softly. "I get up this time every morning." He turned in the bed and they lay face to face. Lauren buried her face in Caleb's chest, loath to let this fantasy end. He said, "I don't want to get up today."

"Caleb, I —" she started.

"We'll figure things out," he said, laying a finger on her lips. She ducked her head to his chest again and this time her lips found his nipple. She kissed it tenderly, then rolled it in her teeth, biting down, exerting more and more pressure until she heard his gasp. She felt his manhood rise up beneath her. She slipped down in the bed and ran her tongue the length of it, culminating with a succulent kiss on the torrid tip. She licked it feverishly with her tongue and then buried her face in the thick, curly hair fragrant with the odor of lovemaking. She covered his belly with little love bites, tasting the saltiness of him.

This time their lovemaking seemed more frantic, more frenzied, as though they knew the day was upon them. Suddenly, Caleb threw back the covers of the bed and rolling onto his back, he gripped her around her waist, lifting her over him. She opened her love-flushed thighs, and he settled her down on that silky spear that was his passion for her come to life. Then he thrust up with his hips, piercing her to her soul, again and again until she thought she would faint with the glorious sensation. At last, the culmination of her desire broke over her. She moaned out loud and slumped forward onto his chest as he filled her fiery femininity with the scalding proof of his satiation.

Lauren lay on Caleb's chest. They held each other, still physically one. Their sweat mingled. When at last he turned out from under her, their parting was painful in the most pleasurable way. They rested for a while, watching the day get lighter and brighter.

Finally, it was time to get up. Caleb showered while Lauren made coffee. The gauze was beginning to lift from her mind, and suddenly she was filled with guilt. What had she done? What had she been thinking? She had never in her life done anything like that before, but then again, she had never been quite so drawn to a man as she was toward Caleb. She had actually been helpless from his first touch. Her body had taken over, responding to his body on some primal level. And now the deed was done. She had cheated. She had cheated on Charles. Could she ever tell him about it? Could she slough it off and go on, like nothing had happened? Something had happened, though. Lauren could not forget the way she had felt when their bodies had melded as one. She could not forget the feel of Caleb's mouth on her mouth, her breasts, on the very center of her femininity.

Lauren's hands began to shake a little as she heard Caleb coming down the stairs. She poured two mugs of coffee to steady herself. He entered the kitchen, dressed in his jeans and t-shirt, his damp hair sticking out in all directions in the most attractive manner. They sat at the kitchen table, looking out across the old garden, silently sipping their coffee.

Finally, Lauren spoke up. "Caleb, I don't know what to say. I don't know what came over me, but I want you to know that I've never done anything like that before." She was embarrassing herself, she thought.

Caleb gave a little laugh as he sipped his coffee. "Well, the important thing is did you enjoy yourself?"

She stared at him, horrified. Had it all been a charade that she had gullibly and willingly taken part in? Had all his pretty words and touches been just totally self-serving? Had that passion that burned between the two of them been nothing but a ruse to get him what he wanted at the moment? Last night she could have sworn to a bond between them. She *knew*. A man couldn't fake something like that. Or could he?

He saw the look on her face. "Look," he said, more gently, "I know you're engaged. I know you're going back to the city. I'm a realistic guy." He set his mug down. Lauren thought he was going to reach for her hand, but instead he folded his arms across his chest. She had seen that body language before. He was shutting her out. He had put up his defenses. He leaned back in the old kitchen chair, away from her. "I want you to know, I haven't ever done anything like that either. I was married before." Here, he stopped and sighed. Lauren didn't tell him what Joan had confided. Instead, she waited.

Caleb continued, in a soft voice, "I met a girl. Her name was Julie. We fell in love. We got married. We bought that little house that I still live in. She was so happy there. So happy. We lived there about a year. Then, she got sick. She got sick and she died. I just didn't want to go on."

Lauren's eyes teared up, stinging as she blinked them back. She reached her hand across the table, but Caleb kept his posture, arms folded, leaning back in his chair. "Oh, Caleb," she said, sincerely touched, "I am so, so sorry."

"That was almost five years ago," he said, looking down at the floor. "And do you know, you are the first woman I've slept with since the last time Julie and I made love." He hung his head. Lauren said nothing. How could she comment on such heartbreak? She waited.

Caleb looked up. He gave a little smile. "My father, he's a good man. He's a smart man, too. He told me he wanted to retire, and he made me take over the business. Just like that, he turned it over to me. He saddled me with the responsibility of eleven employees, fifteen hundred customers, and just as we were expanding into fuel oil. I was so busy, I couldn't see straight. I worked from dawn until way after dark. It saved my life, I think. And my father, he said he wanted to retire, but he was right there with me most of the time, helping me through. I didn't even know it until I look back on it from this angle. Now, he pretty much is retired, but he barely left my side for the first couple of years." Caleb stopped and looked at her, a strange, enigmatic grin on his face. "Maybe you fit the bill because I knew nothing could happen. I knew you'd be leaving and not coming back."

Lauren felt the hurt as her stomach pitched. She knew he was right, but she hadn't wanted to hear it. She opened her mouth to say something, but Caleb kept talking. "Don't get me wrong. You're a beautiful woman, and there was something about you that attracted me the first time I saw you. As for last night, it felt good. It felt good to hold you, but in the cold light of day, I know there can't be anything between us. I know you're leaving. Besides, we're too different. You like the city and your job and your fancy stuff. You said so. I'll be here till the day I die and I love it here. I guess I could go anywhere or buy anything I like, but I like where I am and what I have." He sighed deeply. "Thank you, though. Thank you for…for taking me in." This time he reached out with one hand and laid it over her hand, limp on the table. He squeezed it gently. "To tell the truth, I was afraid to hook up with other women. I was afraid at first with you. I was afraid I couldn't do it. The memory of my wife is still there. I can see her face as clearly as if I saw it this morning. You're different, though, and I wasn't afraid last night. That's what I want to thank you for. Maybe if circumstances were different, we could have had something, but they're not, and we've both got significant baggage."

Lauren just stared at him. She could think of nothing to say.

"Lauren, are you all right?"

She blinked and collected her thoughts. She gave her head a toss and tried to physically shake herself back to reality.

"I'm fine," she said strongly, a bit too loud. She rose to her feet and took the coffee mugs to the sink. "What you say is right, of course. I'm glad you had a good time. I—I did too, but you're right. We both come from such different worlds. So, Caleb, thank you for a fun evening." They both forced a laugh. Lauren continued, still facing the sink, afraid to look him in the eye, "And you have a nice life. You'll find a girl eventually. You're too warm to spend the rest of your life alone. Me, I've got to get back to the city and plan my wedding!"

Caleb stood up. He came up behind her and encircled her waist with his strong hands. He was very close now. His chest just brushed her shoulder blades, evoking memories of the night before. Lauren turned to face him. She felt dizzy, but she couldn't bring herself to break free from his grasp or push him away. He said softly, "I don't really care if I find someone again or not. I can live just fine with my memories, but I would like to kiss you goodbye."

Lauren lifted her face. His soft, full lips sought her mouth hungrily, pressing down until her lips parted, allowing his tongue to meet her own. A thought flitted through Lauren's mind. *This is what I want.* Immediately, she forced the maverick emotion down, down through to her deep subconscious. It was not a quick kiss. They stood locked in each other's arms until she could feel his hardness pushing against her, begging her body as it had the night before. Her thighs quivered under her dress.

Caleb let her go then, touching her cheek with his fingers. He stepped back. "I better go," he said. "I have a busy day. And I'll stop at the garage on my way back to town and send them up to get your car." He backed away from her, his hand reaching out for the screen door handle. "You drive carefully back to the city."

"I will," she said softly. "Goodbye, Caleb."

He smiled, nodding at her. Then he was gone. Lauren sat down heavily at the kitchen table. She heard his truck start up, but she would not, could not, look out the window to see it vanishing down the dirt road.

Chapter Five

Lauren sat there at the kitchen table and tried to remember the name of the garage where hopefully her car was. Nick's? Rick's? Dick's? Something like that. She fumbled through the pages of a five-year-old phone book. Rick's Garage, Anvil Street. That was it. She punched the number into her iPhone.

"Rick's," came the gruff answer.

"This is Lauren Smith. You have my Mercedes, I believe. Have you been able to get it running yet?"

"No."

Lauren waited, expecting an explanation of the problem. There was silence on the other end. Finally, exasperated, she said, "Well, when do you expect it to be ready?"

"Don't know. When the part comes in."

What was with these people and their "parts"? she thought, frustrated. "When do you expect it to be fixed?" She was trying hard to hold her temper.

"Mid-morning."

"Okay, will you call me when it's done?"

"Sure."

Lauren gave her phone number and hung up. She sighed and looked around, deciding to get busy. She was stuck here until the car was done, anyway. She rose and went upstairs, only to stand in the doorway of the small bedroom, gazing at the bed, sheets and duvet all askew.

"Might as well clean up the scene of the crime," she said bitterly to herself. She stripped the sheets off the bed and shoved them aggressively into a big laundry bag. When she arrived back in New York, she would wash Caleb Cochran right out of her life. So thinking, she carefully remade the bed with her grandmother's linens and went back downstairs.

For the next couple of hours, Lauren scrubbed and cleaned various rooms in the house, almost as if she were attempting to wash away the memory of the previous night. At last, she threw the cleaning cloths into the sink and opened the kitchen door for a breath of fresh air.

Lauren meandered out into the yard. Her mind raced and her thoughts were so jumbled, she thought she had better do something or she would go completely mad. She went down on her knees in front of one of the flower beds and began to weed. Even though she had spent most of her adult life thus far in the city, she still knew a weed from a flower.

Lauren worked diligently, concentrating on the flowerbeds, remembering those summers so long ago, when she was a skinny, pony-tailed little girl staying with her grandmother while her parents traveled the country championing this cause and that. It had been a peaceful time then, and it was peaceful for her now. *I guess I still love the old place*, she thought, smiling to herself.

She raised her head when she heard a car pull into the driveway. It was Joan Halloran, the Realtor.

"Oh," she called, waving when she saw Lauren. "You're still here. Where's your car?"

Lauren stood up. "It gave out last night. I'm waiting to have it fixed. It's at Rick's Garage."

Joan didn't miss a beat. "Oh, well, then you can help me write up a brochure for the house while you wait. It's kind of a fixer-up, but I think we can take some good pictures, and with a good description, we'll get it sold. I'm so glad you had the lawn mowed. It looks great." Joan headed up the porch steps. "Uh-oh, we'll have to get rid of these beer bottles."

Lauren hastily scooped up the empty bottles, "Oh, I had a couple of beers last night. It was such a pleasant evening. I just sat out here until late."

"Really?" Joan looked at her skeptically. "You drank a whole six-pack?"

Lauren let out a nervous laugh. "There were only two left in the pack."

"I see," said Joan, looking at her closely. "Okay, then, let's get to work on this."

Lauren followed Joan around while she took notes and pictures. After half an hour, they sat down together at the kitchen table. "Read this back to me," said Joan. "Let's see how it sounds."

Lauren cleared her throat and read out loud, "Charming country farmhouse, circa late 1800s. Four bedrooms, two baths. Center hall. Eat-in kitchen. Two fireplaces and wood stove. Needs some work, but this home is a real find with sixty acres, serviceable outbuildings, ample private water supply, and beautiful southwesterly views. Many perennial beds and borders as well as mature trees, stone walls, picket fence. Priced to sell." She looked up at Joan.

"That sounds good, then, don't you think?" asked the agent, although she made it sound more like a statement than a question.

Lauren ignored her and slowly gazed around the kitchen. "You know, I've only been here for the last two days, and before that, it must have been nearly twenty years ago that I spent any time here, but the more I look around, well, I guess it reminds me of when I was a little girl. My parents used to leave me here with my grandmother when they went to protests and hearings and activist events. I always had such a peaceful time here."

"Maybe you should keep it as a country place," said Joan slyly.

"Hmm," Lauren mused, "I don't think so. I don't think that would work. I—I'd never get up here anyway. I could barely spare the time to get this stuff done."

"Well, I was only suggesting."

Lauren's phone rang. "Hello?... Oh, yes. Thank you. Just a minute, please. Joan?"

"Yes, dear?"

"Could you give me a ride down to pick up my car?"

"Why sure."

It was nearly noon by the time Lauren got on the road. She had planned to start the four and a half hour drive at eight in the morning. *Oh well,* she thought, *only four hours late. I should get to the city just in time for rush hour.*

Lauren proved herself right. At six o'clock that evening, she dragged herself into the lobby of the building on Central Park West. She felt tired and grimy from the long drive and slightly nauseous from getting stuck in traffic twice. The doorman smiled at her as she walked in. "Evening, Miss Smith," he said.

"Oh, Albert, good evening. Is Charles home yet?"

"No, ma'am. I've been here since two this afternoon. Tina's been in and out a couple of times, but that's all. You look tired, miss."

"I am, Albert, I am. I just drove down from New England after a couple of irritating days up there on family business. I'm just glad to get home."

"Well," said the doorman, smiling and pushing the elevator buttons for her, "You just get in a hot tub and relax for a while. I'll give Dennis the heads-up."

"Thank you, Albert," Lauren said as the elevator door closed. Up, up, up she felt the elevator go, and with each floor, she felt a little better. This was where she belonged. She would find out from Dennis whether Charles was coming home tonight or whether he had already left for Singapore. At any rate, she was glad her fiancé was not at home. She would have time to shower and change before greeting him. She would have time to leave Caleb Cochran behind, once and for all.

Dennis met her at the door in the private entrance. "Good evening, Lauren," he said. Impeccably dressed as ever in a dark suit, he reached out and took Lauren's laundry and overnight bags from her.

"Thanks, Dennis," she said. "I'm exhausted."

"Traffic bad?"

"Yes. Is Charles at home?"

"He's not here, no, miss."

"Did he leave for Singapore?"

"Ah, that's the good news, miss. He told me to tell you he would be in a meeting this evening until about eight, but that he wouldn't be leaving for Singapore until day after tomorrow. So, yes, he will be home later this evening."

"Oh, that's wonderful news, Dennis. Thanks. I'll have time to get cleaned up."

"You run along and freshen up. I'll take these things into Tina. She'll make short work of them."

Lauren smiled and went on her way to the master bedroom.

The penthouse really was spectacular. It had been featured in *Architectural Digest* and *The New York Times'* style section. Every time she entered it, Lauren felt awe. The foyer was a dimly lit hall with hidden closet doors. The walls were lined with lighted niches housing Charles's porcelain collection. Charles had worked the Pacific Rim for years and had collected some priceless pieces. Lauren, with her museum experience, had helped him design the display. She was very proud of the way it had turned out. The foyer led to the formal living room, a massive room with a great stone-faced fireplace and four floor-to-ceiling French windows that opened onto a generous rooftop garden planted with pots of colorful flowers. A gardening service came once a week from April to October to care for them. To the right of the living room were the dining room, kitchen, butler's pantry, and staff quarters. To the left was a wide hallway hung with some of Charles's extensive art collection. The hallway led to the master bedroom suite and two guest suites.

Lauren wandered down the hallway and opened the door to the master suite. The bedroom was a large, square room with French windows opening onto a small balcony. The king-sized bed was against the wall facing the balcony. A huge mirror hung over the head of the bed, and there were built-in bookcases and shelving on either side. The room was sleek and contemporary. An original custom-made chandelier hung over the bed. It was designed to look like a meteor shower, and the shiny metal arced out asymmetrically. Reading lights swung out from the cabinetry next to each side of the bed, and at its foot was a red leather bench, upon which Lauren plunked her purse.

For a moment, Lauren perched on the edge of the bed. She stared at the wall where a collection of eighteenth century landscapes hung over a Duncan Phyfe writing desk flanked by two deep wing chairs. Usually, the old landscapes with their sweeping vistas of the

English countryside soothed her, but this evening they had no effect. If anything, their portrayal of stone walls and meadows reminded her of what she had left in Vermont.

The opposite richly paneled wall was hung with a large contemporary storm scape. On each side of the painting was a doorway. The doorway to the right was Charles's dressing room, and beyond that, his private bath. The doorway on the other side led to the dressing room that housed Lauren's wardrobe, her vanity, and her accessories closet. Her private bath, a mirror image of Charles's, lay just beyond the upholstered chaise at the back of the dressing room.

Lauren walked into her dressing room, set her purse on the chaise, and went into the white marble bathroom. She sighed. This would be hers for real, she thought, in just a few short weeks. She started the water flowing into the deep marble tub and shed her clothing. One wall of the bathroom was mirrored, and she stared at herself as if she expected to see something different. She was not tall, but her waist and neck were long, and she curved in all the right places. She looked the same, but Lauren did not feel the same at all. She ran her hands over her breasts and down over her hips, turning her thoughts inward trying to relive the fleeting rapture of the night before. She could feel Caleb's touch on her bare skin. Her thighs tingled with the memory of his caresses, and her face flushed.

Lauren turned away from the mirror and stepped into the warm tub, submersing herself in the water. She took the soap and lathered herself, but try as she might, she could not wash away the memory of her stay in New England. Those tactile feelings remained…his hands, his mouth, his skin. They were imbedded in her body, into her very soul. She had never been touched like that, either physically or emotionally. Consciously, she sought to bury the train of thought. *I will just have to live with it,* she thought. *I will just have to learn to live with it. I can't risk all this. I've worked hard, and I can't risk what I've accomplished.*

Lauren stepped out of the tub and toweled off, then wrapped her fluffy white robe around her. She went into her dressing room, rummaging through her clothes, trying to find something pretty, yet comfortable, in which to greet Charles. Suddenly she felt as though she had been away for a lifetime, but it had only been two nights. She finally decided on wide-legged, black silk pants and a simple white top, cut low over the bosom. She scuffed her feet into black silk slippers and wandered out to the study.

The study was Lauren's favorite room. Unlike the other rooms, it was small and paneled with dark wood. Three walls were bookcases, ceiling to floor, even around the window, which had diamond shaped leaded panes. A small Japanese screen, decorated with a geisha scene, hung over the fireplace. The mantel was deep and held a beautiful old porcelain clock and a bronze statue of two lovers caught in an amorous embrace. A full bar was hidden behind a sliding panel near the fireplace. Lauren walked across the deep, soft Oriental rug to help herself to a gin and tonic.

"I would have gotten that for you," said Dennis from the doorway. He carried in a small silver tray of different hors d'oeuvres and set them down on the butler's table by the sofa.

"Oh, Dennis," said Lauren, "thank you so much. Those look heavenly."

"I think Tina is trying some new things," he said. "I hope you like them. Dinner will be at eight, when Charles gets home. Is there anything you need, Lauren? Are you feeling well? You don't seem quite yourself."

"Oh, I'm fine, Dennis." Lauren forced a smile. He was always so solicitous of her, she thought gratefully, as if he knew, as if he knew her vulnerabilities. "I think I'm just tired. You know, dealing with those people up there in the countryside. It's so frustrating. I guess they don't care about what goes on anywhere else. It took me so long to get things done, and then, well, it just tired me out."

"I understand," said Dennis, smiling. "You just relax for a while. Charles will be home soon. Tina is making something new for dinner, too. I'm going into the kitchen now to sample it." He smiled broadly and left the room.

And it started again. The minute she was alone, visions of Caleb started flirting through her mind. She found herself reliving their tryst, there at the house. *Naked in the grass.* It was unthinkable. How could she have succumbed to that pure animal lust? And yet she had. And now the memory of it would not leave her. Well, she would just have to bear it. She would have to learn to compartmentalize things more efficiently.

Steeling herself, she took a gulp of her gin and tonic. It was then she heard the front door open and Dennis saying, "Good evening, Charles. Let me take that for you. You'll be pleased to know Lauren's in the study, waiting for you."

Lauren heaved a sigh of relief, set her drink down, and stood up to meet her fiancé. Being with him would banish all this nonsense and make her forget her transgression. It would fade into the background of her life, like the memories of those soft summers so long ago. Yes, her guilty secret would evaporate into the foggy past. No one would be the wiser. All the plumbers, fragrant old gardens, and seductive summer nights would go the way of a momentary daydream, and she would be back in her reality, both feet on the ground, her arm through Charles's, protected on all sides by tall skyscrapers, designer clothing, and money in the bank.

She heard the familiar footsteps coming down the hall, and Charles came into the room. Even at that hour of the evening, he was immaculate, unwrinkled, the perfect business man. He held out his arms to her as he said, "Darling! How wonderful to have you back!"

Lauren ran to him. She kissed his mouth. His lips were cool, his face smooth. Lauren wrapped her arms around him, burying her face in his shoulder, feeling the crisp, cool fabric on her cheek. "Oh, Charles, I'm so glad to be home!"

He laughed, and taking her arms in his hands, held her out from him and searched her face. "I would have been home sooner, but the delegate from Singapore was here. I escorted her out to the plane. Certainly the countryside couldn't have been that bad. Are you feeling all right?"

"I'm fine," said Lauren, hugging him again. She tried to clasp him closer. A renegade thought rose up in her mind. *Where was the heat?* She released him. "Can I pour you a drink?"

"Yes, thanks. I'll just sip some sherry. Dennis says we'll sit down to dinner soon. He'll open that new red I bought in Italy. Now, did you get everything taken care of up there?"

"I hope so. The Realtor said it shouldn't take too long to sell the place." Lauren did not want to talk about the house, the countryside, or what might have transpired there. She changed the subject. "I'm so happy you didn't have to leave for Singapore today. I'm glad you're here tonight."

"Well, I am, too," said Charles, looking out the window. Lauren stood beside him. The city was settling into evening. Lights were blinking on, and there was a bluish tint to everything. "I do have to leave in the next day or two, though. That's what the meeting was about this evening. Just lining things up so I can get there, get the business done, and get home. I'll have a stopover in London, but I shouldn't be gone more than a week."

"A week!" exclaimed Lauren. Then she added morosely, "We haven't been together very much lately."

Charles smiled patronizingly. "Do I detect a bit of whining, darling?"

"I'm not whining, Charles!" Lauren was really irritated now.

Charles laughed. "I'm sorry, really. I was just teasing you. You know my business involves a lot of travel."

"Yes, I know," she conceded. "I just want us to spend some time together. I've got a ton of things about the wedding to discuss with you."

"Oh, you don't have to worry about discussing anything with me," said Charles. "I'm sure anything you decide upon will be just fine. Ask your mother about some of that. Make her feel involved."

"My mother!" snorted Lauren. "If my mother and father had their way, we'd be married in a field of daisies by some kind of random preacher. The guests would all get hay fever and we'd be eating tofu salad. They don't understand the kind of life I lead."

Charles laughed. "Well, whatever you decide is fine with me, darling."

Dennis appeared at the door. "Dinner is served," he said.

"Thank you, Dennis," said Charles. "Come along, darling."

Lauren reached for Charles's hand, but he had slipped ahead of her through the door. As she walked behind him out of the study, she noticed the crystal bowl of red roses. Dennis always made sure there were fresh flowers throughout the house in strategic places, but this evening the roses caught her eye. Lauren stopped as she passed them and dipped her nose to them. They were beautiful, but there was no fragrance, no seductive perfume like the aroma that had wafted up from the old roses in her grandmother's garden. Lauren blinked, swallowing down an odd lump in her throat. She looked up, saw Charles disappearing into the dining room, and followed after him.

Dennis served the dinner. Tina had prepared a seared rib-eye on a bed of arugula and roasted peppers with roasted Russian fingerling potatoes. In a separate dish on the side was roasted asparagus with a light balsamic sauce. As usual, Tina had outdone herself. The meal was elegant. Charles and Lauren were still sipping the new Italian red wine when Dennis served the tiramisu for dessert.

Lauren laughed as she picked up her silver dessert fork. "Oh, Dennis! Tell Tina this is fantastic! Charles, this is just decadent!"

"Maybe we should have skipped the main course and gone straight for dessert," Charles said jovially. "Let's take it out onto the balcony and enjoy the night air."

Lauren followed Charles through the living room, out the regal French windows, and onto the rooftop garden. They sat in the comfortable garden chairs and looked out over the city. It was nearly nine o'clock. The well-appointed outdoor lighting, automatically set to turn on at dusk, suddenly flooded the rooftop with soft light. Lauren looked up at the sky. She could not see the stars. Her brow furrowed, and she set her tiramisu down on the little wrought iron table beside her chair. She stood up and wandered over to lean on the garden wall. She could see the traffic below, the lights on the yellow cabs. Sirens blared from different places around the city, and the night was punctuated with occasional shouts and music. The air was slightly pungent with the odor of carbon emissions and something sour. Lauren could not help but focus on just last night, when she and Caleb had sat on the steps of the porch. In her mind, she could smell the roses and newly mown grass. She could hear the bullfrogs. She could taste the heady, grain flavor of the cold beer.

"Something wrong, darling?" she heard Charles say. She turned around. He was lounging in the chaise. He had taken off his jacket and tie, rolled up his sleeves, and opened the collar of his shirt. He was the picture of wealthy sophistication. Nothing could touch him. He commanded respect. No event that was in any way important took place without his receiving an invitation, from long-standing charity dinners to presidential inaugurations. And he had picked her, Lauren Smith, with no background whatsoever, except an old house in New England. She smiled fondly at him.

"Oh, no, Charles," she said, walking over and taking a seat on the edge of his chaise. She played with the gold band of his watch. "Explain to me about your business again. I feel I don't fully understand that part of you, and since I'm going to be your wife, I guess I better understand all of you."

Charles gave a little chuckle and squeezed Lauren's hand. "Don't worry yourself about it, Lauren."

"No, really, Charles, I need to understand your business. Tell me again."

Charles sat up in the chaise and set his drink down. He took both of Lauren's hand in his own. "Nice ring," he said humorously. "Your boyfriend must be rich."

"He is," said Lauren flippantly. "Now you tell me how he got that way."

"Okay," sighed Charles, giving in at last. "As I've explained to you before, I own Beckinsale Industries. Beckinsale is a holding company, meaning that it is the parent company of several smaller companies. This makes it much easier to work internationally, worldwide."

"How many smaller companies is Beckinsale the parent of?"

"That varies depending on what type of business we're involved with at the time, or whoever we're doing business with at the time. We can change our companies to fit a country's specific laws or needs depending on which product or service they buy from Beckinsale."

"What is the product you sell?"

"We sell various products directly, and our brokered sales exceed our direct sales. Some companies sell the actual product, and some companies are brokerages and arrange deals. Their income is based on percentages of sales. Right now we're negotiating a merger between Beckinsale and Chong Industries in Singapore."

"What products do *you* sell?" Lauren rephrased her question.

Charles let go of her hands and adjusted his watch on his wrist. He stood up, picked up his drink, and walked the length of the rooftop garden and back. Lauren sat still, watching him, waiting.

"Well, we broker currency, for instance, all over the world. One of our companies sells bridges."

"Bridges?"

"Yes, actual bridges. All the steel parts you need to build a bridge across any chasm you want."

"And?"

"We sell arms. We broker arms, too."

"Arms? Like guns?"

"Well, yes, American-made arms to foreign markets."

"Is that legal?"

Charles laughed harshly. "Of course it's legal. It's one of the largest industries in the world. Beckinsale owns two arms-manufacturing companies."

Lauren was silent. Money and guns. Finally she said, "I guess I didn't realize I was so close to such a sordid subject." She stood up and gazed off over Central Park.

Charles came up behind her and put his arm around her. "Oh, I wouldn't call it sordid. True, people don't like to discuss money a lot of the time. It's considered, well, gauche, but it is a fact that currency trading and arms sales are two huge businesses. The world is not always a pretty place, but what do you think bought you that ring?" Lauren stared down at her finger. Charles continued, "Look, darling, you've got an American Express card. You can buy anything you want. You've got a great car and a man who thinks you're beautiful." He put his arms out. "You live here—will live here—with me. Let's leave my business interests out of our personal lives, shall we? You know what I want to talk about?"

"What's that?" said Lauren, trying to focus on the here and now of the city rooftop and not think about business. The nature of true love and marriage, so clear a few days ago, seemed to be eluding her. And then there was that business of the prenuptial agreement. She had accepted the process, even when it seemed so demeaning to her. She had accepted it because she assumed that was how sophisticated, successful people managed their lives and assets. Then she'd had that unfortunate discussion with Caleb in the pub, and all of a sudden, she almost felt she'd been duped. She banished the thought from her mind along with the uneasy feeling that went with it.

"I want to talk about how gorgeous you are going to look at the New Yorkers Against Hunger Benefit Ball next week in your Oscar de la Renta and how proud I'll be to have you on my arm! How's that?" He kissed her on the forehead.

"Am I not to be involved in that part of your life, then?" Lauren could not let it drop.

Charles drained his glass. He looked at her, and Lauren was aware that his eyes had changed, becoming somehow shrouded, distant. He answered her question in a voice she hadn't heard him use before, a hard voice. "That's correct. There is no need for you to be involved in that part of my life. In fact, I'll tell you straight up, I don't want you in that part of my life. That's my business. It's difficult enough to keep on top of it without having it spill over into our personal life here. Everything else I'm happy to share." Then, the strange look on his face passed. He smiled his old relaxed smile. "I'm going in to bed. It's getting late. I haven't heard yet when I have to leave, so I need to be ready early in the morning. Come to bed, darling. I'll make you happy to be here."

Lauren knew there was a choice to be made. She could persist and tell Charles she considered it part of a sound marriage for each spouse to be familiar with the other's business interests or jobs. She could tell him it was of the utmost importance that he consider her intelligent enough to know what he did when he flew to Singapore or Johannesburg or anywhere else. And yet she could not bring herself to enter into an argument. After all, she thought as she followed him back inside the penthouse, what he said was correct. Everything was provided for her. Why should she rock the boat? The intricacies of how that provision came about was Charles's game, not hers. In fact, she thought as she struggled to bury that conversation with Caleb she remembered so vividly, that a share-everything, hand-in-hand attitude about marriage was colloquial, provincial at best. Sophisticated couples had a true division of labor, a true separation of business and home life, and kept it that way. It simplified things.

She was lost. That she knew. She had no idea which way to go. All around her was a forest of some kind, an unfamiliar landscape. She knew she was a prisoner and that she had to escape. There were people everywhere, but no one would talk to her.

"Please," she entreated them desperately. "Please, which way do I go?" And they all walked around her. Some looked at her with disdain. She forged on, her feet leaden.

Then, in the very far distance, she saw him. Caleb was standing there, beckoning her. He was smiling, his face alive, his eyes sparkling. She ran, even though it seemed to take every ounce of energy she had. And then she was in his arms. "I love you, I love you," she heard herself saying.

He didn't answer, but bent his mouth to hers. Lauren felt the heat grow between her thighs as his kisses traveled down her neck to her breasts. It was then she realized she was naked and his lips were gently pulling at her nipples. She moaned.

Suddenly, she fell backward, in a sickening spiral. He was yanked away. She tried to get up, but she could not. She looked up to see him dragged away by men. The men had big guns. They were pointing the guns at her.

"Caleb!" she screamed. "Caleb! No! No!" She couldn't see his face anymore, just the men with the guns, dragging him away. She began to scream uncontrollably.

"Lauren!" She was being shaken. "Lauren!" She opened her eyes. It had only been a nightmare. Charles was shaking her shoulders. "Wake up. You were dreaming." His cell phone, always beside the bed, was ringing. Lauren dragged herself up through her unconscious. She heard Charles's conversation as she awoke.

"Yes. Yes. Okay. I'm packed. Call Bob and tell him to get over there. I'll be there in three quarters of an hour… Okay. Thanks… Yes, give them the bonus… See you there."

"Charles?"

"That was Nicholas Jorgenson. The jet is ready to go. I've got to leave now. We want to be in Singapore for a morning meeting. Got to strike while the iron is hot." He was climbing out of bed, shedding his white linen pajamas.

Lauren struggled to sit up. "Charles! You're leaving now? In the middle of the night? It's two a.m."

He leaned over and kissed her on the cheek. "Yes. That's what we wanted. This way we'll get there before this rival conglomerate can get organized against us." He smiled at her. "See why I like to keep business out of the bedroom?"

"Oh. Well. You could have told me before we went to bed," Lauren replied, still fighting the terror of her nightmare.

"Now, now," he chided, smiling at her fondly. "No sulking. Remember what we talked about. Remember what we agreed upon."

Lauren said nothing. She couldn't remember agreeing to anything, she thought a little bitterly.

"Are you all right, darling?" Charles asked as he dressed. "You cried out. Just before my phone rang."

"Oh, I—I had a nightmare." She could still see Caleb's face in her mind's eye.

"Well, it was just a dream." Charles was now dressed immaculately in a crisp white shirt, blue silk tie, and gray suit. He sat on the bed and pulled on his shoes. "You just lie back down and get some sleep. Are you working tomorrow?"

"Yes. I have to go in," she said. "Charles, when will you be back?"

"I'm not sure, darling. We'll be stopping to refuel in London. I'll call you from there."

"Okay," she murmured.

"Goodbye, darling," he said, picking up his bag. "I love you."

"I love you, too, Charles."

Then he turned, a grin on his face. "Sorry to disappoint last night. I was just exhausted. I'll make it up to you when I get back. We'll have some time to ourselves then."

"Oh, that's okay," she said softly. He had fallen asleep before she'd even crawled into bed beside him.

"Goodbye, then," he said, and he walked out the door. She could hear him saying something to Dennis, who had obviously heard, or been prepared for, this eventuality. There was a familiarity, a communication, between Charles and Dennis that she was not a part of. She had the feeling Dennis knew everything. She had the feeling he knew more than she did about Charles's life. It made her feel like an outsider sometimes, despite Dennis's unfailing solicitation of her slightest whim. She heard the big door shut and the snaps and cranks as Dennis locked and bolted it back up.

Lauren rolled over in the bed and buried her face in the pillow, but sleep did not come. The nightmare had upset her. It meant that she had in no way resolved her issues involving her tryst with Caleb Cochran. There, in the dark, Lauren knew she would have to find some way to exorcise the encounter, but it would be difficult. She was glad she and Charles had not made love. She didn't feel she could carry the faking quite that far yet. The episode with Caleb would need to be buried deeper in the past. Instead, it was fresh in her mind, fresh in her body. She laid still, her eyes closed. Her body ached for him, even if her mind could not comprehend the attraction. Finally, moist with perspiration, Lauren got up and got ready for work.

Chapter Six

One, two, three days passed, and Lauren was beginning to feel better. Charles called her every morning and again every evening before she went to sleep. He insisted that she stay at the penthouse and break the lease on her Murray Hill apartment.

"You're never there, darling," he said. "And I feel much better about your safety when I know that you're in my home with Dennis and Tina. I don't know why you've kept it this long."

"I guess I just wanted a place that I knew was my own," she said.

"Well, my home is your home. Do you realize we'll be married in October?"

"I know, Charles. I know. Don't remind me. Please try not to schedule any more business trips between now and then, okay? I know you told me to tend to everything, but there are a few things I need to talk to you about. Or, at least it will make me feel better to talk to you about them."

"Don't worry, darling, I won't schedule anything more."

So, Lauren went about her days finalizing wedding plans, closing out the Murray Hill apartment, and most importantly, putting the finishing touches on several in-progress projects at the museum. It was important that they be completed by the time she stopped working, and her last work day was coming up fast. As the days went by, she found herself only thinking about Caleb on random occasions. When she was alone at night, for instance, or when a handsome young man passed her on the street. Or when she saw a couple embracing or kissing in the park.

That was why, on Friday evening, as she was sitting in the study sipping her gin and tonic and going over the flower arrangements to approve all the changes, Lauren was completely taken by surprise when her iPhone rang. Engrossed as she was with the florist's album, she didn't look at the number that popped up on the screen.

"Hello?" she said flatly, taking a sip of her drink.

"Hi."

Despite the fact that it was full of gin, Lauren's mouth went instantly dry. She knew his voice at once. Her eyes refused to focus on the page. She swallowed hard and set her drink down on the butler's table with a shaking hand. She stood up, but then felt weak and sat back down.

"Hi," said the voice again. "It's Caleb."

"Caleb," she said, trying to sound nonchalant. "This is a surprise."

"Well, I didn't want to give you too much warning. I was afraid maybe you wouldn't see me."

"See you? I'm not there. I went back. I'm in New York right now." Suddenly an unbelievable thought occurred to her. He *couldn't* be!

"So am I."

He *was*. Caleb Cochran was in New York.

Lauren made an effort to steady her voice. "You're in New York City? In Manhattan?"

"Yes. Is that so odd?"

"Frankly, yes. Yes, it is odd. What brings you to New York?"

"I had to see you." He was nothing if not direct.

Lauren was silent. She could think of nothing to say. Her mind was spinning like dry leaves caught in one of those little whirlwinds. Finally she said, "How did you get my number?" She tried to sound angry.

Caleb gave a little laugh. "That was easy. I went to Rick's Garage and asked them for it. Of course, they had it written down."

Hmm, thought Lauren, *that's a small town for you.* "What do you want?"

"I came to talk with you. I have to resolve some things for myself. I'm sorry to bother you, but this is important to me."

"It's—it's not really a good time, Caleb," she said.

"I'm not leaving the city until I see you and talk this through."

"Well, maybe tomorrow sometime, then."

"Your boyfriend there?"

"No, no. He's in Singapore." Damn! Why had she said that! She could have just said she and Charles were going out for the evening.

"Then meet me for a drink."

She felt like she was being sucked into a whirlpool, pulled by a magnet against her will, against which there was no defense.

"Oh, I don't know. I—"

"Look, I'm sorry I took you by surprise. I don't mean to upset your applecart, but I need to talk to you. I need to see you. Just for a little while. Just for a drink. It won't take long. One drink. I've been thinking about you. It's been bothering me, and I don't like to be bothered. I thought if I saw you, I could make sense of it and put it to rest. Please meet me so we can talk."

He felt the same way, she mused. His words were a mirror of her own thoughts. "Well, I guess just for one drink," she said deliberately. "Where are you?"

"I booked a room at the Gramercy Park Hotel."

"The Gramercy Park Hotel? Really?" Lauren was shocked. It was one of the toniest hotels with the hippest bars in the city. Ian Schrager, the famous hotelier, had refurbished the whole thing. Lauren knew him personally and had invited him to the wedding. She'd actually booked functions there for the museum. How would a guy like Caleb know about the Gramercy?

"Yes, is there something wrong with that? They have a bar here. I think a couple."

"Yes, they do. Well, then, let's meet there. Which bar? Rose or Jade?"

"Since I don't know any better, how about Rose?"

"I'll be there in an hour. I have to change, and getting down there from here might take a bit on a Friday night."

"I'll see you in an hour. Bye."

"Bye," she said.

Her heart would not stop pounding. Lauren hurried to the bedroom and stripped off her clothes. She quickly showered, then sat at the vanity wrapped in a towel and carefully studied her face. She applied smoky charcoal shadow with slightly iridescent moon-colored accents. Her mind raced as she brushed blush high on her cheekbones. The thought of seeing him again filled her with excitement and trepidation at the same time. *Calm down,* she told herself, *this is good. We can talk this thing through. What's happened has happened. We slept together. We had sex. Now it's behind us and can't hang over our heads like something waiting to happen. We can talk it through like two rational people. It's not a hope or a fear. It's already done with. Finished.*

"Finished." She said the word aloud and applied a slightly deeper, sexier shade of lipstick than she ordinarily wore.

Lastly, she pulled her hair up in the same sexily messy twist, the same way she had worn it on that night of passion. Finally, she was ready to dress. She flipped neurotically through all her clothes, again and again, trying to decide just what to wear. She wanted to be the most beautiful girl in the room. She wanted to be so sexy he would not be able to keep his hands off her, and yet, she knew she shouldn't lead him on.

I shouldn't be doing this, Lauren thought to herself as she finally picked just the right dress. It was Armani, black jersey with a plunging front, short skirt, and cap sleeves. The waist was gathered with a darkly jeweled belt. Very delicate, very feminine, mysterious. She had just purchased it on her last trip to Bergdorf's, and she hadn't worn it yet. Somehow, that fact made her feel better. She slipped it over her head as she quickly scanned the shoe closet and reached for the Christian Louboutin metallic purple pumps with the five-inch heels. There was nothing like a five-inch heel to give a girl confidence.

Lauren reached up to the shelves over the shoes and brought down a deep purple beaded clutch. She surveyed herself critically in the mirror. Yes, she would make him squirm. Confidently, she hurried from the room, almost crashing into Dennis, who was bringing the tray of hors d'oeuvres into the study.

"Oh, excuse me, miss," he said. Then, seeing her, he said in a surprised voice, "Are you going out?"

"Yes, Dennis," she said nervously. "I just got a call from some old friends who happened to be in the city. They want to meet for a drink. I'm sorry. I meant to tell you before Tina got the dinner going. I guess I was just so excited, I didn't think of it." She rummaged through the foyer closet for her silk wrap, although the night was so warm she doubted she would need it.

"That's fine, Lauren," said Dennis. "You go and have a good time. I'll tell Tina." He started off toward the kitchen, then turned back and said seriously, "Will I see you back here tonight?"

His question totally flustered her. Could he sense something? It was hard to tell about Dennis sometimes. Lauren spoke up, too quickly perhaps. "Oh, of course, Dennis. I won't be late."

"Very good. Have a nice time. I'll call down and have Albert call the car for you."

"Thanks." Lauren smiled stiffly and left the apartment.

It took roughly twenty-five minutes to get down to the Gramercy Park Hotel. The driver pulled up to the portico, and the doorman opened the door for her. She swung her long, smooth legs out onto the sidewalk and stood up, focusing on the door. From behind her, she heard his voice.

"Lauren."

She turned gracefully, calmly, but her heart was hammering in her chest. Caleb stood just to the side of the front entry to the hotel. He smiled as he approached her. "You look beautiful," he said. They faced each other. Lauren was unaware that they were right in the line of foot traffic coming in and going out of the building, unaware of the people around her. The city noises had even receded from her consciousness. All she heard was the sound of his voice. She stared at him.

Somehow, she had expected to see him in his customary T-shirt, jeans, and scuffed work boots. Yet, here he was, urbanely dressed in flat front charcoal pants that fit him oh-so-correctly, hugging his thighs and down his calves to brush against his loafers. A white shirt, open at the collar just seemed to accentuate his muscular build and the healthy, ruddy glow to his skin. He carried a black sport coat over his arm.

She had to smile back at him. "You look very nice yourself."

"You can't smell the fuel oil and soot?" he asked. He grinned, but she felt instantly foolish.

"I didn't mean that, well, I guess I did," she stammered. "At the time. I was crabby that day."

"I was only joking."

Lauren suddenly realized they were getting in everyone's way. "Let's go in," she said, snapping back to reality. He offered his arm, and she slipped her hand through the crook of his elbow, lightly resting her fingers on his forearm. The moment she touched him, Lauren felt like fireworks had gone off in her body. Her heart raced, and she felt a dampness at the backs of her knees. She thought her thighs, that most sensitive part of her, would give way beneath her at any moment. Consciously subduing her passion, she smiled up at him as they made their way into the bar.

They sat at a small table, back out of the way. A tall waiter stood before them.

Lauren said, "I'll have a Hendrick's martini."

"I'll have Scotch. A Dewar's," Caleb added.

"On the rocks, sir?"

"Neat," he said. The waiter nodded and disappeared.

"Whatever made you choose the Gramercy?" Lauren asked.

Caleb smiled a little. "Joan told me it was a good place to stay. She told me what to wear, too. I don't get to the city much. Boston once in a while. I've been to New York a couple of times, but years ago."

"Well, it is a good place," said Lauren, looking around her and keeping the conversation light. "It's one of the best places in the city."

"It's not my taste," Caleb replied, following her roaming gaze. The waiter returned and set their drinks down on the little table.

"Really?"

"Yeah, kinda gaudy, don't you think? This leather chair is nice, though." He lifted his drink to his lips and sipped. Then he said, "You look beautiful tonight."

"Thank you." Lauren felt suddenly shy.

"I wanted to see you in your own environment, so to speak. I wanted to talk to you about what happened between us."

Lauren set down her drink and dropped her hands in her lap to hide the tremble she felt. All her brave assumptions while she had been dressing were out the window. "I thought we were going to let what happened between us fade into our respective pasts."

"I thought so, too," said Caleb. "I thought I could do it, but I keep thinking about you. I keep thinking about that night."

Lauren clenched her fists under the small table between them. "It's just because you hadn't, um, slept with anyone for so long. It's just stuck in your mind."

Caleb's eyes searched her face. She could almost feel his caress. He seemed to ignore what she had said. He rested his elbows on either side of his Scotch and leaned forward over the table, visually devouring her with an almost hungry expression. "Tell me you don't think about that night," he said softly. "Please, tell me it was just a one night stand to you and you don't go over and over it in your mind when you're lying there beside your boyfriend. If you can honestly tell me that, I'll leave here right now, and you'll never see me again."

Lauren picked up her glass and took a large swallow of the mellow gin. She concentrated on the distinctive taste of it going down her throat. Then she put the drink down and studied her fingernails.

"It's true, isn't it? Look at me, Lauren. It's true, isn't it? You think about that night. You think about me."

Lauren looked up. Their eyes met and locked. The irresistible female and the irrepressible male smoldered there, in some time and place that was only theirs, making the magic that was only their own.

Caleb stood up and held out his hand to her. Their eyes never broke contact. She reached up and put her hand into his and felt his strong fingers close around hers. The waiter came back.

"Put the tab on my room," said Caleb, as if he had been ordering random waiters around all his life. He reached in his pocket with his free hand and gave the man a twenty dollar bill.

"Thank you, sir," said the waiter. Neither Caleb nor Lauren saw him disappear into the noisy throng of people in the Rose Bar at the Gramercy Park Hotel.

Caleb led the way, striding through the lobby, his fingers still holding lightly onto Lauren's hand.

"Where are you taking me?" she asked, catching her breath.

"Upstairs to my room," he said, walking steadily to the elevators.

Lauren was powerless to refuse. She felt her blood pounding in her ears as she followed him onto the elevator and he punched the button. They rode up in silence. He never let go of her hand.

When the elevator door slid open, he led her down the hall. It was the corner room. Caleb slipped the card into the electronic key port and opened the door.

Although Lauren had arranged several functions at the Gramercy, she had never been in one of the rooms. This one was large and opulent with tapestry-upholstered chairs around a small table, similar to those in the bar. The king-sized bed was situated on a raised part of the floor, opposite the windows which were hung with heavy, rose velvet drapes. The bed was deep in pillows, a rose duvet that was just a tone darker than the drapes, and several cashmere throws. There was a door to the bathroom off to the right. A pair of men's jeans and a black T-shirt were thrown over the straight chair at the small desk. Small town did not, indeed, reflect a small mind.

Finally, Caleb let go of Lauren's hand. He closed and bolted the door behind them. Lauren stood absolutely still. Caleb turned to her, standing very close, looking down at her with that same hungry, yearning expression in his green eyes. He put a hand on each of her shoulders, then caressed her, his fingers following the line of her collar bone, encircling her neck. His hands traveled lightly up her long neck, his thumbs tracing their way up her throat, coming to rest under her chin. Gently, he lifted her face to his.

It was the kiss that she remembered. It was the kiss that haunted her dreams. It was the kiss that set her soul on fire for him and wiped every other thought from her mind. Lauren let her body melt into his. Then his arms were around her, holding her so close her breasts pressed into his chest. His lips searched her face, covering her eyelids, her cheekbones, her mouth, and her throat with frantic, greedy caresses. She found herself kissing him back, reveling in the taste of him, in the warmth of his mouth, in the softly saltiness of his chest where his shirt was open. She pressed her tongue there, as though she could not get enough of the feel of him. She wrapped her arms around him, under his arms, clinging to him as desperately as she would a life raft. *Save me, save me*, begged the voice in her head.

Finally, he gripped her waist, holding her at arm's length.

"Take your dress off," he whispered hoarsely. "How do I get this dress off?"

She kicked off her heels. They clattered against the front of the armoire. His hands reached downward, finding their way up under the short skirt of her dress, lifting the material around her waist. Recklessly, she pulled at the dress, yanking it over her head, letting it fall in a heap on the floor. She had known, deep in her soul, that this would happen, even as she walked out the door of Charles's penthouse.

Caleb let her go, then, and stepped back. She stood before him in her lacy white briefs and bra. With a lover's knowledge, she knew the effect she had on him. Lauren heard his breath catch. Their eyes met again for a moment, and then he was down on his knees before her, kissing the soft skin of her belly. His tongue tickled her navel. Lauren felt her secret self dampen with desire. Caleb reached around, holding her curves from behind, spreading his hands and pulling her closer to his warm, searching tongue. He dipped his head and paid tribute to her inner thighs which parted, unbidden, at his touch.

Suddenly, her hands were in his hair. Her body arched to his kisses. She moaned, unable to contain the passionate longing within her that he was freeing with his infinite, glorious kisses. He looked up at her, his hands still exploring her round thighs, coming closer and closer to that part of her that was now blazing with desire.

"Lauren," he said.

"Please," she begged, lost in the sensation of his touch, "please, let me feel you. Let me touch you. Let me taste you, too."

Caleb stood up quickly, and before she was fully aware, he scooped her up in his arms as easily as he might have held a kitten, and carried her to the bed. Gently, he laid her down.

"I'm going to love you, Lauren. I want to explore you, discover you." He was tearing off his shirt, stepping out of his pants. Suddenly he was naked on the bed beside her, all there and all male. He stripped off her panties and released the front closure on her bra.

"Oh, Caleb, let me kiss you, too," she said, entwining her fingers in the curly light brown hair of his chest and pushing him down on the bed. She knelt over him for a moment, smiling, before she bent down, taking his nipple in her teeth in a tender love bite. She heard him groan with the pleasant pain of it and felt his hips thrust upward against her. His hands went around her waist, but she took him by the wrists. "Not yet," she whispered. "Not yet. I need to, I need to look at you, taste you, touch you."

Lauren bent her head again, trailing a line of kisses down his middle, over his hard stomach, down to that graceful line of muscle that defined his groin. Then, with the most delicate touch, she stroked the length of his erection, wondering at the beauty of it. She began to cover the shaft with little licks and kisses until he was moaning and arching his hips.

Suddenly, she felt Caleb's hands around her waist. He could wait no longer. He lifted her, wrapping his arms around her, fairly smothering her as he crushed her to his chest, rolling over on top of her. She felt that feminine place between her thighs tingle and swell in an invitation to him. Her thighs relaxed and embraced his hips. She opened herself to him, enticing him, and finally, sheathing him with her heat.

His thrusts were slow at first, and Lauren felt she might die, dangling as she was on the brink of her ecstasy. She raised and lowered her hips, meeting his thrusts, urging him. His fingers found the place where they came together, working their way between the folds of her flushed silken skin. Lauren gasped and moaned, giving in, letting the intensity of her climax wash over her, transport her. Caleb felt her thrill and released his pent-up passion, meeting her rapture stroke for stroke until he collapsed, throbbing, on top of her.

They lay like that for minutes, arms around each other, their sweat mingling, each listening to the beat of their own heart echoing in the other's body, waiting for their breathing to return to normal.

"Am I too heavy? Can you breathe?"

"You're not too heavy. I love the feel of your body on mine."

Caleb rolled off her, yet never let go of her. "Well, I like to look at you." He trailed his hand over her chest, circling her breasts with his fingers. He ran his warm hand over her belly, tickling around her navel. "You feel cool," he said. "Let's get under the covers." He threw a few of the extra pillows on the floor, pulled back the heavy comforter and they slipped between the crisp linens. They snuggled together. Lauren dipped her head and nuzzled his chest, drinking in the feel, the scent, the strength of him. She felt his arms cradling her, warm and protective.

Lauren whispered into his body. "Why do I feel so safe with you? I barely know you. You barely know me."

"How long does it take people to know each other?" answered Caleb, burying his head in the masses of her blond hair on the pillow. "I know some couples who've been married thirty years and don't know each other at all and people who meet and have an instant understanding of each other. That's what I think happened with us. For whatever reason. For no reason at all." He showered the top of her head with kisses and clasped her tighter to him.

Then, as it was every time she was with him, Lauren sighed contentedly. She relaxed into an animal-like state of mind, giving herself over to physical sensation alone. She wriggled in closer to him, leaving no space between his skin and hers, and, lulled by his rhythmic breathing, she fell asleep.

It was just after four in the morning when Lauren awoke. She was still in Caleb's arms, but her heart was pounding. Her eyes flew open. *I shouldn't be here,* she thought, suddenly panicked. *I'm engaged to someone else. Why does this man hold such power over me?*

As if he could read her mind in his sleep, Lauren felt Caleb stir. She felt the gentle tightening of his arms around her, felt his kisses in her hair, felt his desire rising up against her. He ran his hand down her arm, caught her fingers in his and lifted her hand to his lips. He kissed her fingers one by one, then pressed her hand above his heart. Lauren could feel the beat of the passion that was defining itself within him. She entwined her fingers in the curly hair of his chest. With a gentle sigh, Lauren closed her eyes again and allowed herself to be carried away with the sensation. She kept them closed. Opening her eyes would mean she might see the clock and be aware of the passing of time. Or she might see the window and be aware of the world outside. No, she would keep her eyes closed and savor this warm, safe womb of love in which she found herself with this remarkable man.

Involuntarily, her hips moved against him. Her thighs opened slightly and he slipped between them. Lauren raised her chin until she felt his lips on her own. She kissed him hungrily, arching her body against his. He was steel to her magnet. She enveloped him in that wet and warm place where her desires smoldered, waiting to burst into flames of passion. She heard his groan of pleasure. They made love furiously, face to face. Then, just as the waves of her ecstasy began to wash over her, just as her fire was reaching incredible heights,

Caleb slipped out. He placed his hands on her hips and turned her over, kneeling between her quivering thighs.

Lauren buried her face in the pillow and moaned as his hands slid slowly down her back, caressing, teasing, fondling. She should have felt vulnerable, naked as she was and unable to see him. She should have felt exposed or defenseless. Instead, she felt empowered. She felt liberated, free to express her own incredible and indescribable feelings. Free to revel in her own body, and his. She arched the curves of her buttocks and felt his hands cup them, slide down them and catch her thighs. He lifted her up and back. Lauren cried out loud with the abandonment of pure lust as he brought her down upon his steely erection. The darkness was pierced with her cries of delight as she opened herself to him, meeting his thrusts, pushing back into his hard belly. He reached under her, his fingers searching until he found that place, that usually soft button, grown harder with its erotic exercise. Ever thrusting, he pressed it, caressing it between his thumb and forefinger. And now Lauren was lost in her lust. She felt herself go over the edge, past the point of no return. Her body shuddered with her climax as she felt Caleb's own explosion of his pent-up longings.

They collapsed into the soft bedding, awash in the sweet sweat of their mutual desire. He did not move from inside her, but covered her with his body while she shivered with the last delicious spasms of her orgasm. Finally, as their breathing slowed and their sweat cooled, he slid gently off her.

"Lauren," he whispered her name. "Lauren." His arms were around her, holding her close to his body. She wriggled into the curve of him. It was so lovely to hear the person you loved say your name. The thought struck her like a thunderbolt. *The person you love.*

Caleb bent his lips to her ear. "I love you, Lauren," he whispered.

Lauren's heart began to beat faster, and before she thought, she whispered back, "Oh, Caleb, I love you, too. I love you so much!"

They fell asleep in each other's arms, the words echoing in their ears.

They awoke at eight o'clock. It was Caleb's phone that woke them. He reached over to the bedside table and picked it up. "Hello?... Yes, I was sleeping. I'm on a little vacation here. What's up?" As he listened, he eased his arm out from under Lauren's shoulders and sat up in the bed.

"Son of a bitch!" he exclaimed. "What an idiot! Did any fuel leak out?... That's the important thing. Well, good. Was the foundation of the house damaged?... They'll have to get an adjuster out there and tell them to let us know. Son of a bitch! I try to get some time, and things go to hell. Well, call Rick and have him get over there. He may have to call L-and-L Truck Service because you can't be hauling those fuel trucks around on a winch. They'll lose it and we'll lose fuel all over and then we'll be in big trouble." He stopped, apparently listening to the person on the other end explain something at length. "Yes, I know. I know. Look, do that and do it right now. Call me as soon as you can and let me know what's happening. Thanks, Kathy... Yes, actually I am having a good time." He looked over and smiled at Lauren, who was lying back on the pillows, watching him, the memory of their lovemaking still fresh in her mind and body. "Okay, okay. Yes. Yes. Thanks, Kathy. I'll talk to you later. Bye." He placed the phone back on the bedside table.

"It's none of my business," said Lauren, "but what happened?"

"Anything I do is your business," said Caleb, nonchalantly. "Actually, that's what happens when you run your own business. You can't turn your back for a minute. Kyle, our newest fuel truck driver, was making deliveries and left the truck on the incline and tried to short-cut across the lawn. Kathy said the emergency brake failed, the truck slipped backward, took out their picket fence, and crashed down the lawn bank into the house. Now it's wedged there against the foundation."

"Oh, no! That sounds serious!"

"Not half as serious as it could have been if oil had leaked all over." Caleb sighed. "My guess is he just forgot about the emergency brake. Oh well, Kathy will just have to take care of it."

"Who's Kathy?"

"She's my office manager. Fairly competent, although I have to keep all the bases covered all the time."

"Do you work out in the field, too?"

"Most of the time. Kathy does the bookwork and everything like that, but I still have to check it and follow up, things like that. It's just a part of running a small business."

"It doesn't sound so small to me." It was refreshing, thought Lauren, to ask a question and have it answered, and to have your opinion valued.

"I'm hungry," said Caleb suddenly. "Let's have some breakfast."

"I could use some coffee," Lauren replied.

"Don't you eat breakfast?"

"Not usually. Mostly just coffee or a latte."

"Well, you'll need more than coffee this morning, after the work-out we've had!"

Lauren blushed, and Caleb laughed as he climbed out of bed. Walking over to the window, he drew back the heavy curtain and stood for a moment, naked, looking out. The morning flooded into the room, illuminating everything with a golden wash, a surreal glow. The light glistened through the curling hairs on his arms and legs, giving his body a subtle sparkle. His back was to her, and Lauren thought she had never seen a more beautiful body on any man. She recalled the strength of his arms from the night before. How could they be so rugged and yet so tender, so gentle, at the same time? He turned to face her, and she caught her breath at the sight of him, relaxed now, satiated, the muscles of his stomach rippling smoothly down into his groin.

They showered together, taking turns soaping each other's bodies, exploring. Lauren reveled in the tactile sensation of touching him. She ran her hands over his chest and back, feeling the firm strong muscle sheathed in the smooth, supple skin. Caleb reciprocated, tenderly massaging her back, covering every inch of her body with his open hands, cupping her breasts. He bent his head and kissed each of her nipples in turn.

"Hey," she giggled. "No taking liberties!"

"I couldn't resist. They were begging for it."

"And what gave you that idea?"

"Well, just look at them, pointing right at me, all at attention."

Lauren laughed. "I think we'd better get out of this shower and order some breakfast before everything stands at attention!"

Caleb stepped out of the shower. He wrapped one of the thick white towels around his waist and wrapped her in another, patting her dry. They put on the luxurious robes provided by the hotel. Caleb called room service, ordering coffee, pancakes, scrambled eggs, melon, bacon, toast, and orange juice.

"Wow! That's quite a breakfast," said Lauren, fluffing out her hair. "You must be hungry."

"You're going to help me eat it," he said.

When room service delivered the food, they sat at the table in front of the window, sipping their coffee and looking out over the city.

Caleb set the coffee cup down and cut off a big fork-full of pancake dripping with syrup. "I couldn't live here," he said matter-of-factly.

"Oh, it's exciting to live in the city," Lauren replied. "There's always something to do. You can walk to get anything from groceries to a doctor."

"Well, I'm primarily an outside person," said Caleb, chewing slowly. "And here, even when I'm outside, it feels like inside. It's hard to breathe. I like to live in a place where I know almost every person I see on the street. I bet you don't even see your own friends on the street."

As they finished breakfast, Lauren suddenly began to feel agitated. The daytime hours had a way of putting everything under a microscope. Lauren could see clearly, almost too clearly. There was a knot of guilt in the pit of her stomach. Guilt because she was lying to Charles. Guilt because she was lying to Caleb. And mostly, guilt because she was lying to herself and knew she must persist in this lie because this was what she had chosen. Situations and options were so muddled in her head, she felt she might explode.

Caleb frowned. "What's wrong?"

Lauren stood up, gathering the robe around her, abruptly aware of her own nakedness underneath. "I—I—I have to run back to the apartment and get to the museum. This was to be my last day, and I need to organize things for the person who'll be taking my place."

She scooped up her clothing and the little evening clutch, which, thankfully, held mascara and lipstick, as well as a small hairbrush. She hurried into the bathroom. Through the door, she could hear Caleb talking to her.

"Will you meet me for dinner? You pick the place," he said.

"I don't know, Caleb. I — this might not be a good evening."

"It has to be tonight, or even today sometime because I'm going back home tomorrow. We have to talk. Somehow, we never to seem to get to that part."

Lauren pulled the brush through her hair and twisted it back into a bun suitable for daytime. Her mind was racing. It was the most foolish thing she'd ever done, she thought to herself, to become involved with this — this plumber from the sticks. Yes, he was sweet and certainly the most handsome man she had ever seen. Yes, she was wildly attracted to him, but she was leading another life. She threw open the bathroom door and stuffed her feet into her shoes. Caleb had pulled on his jeans and a T-shirt, but she could still see that extraordinary body.

"We have to talk," he said. "Something happened between us." He approached her and took her hand. "Something exists between us. You can't deny that, Lauren." He held up his hand, palm out. Then he took her wrist and lifted her open hand, pressing it into his own, so that they were palm to palm. "Tell me," he said quietly. "Tell me you can't feel that energy. Tell me you can't feel it when we touch."

Tears burned at the backs of Lauren's eyes. She blinked hard to keep them from splashing down her cheeks. "Caleb, I — " she started.

"Don't speak right now," he said, kissing her ever so lightly on the temple. "Just meet me here after work."

She nodded, then smiled up at him. "I'll be here at six."

Caleb put a hand on each of her shoulders and kissed her tenderly on the mouth. "I'll be here, too."

Lauren reached up to touch his face. The green lights in his eyes flashed darkly. She kissed him on the cheek. "I'll see you then."

Chapter Seven

Lauren finally made it into work at noon. Nearly everyone had gone to lunch except the doyenne at the front desk. Lauren skipped up the short marble stairway that led to her office on the mezzanine. She opened the door a crack, scooted in, and shut it quietly behind her.

Since she had left Caleb at the Gramercy, her mind had been in a tumult; her brain was whirling in an agony of effort to figure it all out. Her thoughts were like moths, trapped inside a jar, beating their wings against the glass to try to find freedom once again. She felt as if she were two people: the Lauren she knew who was curator of one of the finest museums in the city, who appeared in *The New York Times* and *Town & Country Magazine*, who shopped at Cartier, who was engaged to one of the most prominent businessmen in the world…and then…then there was this new Lauren—or was it the old Lauren?—pushing up from somewhere she had forgotten existed, dropping in from nowhere. Lauren, the small town girl, drinking beer on the porch steps with the man of her dreams. Lauren, the girl in the gauzy sundresses who mopped old kitchen floors just to see them shine. Lauren, whose unbridled passion was so earthy and vibrant, she could make love to her man, naked, in the grass on a warm, spice-scented summer night.

Lauren sat down heavily in her green velvet upholstered chair and laid her head in her arms on her desk. The sound of the door opening brought her out of her reverie.

"*What* is going on with you!" Kelly's dark, always attractively disheveled curls fairly quivered with indignation.

"What do you mean?" Lauren tried to sound cool.

"You know what I mean!" Kelly bent over the desk, looking into Lauren's eyes. "Something's up. You're three hours late to work! I've been trying to call you. You turned off your phone. You *never* turn your phone off!"

Lauren opened her mouth to speak, but Kelly continued with her tirade. "And don't you lie to *me!* Dennis said you met friends from out of town last night at the Gramercy. What a crock of crap! You don't *have* any friends from out of town. In fact, I'm not sure you have any friends at all. You're either here, or being arm candy for Charles, or you're with me!" As she spoke, Kelly stomped across the floor and picked up the priceless Queen Anne chair that sat by the door. She plunked it in front of Lauren's desk and sat down determinedly on its white satin cushioned seat. Lauren winced when she considered that probably no one had sat in the chair for two hundred fifty years, but there was no stopping Kelly now. "So you tell me—and tell me the truth—*now.*"

Lauren looked up at her friend, her soul in her eyes. "I was with the plumber," she said.

Kelly slapped both hands down on the desk. "*What?*"

"The plumber. I was with Caleb Cochran, the plumber."

"The *plumber?* The plumber from up in New England? The same plumber from the erotic dream?"

Lauren nodded. "Yes."

"Whooooooooeeeeee!" Kelly exclaimed, exhaling loudly. Then she dropped her voice. "What's going on, Lauren?"

"I don't know, Kelly. I can't resist him. He says he's in love with me. He says we're in love. How can you be in love after just a few hours? Oh, what am I going to do?"

Kelly straightened up in the chair and folded her hands primly in her lap. "Well, I guess you *do* have friends from out of town," she murmured. "He says you two are in love? He can't speak for you, Lauren. How do you feel?"

"I can't resist him. He's like a magnet or something. I go all to pieces whenever he touches me. I get all…all *squishy.*"

"Hmm. I'd like to see that. The ice queen melts."

"What am I going to do? It's just a weird physical thing with Caleb. Some chemical attraction or animal instinct."

"Magnets. Chemicals. Animal instinct. Sounds like love to me."

"Be serious."

"I *am!* I'm just trying to get my head around it. Does he know about Charles?"

"Yes," said Lauren, "I told him everything right up front."

"And he's not letting that get in his way," said Kelly, more to herself than to Lauren. "Sounds like a man to me."

"I have to tell him any relationship between us is impossible. I'm marrying Charles."

Kelly mumbled under her breath, "You keep telling yourself that." Then, looking Lauren straight in the eye, she asked more loudly, "Then what's the problem?"

"I've *never* felt like this with anyone before!"

The obvious pain in her friend's voice softened Kelly's attitude. She stood up, walked around the corner of the huge old desk, and hugged Lauren. "Don't worry. Things will work themselves out. You'll know the right thing to do." She sat back down in the Queen Anne chair.

"He's got all kinds of baggage, too. He was married, and his wife died. How do you compete with that? How do you lay a ghost to rest?"

Kelly answered her without joking. She met Lauren's gaze and said, "With honesty. And love." The two friends looked at each other for a long moment. Lauren saw the concern in Kelly's sweet, round face, the gentle brown eyes worried now, the pink lips frowning. Kelly was the first to speak.

"Look, see him here, in your office, tonight. You'll be on your turf. Things will be clearer to you. And it's private. You can say what you want. Only the watchmen will be here. And they won't say anything. And there won't be a bed in the room to — to distract you."

Lauren wasn't so sure. "What if someone does see us and says something to Charles?"

"No one here likes Charles, Lauren," said Kelly bluntly.

"Hey!" Lauren protested. "Charles has been very, very generous to this museum!"

"Oh, please, spare me," scoffed her friend. "It's the easiest thing in the world for Charles to write a check. It's good for the museum, and it seems to impress you, but it doesn't mean we have to like him. He's a stiff." Then Kelly waggled her hands back and forth in mid-air. "Anyway, that's not the point. We're getting off topic. Invite Caleb here. Tell him how you feel and that you're engaged to Charles and you're going through with the wedding. That's your only option." Kelly paused. "If that's the way you feel about things."

"What's so bad about Charles, anyway?"

"Charles eats, sleeps, and breathes power. It's not even the money that interests him. That would be understandable. No, Charles likes the power he has over people. The only people he fraternizes with are his business associates, people he pays, and you. He doesn't have any real friends. He doesn't hang with anyone who isn't dependent upon him for their living."

Lauren knew this was true. "Well, he can't. He doesn't have time for friends."

"He doesn't *want* friends. He doesn't want people to get close to him. It compromises his power over them. I bet you'll find out he'll keep even you out of certain places in his life."

"Charles tells me everything," said Lauren, lying through her teeth. Kelly didn't know about her conversation with Charles the night he left for London.

"That may be so, or not," said Kelly cryptically. "Anyway, in my opinion, Charles sees himself as superior to the rest of humanity, and I think it will lead to trouble for you." Lauren shook her head slowly until Kelly spoke again. "Look, I'm sorry. I didn't mean to come in here to trash Charles. I just want to make sure you're all right and happy with your choices."

"You're entitled to your opinions, Kelly. I'm not saying you're not," Lauren said edgily, "however, I will tell you that I am going through with my marriage to Charles. I...I love him. And we are going to have a wonderful life together. This...this infatuation is just some kind of pre-wedding jitters or something. I'm going to tell Caleb that. He's a reasonable man, and he'll understand. I'm just going to be honest."

"Are you, Lauren?" asked her friend, and before Lauren could answer, Kelly left the room, shutting the door with slightly more force than necessary.

Lauren pushed away from her desk, laid her head back against the cushioning of her chair, and stared at the ceiling. There was really nothing left to do except make sure Kelly could find everything she needed when she took over the job. The day dragged on. Finally, she looked at the clock. It was four; it was time to call Caleb and tell him the change of plans. She was prepared for him to be upset, but he was perfectly calm.

"That's fine," he said. "Just give me the address, and I'll be there. I'd like to see where you work, anyway."

After he hung up, Lauren paced up and down the long room, agitated. Nearly a half-hour passed and she finally called Kelly. "Can you come in here for a moment?"

Kelly came through the door two minutes later. "What?" she said flatly.

"Are you angry with me?"

"Of course not!" said Kelly. "Just exasperated, I guess. I don't know, Lauren. I guess I have to just tell you straight. Nothing like this would have happened if you were truly in love with Charles. Bottom line. That's the fact."

"That's not true!" Lauren argued indignantly. "You can have an attraction to another person, even when you're in love with someone else."

"Not an attraction that's such a *distraction*," persisted Kelly. "And, Lauren, whatever you do with your life, I will support you and be there for you, but I've told you from the start, I don't think Charles is the man for you. But I'm not marrying him; you are. You'd better search your soul, though, and make the right choice."

There was a knock at the door.

"Come in," Lauren called out.

The door opened, and Caleb walked in. He had the dark gray trousers on and a light blue linen shirt. The sleeves were rolled above the elbow, exposing his powerful forearms.

"Oh," he said easily, "I didn't mean to disturb you. I'll wait out here."

"Don't, no, don't worry," said Lauren nervously, coming around the desk. "This is my friend and colleague, Kelly Russell. She was just leaving anyway."

Caleb extended his hand and shook Kelly's politely. "Pleased to meet you."

"The pleasure is mine," said Kelly, smiling. "Well, I'll be going now. Oh, Lauren, could I see you in the hall a minute, please?"

Lauren followed Kelly out of her office, shutting the door behind her. Kelly's hand snaked out, and her fingers closed around Lauren's wrist.

"Is that him?" she hissed in a stage whisper. "Is it? Is that the plumber?"

"Yes, that's the plumber."

"Plumber! He's not a plumber; he's a goddamn movie star! What's going on here! You are *crazy*, girl! You better think about this hard. Call me later." She dropped Lauren's wrist and skipped down the curved marble stairs toward the front door.

Lauren stared after her for a second, then returned to her office. Caleb was standing where she had left him, looking around the opulent room.

"Sorry about that," she apologized.

"Oh, no problem," he said. "Your office certainly isn't like mine." He laughed.

"Well, we use some of the antiques and artwork in the offices. It makes a good impression when we entertain potential supporters. We get very little government funding. We depend mostly on gifts from wealthy donors."

"Hmm," said Caleb. "And you're leaving this job? Don't you like it?"

"Oh, yes, but…Well, sit down, Caleb." She gestured to the Queen Anne chair Kelly had vacated and went around to sit at her own chair.

Caleb remained standing, a small smile on his face. Lauren looked up, surprised. "Something wrong?"

"I'm not a patron," he said. "I'm not going to sit across this massive desk from you to discuss our private lives. Let's sit over here." He pointed to an intimate grouping of a small loveseat and two overstuffed chairs against the far, book-lined wall.

Lauren stood up slowly. "Well, okay. Yes, we can sit over here." Her heart was pounding. She was trying to keep a physical distance from him. She knew what she had to do, and she knew that any touch from him had the power to erode her convictions.

Caleb sat down on the loveseat, legs apart, leaning forward, his arms resting on his knees. Lauren sat in the big chair facing him, her shoes left on the floor as she curled her legs up under her. She pulled at the hem of her khaki skirt, trying to cover more of her shapely legs. Nervously, she fussed with the cuffs of her white blouse. Caleb spoke first.

"I came to ask you to break off your engagement, or at least postpone the wedding. Just until we can figure out what to do. I don't think you're ready to get married, Lauren, at least not to that guy, and I'm in love with you. I'd like to give us a chance."

Lauren looked at him, sitting on the loveseat, the poster boy for masculine virility. She could hardly repress the temptation to reach out and touch him, just to feel those muscles rippling under her fingers whenever he moved. For a moment, her mind stuck and all she could think of was his hands on her throat, stroking her, caressing her breasts, opening all her physical and emotional floodgates. For all his animal strength, he was gentle with his touch, yet he could stir the flame in her until the resulting fire between them transported her to unexplored heights of passion.

"Lauren?" He looked at her with that dear, open and honest face. The green lights in his eyes smoldered now with emotion, with that passion she had come to know so well.

"Caleb," she said, standing back up, "I have to say this. Please hear me out. I've never met anyone like you. I'm drawn to you like a moth to a flame. Everything we did together, I—I have never experienced with anyone, but I'm engaged to someone else. Someone who leads the life I do." Lauren began to pace. Caleb remained motionless on the couch. "I intend to go through with my wedding to Charles. I intend to continue with my plans, with my goals for my life." She turned her back to him, pretending to concentrate on the books on the shelves. She was trying to forget how safe he made her feel. Why couldn't she just let go? She was trying to forget his charming way of speaking so honestly and openly about everything. She was trying desperately to forget what he looked like when he leaned over her in bed. She heard him stand. In a moment, she felt the heat of his body as he stood very closely behind her. His arms went around her.

"You will regret it," he said simply. "Just postpone things. Come back to New England with me. You can stay in your grandmother's house for a while. You said you had such good memories of your time there, that you loved that house."

Lauren melted back into his chest. She felt her resolve weakening, and she struggled to maintain her stand. She said defiantly, "I do love the house, but that was a long time ago! That was the old Lauren. I've made it, Caleb. I'm where I always pictured myself. I worked to get here. Maybe if I did live there and I wasn't engaged, then there would be something between us. I mean, there *is* something between us, but I won't let it interfere. I won't let it happen and spoil my plan!"

He spun her around then, and kissed her hard and long. She slumped forward into his embrace, her lips opening involuntarily, inviting his probing tongue into the warmth of her body. His hand was on the small of her back, then up under the blouse, on her bare skin. She could feel the thrill between her legs as he clasped her tightly.

"I love you, Lauren," he whispered.

Suddenly, she pulled back and away from him. "No, no. Please! Please don't touch me! I love you, too! I do." Tears gathered at the corners of her eyes.

He stood there, motionless, arms at his sides. Her own heart was aching. She had better get this over with. She smoothed the sides of her skirt. "I'm sorry. I'm sorry you came. I wish you hadn't. I want you to leave now. Please." Caleb's image blurred as those tears scalded her eyes. She blinked hard, and they spilled down her cheeks, but she stood her ground, determined.

Caleb gave a little sigh. Lauren saw him recover, and he spoke quietly. "I'm not sorry I came. We had to work it out, and it looks like we have. I'm worried for you, Lauren, but I'm not going to stand here and beg. You know how I feel, and you've made it clear what you want. I see what's important to you, but I've got things that are important to me, too. I've got some standards that I don't compromise. I guess I thought you were that kind of person, too. Actually, I think you are. I think you're afraid to look yourself in the face, to see the real Lauren. For some reason, you think you're more in control behind this smoke screen you've created for yourself. I'll leave, but I will always remember the time we had together. Like I said, I'm pretty good at living with my memories."

"Oh, Caleb," she cried, "I love you, but can't you see how much I would have to change? How much I would have to give up for this love of ours?"

Caleb gave a little, quizzical laugh. "You don't give up anything for true love," he said. "Love gives you everything." He said nothing more. He turned, and with his easy, unconcerned demeanor, left the room, closing the door softly behind him.

Lauren stood, shocked at what she had instigated. She felt as though someone had sucker punched her in the stomach. She felt sick. She heard the soft voice of the watchman, the big front doors open and close. Then silence. She collapsed in a small heap beside the chair and wept.

The surge of emotion exhausted her, and after her sobs had subsided to whimpers, Lauren must have drifted off to a fitful sleep, for she awoke in a panic to the click of her door opening a half hour later. She tried to scramble up from the floor. Her legs were leaden, cramped by the position in which she had crouched in her despair, and she nearly fell over. The room was dark.

"Lauren!"

It was Kelly. "Here I am," Lauren said weakly, pulling herself to her feet. Her face felt puffy, and her eyes burned. Kelly crossed the room and switched on the desk lamp. The two friends stood staring at each other.

Kelly gasped. "Lauren! What happened? I came back to the office to get a paper I forgot and then I heard something in here when I was leaving. Tell me, what went on?"

Lauren sat down heavily in the big chair. "I told Caleb there couldn't be anything between us. I told him. I told him I was going through with my marriage to Charles and that was it."

"Oh, dear," breathed Kelly, sitting on the arm of the chair. She took Lauren's hand in her own. "Did he freak out?"

"No." Lauren sniffled. "No, he didn't, not at all. He just said he was good at living with his memories, and he left. Just walked out."

Kelly sighed. "Well, what did you expect? That's what you wanted, wasn't it?"

Lauren said, "I was fine. I was fine until he left. Then I came undone. I just couldn't stop crying"

"Oh, honey!" Kelly reached around Lauren and gave her a big hug.

"It's better this way, though. Really. This is where I live. This is my life. I'll be fine. Caleb will be fine. It was just a—a kind of glorious interlude." She put her face in her hands.

"I'll say," muttered Kelly. She rose from the chair and went into the small powder room behind Lauren's desk. Inside there was a sink, toilet, and a little shelved alcove in the wall that held Advil, some cosmetics, hair and tooth brushes, and some fluffy small towels and washcloths. Kelly took one of the washcloths and soaked it in cold water, taking it out to Lauren.

"Here, honey," she said. "Wipe your face off with this."

"Do I look bad?"

"I've seen you look better."

"My face feels all puffy. My eyes are burning."

"Hold that cold cloth to your face for a while." Kelly went back into the powder room and returned with two Advil and a small bottle of water. "Take these," she ordered.

Lauren obeyed, sipping pensively on the water, twirling the bottle slowly in her fingers.

"Too bad to end the last day of your job like this," Kelly said.

"Oh, it doesn't matter. I haven't been here in spirit for a while. You've done more work than I have here lately."

"You've been preoccupied," remarked her friend indulgently. "Now pull yourself together, and I'll walk home with you. Or maybe we should call a cab. It looks pretty gloomy out there."

"You don't have to come with me. It's only six blocks. I'll be fine. I'll call you later."

Kelly looked at her, askance. "Well, okay, I guess. I'll get a cab downtown, then. Are you sure you'll be okay?"

Lauren managed a smile. "Yes, I'm sure. And thank you, Kelly. You are a real friend."

They hugged each other closely for a long moment and then left the office, walking down the curved marble steps arm in arm.

Out on the street, it was just getting dark and had started to rain. Kelly hailed a cab.

"You sure?" she said before she got in. "You don't even have an umbrella."

Lauren smiled and nodded. "Yeah. I'll be fine. I'll talk to you later." Maybe the rain would wash away her obvious emotional trauma, she thought, and hide it from the ever-observant eyes of Dennis. She started down the street.

Entering the building, she managed a small smile for the doorman and punched the elevator button. The door slid open, and she went in, feeling the elevator take her up. At last it stopped, at Charles's penthouse private entrance. She got out, and Dennis was standing there.

"Oh, you didn't have your umbrella with you, I see," he chided her. "Here, give me your briefcase and go change before you get a chill."

Lauren had to smile. "You sound like a mother hen, Dennis."

"Just looking after you," he said, smiling back.

Gratefully, she handed him the briefcase. It felt as though it weighed a ton. "I'm fine, really. I'm not that wet. I think I'll just go into the den and have a drink."

"Very well. I'll bring a snack."

She let her thoughts run. *I did what had to be done*, she thought. *I'm engaged. I've established my life. One fling can't jeopardize that. I have to put it in the past and forget about it. At least I know Charles. I don't even know Caleb. Maybe Charles and I just need to be together more, that's all.* She mused, looking out the window at the city, lighting up as dusk fell. She was so engrossed in her thoughts, she jumped when her iPhone rang. She looked at the caller ID and answered immediately.

"Charles!"

"Hello, darling."

"I was just thinking about you!"

"And I, you. That's why I called. I was going to congratulate you on your last day in the salt mines. Did it go well?"

Lauren's voice nearly caught in her throat. "Oh, oh, yes, it did. Thank you, Charles."

"And did they present you with a gold watch?"

Lauren laughed. "No, they didn't. Guess I wasn't there long enough."

"Well, I'm calling to say that I'm taking off from Singapore in a couple of hours."

"Oh, Charles! You're coming home early! I'm so glad. I miss you so much."

"And I miss you, too, darling, but I have a stopover in London. A business colleague here in Singapore is headed to the London office. I thought it would be a good time for me to visit that office too, explain things that transpired here, and then come home to the States. It won't be a long stopover, just a couple of days or so."

"Oh, Charles…"

"Now, this is business. Remember, I promised to devote my whole attention to you and our wedding when I get back."

"I know. Really, I'm fine. It's just…it's just that I miss you."

"I'll be staying at the St. James's, then."

"The same suite as always? We had such a wonderful time there when I went with you last fall."

"That's where I'll be, darling. I'm at the airport now."

"Call when you get to London, please. I miss you so much, Charles."

"I'll call."

"Charles?"

"Yes?"

"I love you."

"Yes, darling, well, get a good night's rest. I'll call when I get to London. Bye for now."

And he hung up. Lauren felt hollow. She wished Charles would just get home. Spending time with him would alleviate this awful void and banish any residual feelings she might harbor for Caleb Cochran.

Lauren listlessly ate the snack that Tina prepared for her. Dennis came in to take the plate away. "Thanks, Dennis. That's all I'm going to eat tonight. I don't feel that well."

"You do look a little drained," said Dennis. "Why don't you just relax here, then. I'll be in my quarters. You can ring me for anything at any time. Would you like some Advil? Pepto-Bismol?"

Lauren smiled wanly. "Oh, no, Dennis, thanks. I guess I'm just tired. I think I'll get into bed, watch a little news, and try to sleep."

"Very well. Feel better. Goodnight."

"Thank you. Goodnight," said Lauren as Dennis left the room. She set her glass on the bar and glanced at the antique clock on the mantel. It was eight o'clock. She heaved a long, shuddering sigh and wandered down the hall to the bedroom. Functioning almost by rote, she went into the bathroom, brushed her teeth and washed her face, undressed, and took a hot shower. After she had let the massaging shower head pummel her tense shoulders for a while, she toweled off and slipped into a long black silk nightgown that hung on the hook on the bathroom door.

Lauren meandered back into the bedroom and stood for a moment, looking out the huge windows with unseeing eyes. Then she pulled the heavy drapes and got into the big bed. She tried to read, but she couldn't focus. She couldn't shake the image of Caleb's back as he left her office. Even in his distress at her refusal to postpone her wedding, he still walked with the confident grace of a healthy young animal. He had not even so much as glanced over his shoulder. Nor should she have expected him to. Their time had been, and now was over. She would never see him again. Her life was here with Charles.

It was then that the thought struck her like an epiphany. That was it! Her life was with Charles! She belonged with him! After all, it was loneliness that fueled her confusion that had led to her careless transgression with Caleb. She needed to be with Charles. Wherever he was. If he was in Singapore, she would be in Singapore. If he went to London, she would go to London. Lauren sat up straight in the bed, excited, and reasoned it out logically. She wouldn't have to trespass on his business life. She could just be there when he finished with the day, no matter how late it was. There was plenty to do in the various cities he frequented, and she had always been good on her own, good company for herself. As long as they were in close proximity. As long as they could spend a bit of each day together.

Lauren leaped out of bed, hurried into her dressing room, and rooted out her carry-on bag. Almost frantically, she began going through her drawers and the clothes that hung at various heights against one whole wall of the room, picking this item and that item, hurriedly folding things and stuffing them into the tote. She would go to London, surprise Charles, and fly home with him. Her mind raced. He would be thrilled. She couldn't wait to see him, looking so handsome in his starched shirts and impeccably tailored suits. His coolness would calm her. She missed his sophistication. She loved to watch people's faces when he entered a room. People fairly danced attendance on him, and he treated them with a detached politeness that maintained his dignity and set him apart.

Lauren sat on the edge of the chaise in her dressing room and hauled her iPad out of her briefcase. Within minutes, she had booked her first class ticket on American Airlines for the next evening. She would arrive at Heathrow at about six a.m. London time. She could get to the hotel before Charles left his room! Her plan was coming together. She smiled to herself as she picked up her phone to call Kelly. Her friend answered.

"Hello."

"Kelly!"

"Lauren, are you all right?"

"Yes, yes, I'm fine. Listen, I've figured it out!"

"Really? And?"

"And I have a plan!"

"I'm waiting."

"Charles and I need to be together on a more consistent basis. You know, like daily, most of the time. For at least part of each day."

"I'm not going to argue with that. That's what most married couples do."

"So, when he has to travel, I'm going to start traveling with him! And here's the clincher! I'm starting tomorrow. I've booked a fare on American, and I'll be there early in the morning to surprise him before he even leaves his hotel room!"

There was dead silence on the phone.

"Kelly?" Lauren asked tentatively.

"I'm here."

"Well, isn't that a good idea?"

She heard her friend draw a deep breath. "Lauren, I don't know. Are you going *to* Charles or *away* from Caleb?"

"Damn!" exclaimed Lauren. "Kelly! Of course I'm going to Charles. The Caleb thing is over. Please, let it drop!"

"I'm sorry," said Kelly. "I just want you to be sure. Also, Charles doesn't seem to be the kind who likes to be surprised."

Lauren snorted through her nose. "Maybe not in a business situation, but it's *me* we're talking about, the person he's going to *marry*."

"I'd still tread a little lightly. It seems to me if this is something Charles wanted, he would have suggested it himself."

"Kelly, I don't know what you're talking about."

"It's just that I… Well…" and here, Lauren was surprised to find that her usually garrulous friend seemed to be at a loss for words. She waited. Kelly continued, "It's just that Charles is a very *specific* person. Think about it, Lauren. He's a cool customer. He keeps everything, *everyone*, in their place. He's very organized in his business dealings, in his thought patterns, in his day-to-day life with you. All I'm saying is that he may not be into surprises, even from you."

Lauren laughed. "That's all you know! He'll be delighted. He always likes to see me. And if he isn't, well, he'll just have to get used to it!"

Kelly let it drop and reverted to more practical matters. "When will you leave?"

"Tomorrow, late afternoon. I'll be in London by six the next morning and at the hotel by seven-thirty. It'll be fun to see his face!"

"I only hope so," said Kelly, giving in at last, having made her point. "Have a good time, Lauren. You deserve it. I'll hold the fort here. Call me and let me know what's happening. Do you have any idea when you'll be back?"

"Oh, I imagine in a couple of days. This was only going to be a stopover for him, anyway," explained Lauren. "We've still got a lot to do to plan the wedding. You better call the girls and remind them there's a fitting next week."

"I'll do that," said Kelly. "Have a safe trip, Lauren. Bye-bye."

"Bye, Kelly. And thanks for being there for me."

"Any time, honey."

Lauren smiled fondly at the phone as she ended the call. She surveyed the start she had made at the packing. "I'll finish up in the morning, and get to airport by two," she said to herself, and she went off to bed.

Lauren lay there in the big bed, pleased with herself at finding such a practical solution to her problem. She was glad that her self-analysis had opened that particular door and she was able to identify what had made her act in such an unorthodox way when she had been in Vermont. The fact that it had been pure loneliness was so simple. Charles had not been around much since he had proposed and she had accepted. After that, his business responsibilities had ramped up considerably and he was away most of the time. In fact, Lauren thought as she lay there, staring at the dark wooden beams that crisscrossed the ceiling, he had been gone almost four of the last six months, mostly to Singapore and London. Of course, she'd had a job, too, which precluded her accompanying him. However, now she was free. She could be there with him, *for* him, and wasn't that what a wife was supposed to do? She closed her eyes and drifted off to sleep.

Lauren looked around her. She was standing in a meadow. The grass was up to her knees. Buttercups and daisies surrounded her. The sun shone brilliantly. Suddenly she saw a figure standing on the edge of the meadow. It approached her. As the figure grew nearer, she could see that it was a man. Nearer still and she could see that it was Caleb, dressed in his customary black T-shirt and jeans. She saw his biceps flex as he raised his arms up and out, reaching.

"Caleb!" she called and tried to run toward him. The buttercups and the daisies seemed to wind themselves around her legs. Instead of parting as she ran through them, they seemed to weave themselves together to make an impenetrable wall. She felt as if she were running through waist-deep water. "Caleb!" she called to him again.

She saw him smile. He was walking faster now, coming closer and closer. She reached out to him, and he was looking beyond her. She could not catch his eye. He didn't acknowledge her, but walked determinedly right past her.

Indignant, Lauren turned to follow him. He was walking into the arms of a girl. A beautiful girl in a white dress, her long thick dark hair shining in the sunlight as she raised her lips to be kissed and wrapped her arms around him.

Lauren tried to run faster, harder, but she was held fast by the plants. "No!" she cried. "No! No! Here I am! Kiss me! Kiss me!"

Finally, they turned to face her. They stood holding hands, smiling at her. She could not move for the grass and plants around her feet.

The girl approached her then. She came very close, a wide, bright smile on her face. Her eyes were large and dark. They sparkled as she spoke to Lauren. "I will give you my wedding veil," said the girl happily. "Yes, that's what I'll do. You need it. I will give you my wedding veil." She lifted her arms, and in her hands were what seemed to be yards and yards of gauzy white, cloud-like material. She fluffed it out and it settled heavily over Lauren's head, then over her face.

Suddenly, she couldn't see. She gasped. It was hard to breathe. She tried to scream, but couldn't. She tried to tear the veil from her face, but it clung even harder, resisting her efforts. The girl was laughing happily. Lauren couldn't breathe. She was having trouble seeing.

Lauren woke with a start. The sheet was over her face. Her heart was beating as though it would come right out of her chest. She could feel her temples, the back of her neck, and down her cleavage soaked with salty sweat. In a frenzy, she tore at the sheet, ripping it away from her face. Tears streamed out of the corners of her eyes, although she wasn't crying. Her mouth was dry. Shakily, she climbed out of bed and went into the bathroom. She leaned on the sink, staring at her reflection in the mirror. Her face was pale. At last she could feel her heartbeat slow, her body cool a little.

Lauren knew what that dream was. She had dreamed that Caleb's dead wife was not dead. She had dreamed that Caleb had not even seen her, even as she called out to him in her dream. And the action of the dead wife, giving her the wedding veil. So frightening. Lauren could still feel the gauzy film as it settled over her like a shroud.

Still shivering, Lauren wandered back to bed, slipped under the covers, and straightened out the sheet. As a little girl in her grandmother's house, Lauren would sometimes have nightmares. She could remember her grandmother coming in when she cried out, sitting on the edge of the bed, comforting her. Her grandmother had always told Lauren that dreams were the true expressions of feelings you kept repressed in your conscious mind. Dreaming, Gramma had said, was your mind working things out. They were representative of things you either hoped would not happen or things you wished would happen. Which was this, she wondered.

Lauren did not sleep the rest of the night. She dozed fitfully off and on and finally got up at five o'clock. *Oh, well,* she thought groggily. *All the better. I'll sleep on the plane, and the flight will go faster.*

Lauren showered, applied her make-up, and dressed in a summer khaki shirt dress. She slipped her feet into little gold flats and finished packing. There was no reason to wake Dennis any earlier than usual. She didn't have to be at the airport until three, and she would probably go there a little bit earlier. Even though she had booked a first class ticket, which allowed her first-on/first-off privileges, Lauren liked to try to relax before any flight. A cocktail in the VIP lounge would allow her to settle her thoughts. She had taken the American Airlines Flight 100 aboard the Boeing 777 to London before. Being a morning person anyway, it agreed with her, arriving usually on time at six-thirty the next morning.

It would be Sunday morning when she landed in the U.K. Charles would not be hurrying to any breakfast meetings. She smiled to herself as she opened the door to the bedroom. In the nether regions of the penthouse, she could hear someone was awake. It was either Dennis or Tina. Lauren wandered back through the living and dining rooms to the airy kitchen. After the small study, the kitchen was Lauren's favorite room in the penthouse, although she didn't spend much time there. It was a bright, sunny room, sleeker and brighter than the rest of the home. The floor was tiled in paving stones. The cabinetry was white, and the counter tops, except for the chopping block in the island, were black marble. The appliances were all state-of-the-art stainless steel. China and glassware sparkled and winked behind glass-doored cabinets in the butler's pantry. Attached to the kitchen was a small breakfast nook with big windows that looked out over the park. Whenever she woke before Charles, or when she was there alone, Lauren liked to drink her coffee here early in the morning and watch the city ramp up to its daily fervor of activity.

"Good morning, Tina," she said as she came through the swinging doors.

"Oh, good morning, Lauren," said Tina, reaching for a cup. "Coffee this morning, or latte?"

"Coffee, please," she replied, taking her seat at the small table. She watched as Tina, a stout, pleasant-looking woman with short thick salt-and-pepper hair, poured the fragrant liquid into the cup. She set it before Lauren, then put the crystal sugar bowl and creamer in front of her. Lauren stirred her coffee, feeling the heat travel up the silver spoon. She raised the cup to her lips and sipped. The hot liquid felt so good going down. There was nothing like the taste of the first sip of coffee in the morning. Without warning, her mind wandered back to that magical morning in New England when she and Caleb had drunk their coffee together after that first amazing night in each other's arms.

Quickly, Lauren put her cup down. Her hands had started to shake. She fought to crush the thought, the image of him that had suddenly come, uninvited, into her brain to taunt her.

"Would you like something to eat this morning?" Tina asked.

"Yes, yes, I would, Tina. Thank you," said Lauren quickly. She had better put something in her stomach. Airplane food, even in first class, was not the best.

Within ten minutes, by the time Lauren needed a refill of her coffee, Tina had set fluffy French toast, bacon, and sliced cantaloupe in front of her. Lauren poured the maple syrup over the sugar-dusted toast and ate it with relish. It did make her feel better. She took a final sip of coffee and stood up. "Thank you for breakfast, Tina," she said. "It was delicious. I'm going…I'm going to visit friends tonight, so I won't be home until Monday."

"Where are you going?" It was Dennis. He had just come into the kitchen. Something happened in that moment. For the first time since she had known him, Lauren felt uneasy. Almost as if she didn't quite trust him. She decided not to tell either of them her plans. Dennis might have an attack of loyalty or brotherhood, call Charles, and ruin her surprise. There was nothing to confirm this suspicion; it was just a feeling she had.

"Oh," she lied, "I'm going to visit Kelly's family in Connecticut. We'll be back on Monday morning. I'm going to finish packing." She left the room quickly.

As Lauren tended to the last details of her packing, she wondered why she couldn't shake this slightly queasy feeling of nervousness. And why her sudden distrust of Dennis? Lauren shook her head as if to physically expel the feeling. She zipped her tote and went through her checklist one last time. It was such a bother now to travel, especially overseas. Everything had to be in little plastic bags. Everything, including the passenger, was scrutinized intensely and subject to so many rules and regulations, Lauren could not keep track. Oh well, she was traveling light, just bringing a couple of changes of clothes, an extra pair of shoes, and her make-up. She would buy personal toiletries when she got there. It was such a pain to pack them.

She brought out her large Tory Burch bag and stuffed it with her passport, credit cards, cash, a couple of pieces of costume jewelry, hairbrush, lipstick, phone charger, iPad, and a paperback mystery. She sighed. "Ready," she said aloud, looking at her watch. It was ten-thirty in the morning. The hours crawled by. She skipped out once to buy a few magazines to read at the airport and on the plane. She tried to watch television. She Facebooked all her friends. Just as she thought she might go crazy, Dennis stuck his head in the study door.

"It's two o'clock, Lauren. Would you like me to call a cab now to take you to Tribeca?"

"Oh, yes, Dennis, please," she said eagerly. Her plan had kicked into action. She was feeling much better. Tribeca was where Kelly lived with her boyfriend, Brian, in their loft.

Albert called up from the lobby. The car was there. Lauren grabbed up her purse and went through the foyer to the elevator door. Dennis followed, carrying the tote. She found that she had to subdue her enthusiasm. Dennis might grow suspicious to think that she was this excited to be going to Connecticut with Kelly, where she had been so often before. Lauren couldn't lose the feeling that Dennis would call Charles if he suspected anything. Kelly's words echoed in her mind. "Charles doesn't strike me as the type who likes to be surprised." *Be that as it may,* thought Lauren determinedly, *I will surprise him, and Kelly will just have to eat her words!*

Dennis walked her out of the building. The driver opened the back door, and Lauren scooted in. Dennis smiled and waved to her. "Safe travels," he called as the car pulled away from the curb.

Once in the car, Lauren said to the driver, "American Airlines terminal, JFK, please."

"I thought the dude said Tribeca," grunted the driver.

"He got it wrong," said Lauren.

It was Saturday afternoon, and the airport was a crowded mess. "Good thing we left a little early," the driver said.

"Yes, it is," replied Lauren. "Look at this traffic!"

"Not to worry, miss," the driver replied. "We'll get through to the American Airlines terminal in plenty of time. Your flight's at six, right?"

"That's correct," said Lauren. She was grateful for the experienced driver who slipped expertly in and out of the confusion of cars, buses, and cabs to get to her terminal. He pulled up to the door and helped her out, then retrieved her travel tote from the trunk.

"Have a good flight," he said as she collected her things.

"Thank you, I will," Lauren said, smiling. She paid him and made her way into the terminal.

When Lauren traveled with Charles, they always took the private corporate jet, but at least when she had to fly commercial, she could fly first class. The best thing about flying first class, reflected Lauren, was the absence of lines. She quickly checked in at the first class desk, then made her way through security. With only two men ahead of her, Lauren went through the check-in in record time and made a beeline for the Terminal 8 mezzanine and the Admirals Lounge.

A tall, graceful woman graciously greeted her just inside the door, checked her membership, and opened the inner door for her. Lauren found a quiet corner and sat down where she could check her email and read for a while. A waitress came by.

"May I get you anything, ma'am?" she asked, smiling.

"Oh, yes, thank you," replied Lauren. "I'd like a Bloody Mary, please. Oh, and could you bring me a turkey sandwich, please? Just turkey, lettuce, and mayonnaise."

"Certainly, ma'am. And the vodka would be?" acknowledged the woman.

"Grey Goose, please."

"Very well."

Lauren opened her iPad. In ten minutes, the server had returned with the drink and sandwich on a small silver tray. "Anything else I can get you?"

"No, no, thank you," said Lauren. She realized now how hungry she was. She bit into the sandwich and took a sip of the Bloody Mary. Lauren always drank Bloody Marys when she had to fly. The spiciness of the drink settled her stomach, and the vodka relaxed her. She took a deep breath. Soon she would be with Charles. This was the way things should be.

By the time Lauren had finished her drink and sandwich and had dashed off an email to Kelly, they were calling her flight number for first class passengers. She gathered her purse and tote and walked out to board the plane. Lauren settled into her ample seat, letting the steward stow her carry-on. She looked out the window across the tarmac. She could see into the terminal, see the lines of passengers slowly boarding the Boeing 777. Off to the side, she saw a young couple. The man was dark haired and handsome. The girl was blond and wore her hair twisted in a clip. They were facing each other, holding hands. Even through the airplane window, the distance across the tarmac, and the huge windows of the terminal, their mutual desire was easy to see. The man bent forward and kissed the girl fully on the mouth. She reciprocated and embraced him around the neck, holding him close. His arms went around her.

Without warning, Lauren's eyes filled with tears, and she had to look away. Memories of Caleb flooded her thoughts. She leaned back in her seat with an audible groan as she recalled those nights of passionate lovemaking. She closed her eyes. His gaze bore its way through her memory until she could see those flashing green sparkles of his hazel eyes in her own mind's eye. She had the overwhelming urge to sit with him again on the steps of the porch and just listen to him talk. The timbre of his voice had been so soothing, and his quick smile had warmed her soul. In her mind, Lauren could feel the touch of his hand. His hands, strong and callused by work, and yet so gentle they could raise her desire with feather-light caresses wherever they touched her. They were hands you could trust your life to. That's how she had felt. *This is what I want.* She gave a little gasp.

"Are you all right, miss?" It was the steward.

Lauren's eyes popped open and a tear slid down her cheek. Embarrassed, she quickly wiped it away. "Oh," she stammered, "Oh, I'm fine. Just a little nervous, I guess. Could I please have a Bloody Mary?"

"Most certainly," said the steward sympathetically.

While he mixed her drink in the first class galley, Lauren turned her head to look out the window again, but all the people had boarded. The couple wasn't there. She sighed. A good thing. She didn't know why she would want to torture herself like this. She needed something to banish these thoughts or she would go crazy by the time she reached the other side of the Atlantic.

The steward returned with her drink.

"Thank you so much," said Lauren gratefully.

"No problem at all," the steward replied. "If you want anything at all, just let me know. We should be airborne in about twenty minutes." He smiled kindly at her and disappeared down the aisle.

Twenty minutes. *There's time to call Charles,* thought Lauren, *just speak to him. It will make me feel better.* She took her phone out of her bag and punched in Charles's number. It went straight to voice mail. Lauren automatically calculated the time in her head. It was about eleven-thirty at night in London. Charles was either out where he couldn't take a private phone call, or, if it had been a particularly grueling day of meetings, he might be sleeping. Lauren decided he must still be out because he always called her before he went to bed. This was good, because she could give another try just before take-off.

She waited impatiently, sipping her drink and watching the crew. Lauren was an experienced traveler, and she recognized take-off as imminent. The flight attendants were putting things in order. The captain and the co-pilot were seated in the cockpit. Now the steward who had brought her her drink went to the cockpit door. The captain stood up, said something to him, and closed the door. Lauren heard a series of locks click. It was her last chance to call Charles before they were airborne.

This time he answered. "Yes?"

Lauren was delighted. "Charles! I just had to talk to you."

"Is everything all right?"

"Yes, I just miss you. Are you all right? You sound out of breath."

Charles's voice lowered. "No, I'm fine. Just running out from a late dinner meeting back to the hotel."

The flight attendants were checking all the overhead compartments. The friendly steward winked at Lauren and made a flip with his hand, signaling her to cut the phone call. Lauren smiled back at him.

"Charles, I'm…I'm on way to Kelly's in the countryside. I've hit some traffic here. Can I call you back?" There was silence, followed by a rustling sound. "Charles? Are you there?"

"Yes, yes, I'm here. What did you say?"

Lauren was irked. Something was taking his attention. "Never mind, Charles. Just wanted to say hi and I miss you. I'll see you soon."

"Fine, darling, fine. I'll call you later. Bye now." And he hung up. Lauren thought that was strange, but he was probably with a group of people, trying to get back to the hotel. He really should take better care of himself when he traveled. Well, when she got there, she would see to that. She would make him realize that traveling with her was much more pleasant than leaving her at home.

"Flight crew prepare for take-off," the captain's voice announced over the intercom. Lauren watched as the crew went through the usual precautionary instructions, checked the seat trays and seat belts, and strapped themselves into their own seats. She leaned back and closed her eyes as the engines hummed and they taxied out onto the tarmac. The engine noise escalated as the plane gained speed, and then they were airborne, heading out across the Atlantic. Soon she would be far away from Caleb Cochran and seductive summer nights.

Chapter Eight

The Boeing 777 droned across the Atlantic like some huge, migrating bird headed for home. Lauren tried to sleep, and she dozed on and off, but thoughts of Caleb Cochran popped up randomly, disturbing her rest. She could not get over the feeling that she needed to talk to him one more time. For some reason, even though she meant to break it off with him unequivocally, it did not make her feel as free and as powerful as she had imaged it would. Instead, there was a nagging feeling of something unfinished hanging over her head, along with an unpleasant void in her heart, as though she had lost something irreplaceable.

Lauren straightened up in her seat, determined to banish any thoughts of Caleb by meticulously reviewing all the details of her upcoming nuptials. She leaned forward and took the wedding file from her purse. She smiled as she opened it. It was a small yellow folder stretched to capacity with notes, newspaper clippings, schedules, appointments, plans, and the names and numbers of everyone the wedding planner had on board.

Lauren started with her dress. It was strapless with a tulle ball gown skirt over an organza insert. The fitted bodice was appliqued Chantilly lace, and the waist was girdled with a wide grosgrain ribbon. A twelve-foot tulle train embroidered with Swarovski crystals trailed out behind the dress. It was beyond expensive, which made Lauren proud. Money was no object, Charles had said. The eight bridesmaids would wear simple, strapless deep purple satin mermaid dresses, which flared out gracefully around their feet. Charles and the eight groomsmen would wear black tuxedos because there was nothing more handsome on a man, Lauren thought.

The rehearsal night dinner was to be held at the Plaza. It would be a much smaller affair than the wedding, no more than sixty people, only close friends and family. The menu was still up in the air. Lauren wanted something simple, so that people would not be distracted by what they were eating and could enjoy each other. The wedding planner on the other hand was insisting on escargot with burgundy wine reduction and shrimp sautéed in basil sauce to start, followed by two entrees. There would be jumbo Portobello ravioli tossed with mozzarella and artichokes for the vegetarians, or Chateaubriand. Dessert was to be chocolate pyramids filled with raspberries and apricots and served on little gold plates. It would be spectacular.

Fully six hundred fifty guests were expected at the ceremony the next evening, among them both New York senators, several members of Congress, Michael Jordan, Michael Douglas and Catherine Zeta-Jones, Jay Leno, Patti LuPone, and Mick Jagger to name a few of the popular notables.

The wedding and reception were to be held in the ballroom at the museum. Lauren had chosen a woodland fantasy theme. The high ceilings were to be swathed with deep purple velvet studded with tiny lights, to simulate the star-strewn night sky. A huge round chandelier, custom made for the event, would look just like the real moon. Live trees in pots, sprinkled with more tiny lights, would be brought in and placed in strategic arrangements like thickets around the huge room. At the far end of the hall, through a fabricated tree-lined path, was the tinkling waterfall, all pumps and pipes hidden, of course, in front of which Lauren and Charles would become man and wife. It would be the most magnificent wedding anyone had ever seen. Lauren's brow furrowed a little when she recalled her mother's reaction after Lauren had described the event to her.

Immediately following her engagement, Lauren had made a special trip to San Francisco, rented a car, and driven up into the bucolic little valley where her parents lived. Three dogs had rushed out to greet her. Her mother was planting the garden, and her father was constructing another bank of solar panels. They were thrilled to see her. Lauren loved them both very much, but their hippy lifestyle had always rather embarrassed her. Their activist days primarily behind them, Lauren's mother concentrated on her pottery and her father his music. To her, their life was so quiet and boring, Lauren wondered about their sanity. She preferred the intensity of city life. When Lauren's grandmother had been alive, her parents had visited her in the city or she would take a quick trip up to New England to see them, but now they didn't get back east any more often than Lauren went west.

Lauren had showed them the ring and told them about Charles. They had met him once, when Lauren was first dating him. They'd oohed and aahed appropriately, in a somewhat detached manner, over the ring. Then Lauren had described the wedding plans. Lauren's mother had laughed spontaneously, right out loud.

"Oh dear, honey! What a waste of effort! Why don't you just opt for the real thing and find a place in the country to get married?"

Lauren shut the wedding file and settled back in her seat. It was that hippy mentality again. She closed her eyes and began to drift between waking and sleep. Her thoughts began to wander.

I wonder what kind of wedding Caleb had? Probably small town bourgeois. In the village church with the reception at the American Legion hall in town. Catered by the same guy who did the school lunches. That laughing girl in the white dress in the picture in his kitchen. Undoubtedly his wife. She was very beautiful. Had that been her wedding dress? He must have loved her very much. Could he ever move on? Had she been buried in that dress? And her wedding ring. Had she been buried wearing her wedding ring?

The vision of a disembodied skeletal hand, a gold ring rattling on one of its fingers, reached out toward Lauren through the void of her subconscious.

"Excuse me, miss?"

Lauren's eyes popped open. It was the steward, bending over her with a plate of breakfast in his hand. Her heart was pounding. She realized she must have fallen asleep.

"You cried out, miss," he said gently. "It's breakfast time, though. Here is an omelet and some coffee for you." He was sympathetic, but totally professional, sparing her any embarrassment. He set the plate and utensils on the tray and went about his business.

Lauren straightened up in her seat. Coffee would do her good. They were probably about an hour or so out from London. Soon she would be with Charles, and these dreams and dark thoughts would disappear. She sighed and stirred the cream and sugar into her coffee.

They were closer than Lauren had thought. Within minutes of her finishing her coffee and deciding to leave the omelet untouched, the steward came sweeping through, picking up the plates, speaking to each first class passenger. "We are entering our descent and will be preparing for landing in a short while." Lauren's ears popped as she felt the plane slide easily down into lower altitudes. The steward was speaking over the address system. "We will be landing at Heathrow, London, England, in a few minutes. Please see that your trays are in the locked position and your seats are upright with seat belts securely fastened. All handbags and packages should be stowed under the seat in front of you. All electronic devices should now be turned off. Thank you for your cooperation."

Lauren did it all automatically. She felt the plane shift as the engines adjusted speed for landing. She heard the click and slow grind of the landing gear dropping into proper position. She glanced out the window. Bits of gray cloud flew past the window, and through the fog she could just glimpse the countryside surrounding the airport. She heard the captain say, "Flight attendants, take your seats for landing, please."

Now the plane was descending fast. Any visibility from Lauren's point of view was lost in the morning mists that habitually enfolded all of London every day at this time. She could not tell how close they were to landing. Then she heard the flaps on the wings dragging against the pull of the sky. The engines subtly changed tone once again, and finally she felt the tires on the tarmac and the plane braking to come to a taxi speed.

The steward's voice was again on the address system. "Folks, we've landed at Heathrow, London, England. We hope you enjoyed your flight, and we appreciate your patronage. Please remain seated until the aircraft has come to a complete halt. Thank you for flying with us."

This was the hardest time for Lauren. All she wanted to do was jump up, grab her bag and her tote, and head out for the St. James's Hotel. She knew she would still have to make it through customs, and these days, the customs officers didn't care whether someone was in a hurry or not. They stoically and carefully did their job.

At last the plane came to a full stop at the terminal. Lauren unbuckled her seat belt and collected her things. She was the first person in line as the steward was opening the door.

He smiled at her. "In a hurry, miss?"

Lauren smiled back. "I'm meeting my fiancé."

There was concern in his voice as he said, "Oh, I would have guessed something else." But then he laid a hand on her arm and remarked honestly, "How nice. Have a good time in London. Bye-bye."

"Thank you," said Lauren, and she exited the plane.

Heathrow was a huge airport and very busy even though it was only six in the morning. Forty-five minutes later, Lauren was finally through customs and on her way in search of a cab. She followed the Ground Transportation signs and found the line of London cabs idling outside, waiting for fares. A driver jumped out of his vehicle.

"Right here, miss. Where to?"

"St. James's Hotel. Near Mayfair."

"I'm familiar," he said, taking her bags and putting them in the back. Lauren climbed into the funny little car, and they were off.

"Traffic's not too bad this time in the morning. We'll be there in no time."

He was right. At 7:25, he was pulling up to the front entrance of the magnificent St. James's Hotel. The doorman opened the cab door, and Lauren climbed out. The cabbie handed her her tote, and she tipped him generously. "Thank you, ma'am," he said, tipping his hat. "And enjoy your stay."

Lauren was smiling in happy anticipation as she entered the lobby. She knew just where to go, and it was a good thing. If the concierge got wind of a visitor or was even asked about a certain guest, that guest would be notified instantly. They were very protective of their clientele.

Charles always stayed in the deluxe suite on the fifth floor. Lauren slipped unobtrusively into the elevator. Suddenly, she felt lighter, more cheerful and carefree. At last she would be where she was supposed to be. At Charles's side. She couldn't wait to put her arms around him and kiss him and tell him how much she loved him.

The elevator stopped, and she stepped out into the lovely wide corridor. It was very quiet. Sunday morning, after all. Her footfalls were totally absorbed by the plush carpeting as she approached the door to the suite. Mischievously, she stood off to the side of the viewing port and knocked on the door. There was no immediate answer. She could hear voices—the television. Charles would be watching the news, probably still in bed. She knocked harder. Now she heard his voice.

"That would be room service." Charles must really be lonely, thought Lauren. It wasn't like him to talk to himself. She could hear him unfastening the bolts, and then the door swung open. Charles stood there in his knee length silk dressing robe.

"Charles! Surprise!"

For the past two years, Lauren had spent every moment she could with Charles. She had experienced his array of emotions. Anger, affection, humor, impatience. He faced them all with a cool detachment, his face impassive save for the slight smile that covered his actual thoughts. So Lauren was completely unprepared for Charles's reaction.

All the color drained from his face. His lips went white. He opened his mouth, shut it, and then opened and shut it again. He made some kind of sound. Then he stepped into the hall and closed the door. He grabbed Lauren's upper arm with uncharacteristic force.

"What are you doing here?" he said in a hoarse voice.

Lauren was shocked. It was obvious he was not happy to see her. She was so distressed by his actions, she couldn't speak.

"I have a breakfast meeting going on here. I thought I told you that my business life was to have nothing to do with our personal lives!"

Lauren struggled to fight back tears, to find her voice. "A breakfast meeting in your dressing gown? Charles! I came to surprise you. I—I thought you'd be happy." She had never been so confused.

Charles's grip tightened uncomfortably around her arm. Instinctively, she drew back. Charles opened his mouth to speak, but the door clicked behind him. He dropped Lauren's arm.

"Darling?" Lauren heard the soft voice from inside the room. It echoed in her head. Somebody else was calling Charles "darling." All at once she knew. If someone had hit Lauren in the chest with a sledgehammer, it couldn't have stunned her more. She stood as one turned to stone, not thinking, just watching this unimaginable scene unfold before her. She knew she was being sucked into some appalling drama, and she could do nothing about it. She looked at Charles. He met her gaze, but he offered nothing.

The woman who belonged to the voice stepped out into the hall. She was tall and obviously of mixed Asian and European descent. She wasn't young, much closer to Charles's age than Lauren's, but she was exquisitely beautiful. She was dressed in a long black silk peignoir. Her jet black hair cascaded down her back. Her skin was ivory-colored, and her slightly tilted dark eyes shone with the understated luminescence of highly polished ebony. She wore a strand of graduated pearls around her long neck.

She alone seemed to be in control. She gazed at Lauren. "Is this the girl?" she asked simply with no particular emphasis in her words.

Charles nodded. "This is Lauren Smith. Lauren, this is Sally Chong."

"Please," said Sally Chong, "come in. We shall discuss this. You should understand." She didn't smile, but her suggestion was not unfriendly.

Lauren's first reaction was to slap Charles as hard as she could and turn and run out of the St. James's Hotel as fast as she could, but she was recovering her dignity. The feeling was returning to her limbs, and she felt her face cool. Charles gestured with his hand. Still in shock, Lauren walked ahead of him into the room.

"Please," said the woman again. "Sit."

"I'd rather not," said Lauren stiffly, finding her voice at last. She set her tote down slowly and stood, as if trapped in some nightmare.

Charles went to the bar and poured himself a Bloody Mary out of the crystal pitcher. "Would you like a drink, Lauren?" he asked her.

Suddenly, Lauren's shock was gone, and her anger replaced it with a vengeance. "No!" she said viciously. "No! I do not want a drink, Charles. I want you to tell me what's going on! Who is this woman? It's obvious this is no breakfast meeting!" Lauren whirled to face Sally Chong, who was sitting comfortably on the pale blue sofa, seemingly completely unruffled. "Who are you? Tell me. Tell me now!"

It was Charles who spoke. "Sally and I have been friends for years. She is a business woman from Singapore. We've been working on a merger for quite some time. A communications conglomerate. And no, our relationship is not platonic and hasn't been for years, but it had — *has* — nothing to do with our relationship. Sally has always known about you and my plans for our marriage. I wish you'd not made the choice you did, Lauren, to come here. If I had wanted you to accompany me, I would have asked you to come. I didn't mean for you to get hurt or discover something you're not sophisticated enough to accept."

His last statement put Lauren right over the edge of her emotional cliff. Psychologically, she jumped, and in that split second, she felt as though she had landed in a clean, clear place. Suddenly, she was devoid of all feeling, and she gave way to her logic and reason. She stood straight and strong. She was able to speak without hysteria or tears.

"I thought I was sophisticated, Charles, but it appears, according to your standards, I'm not. I don't care. Whatever I am, I can tell you I am horrified by this. *Horrified.* In any relationship, there are deal breakers, and this is mine. Not so much the infidelity — " and here Lauren paused to give her words emphasis " — which is terribly common of you, Charles. What is disgusting to me is the *coldness* and *acceptance* of it as…as simply a part of doing business. I *will* not, *can* not, be a part of it for one moment longer. Being in this room with you is making me sick. It's a sick and twisted situation." Lauren struggled with her ring, wrenching it off her sweating finger. She held it up for a moment. "Find something else to do with this, Charles. When we were standing out there in the hall, I wanted to ask you why, or get an explanation, but I don't really care. There's a certain power I find from finally realizing I don't care. So you can continue working on your merger for as long as you want to, but you will not see me again. Ever." She placed the ring on the coffee table, which was the nearest piece of furniture to her. "Please don't come back to New York for two more days. It will take me that long to remove my things from your place. I ask that you respect me that much, at least."

Charles spoke, smoothly, coolly. "You gave up the apartment in Murray Hill, Lauren. Where will you go?"

Lauren stared at him for a moment before she spoke. "That is of no concern to you."

"I have several properties around the city. Nice properties. Please, relocate to one of these. A phone call from me, and you can move in. We can discuss things later."

It was all taking a very surreal feel. Lauren struggled to keep her mind focused. "Charles, stop talking. You sound like some sort of old movie. I am perfectly capable of taking care of myself. I am no longer a part of your life and certainly not your responsibility."

Then it was Sally Chong who spoke. Her voice was calm and melodious. She spoke with a British accent as she met Lauren's eyes. "Charles, darling, would you pour me a drink, and one for Miss Smith, also. Miss Smith, I ask you to listen to what I have to say."

"I said I will not have a drink," Lauren repeated emphatically. "And what could you possibly have to say to me that I would want to hear?"

Sally Chong stood up and took the drink that Charles handed her. Without taking her eyes off Lauren, she sipped it thoughtfully. Then she spoke in her clear and musical voice, walking slowly, elegantly up and down the room.

"I am surprised by your emotional outburst. Charles has always portrayed you as a level-headed pragmatist, wanting the same lifestyle he keeps, interested in being on top of the social heap, so to speak, and representing his best interests on the social scene. Charles has always wanted a child, also, and this is something I cannot provide for him. I am not interested in marriage or child-bearing. You, however—" and here Sally Chong paused and looked at Lauren critically, up and down. "You however," she continued, "would probably have no objection to conceiving and bearing a child or two. Of course, we would see to it that you have plenty of help to raise the children. You would not be inconvenienced. I urge you to reconsider Charles's offer of marriage. I can assure you that he does care for you and I would in no way interfere with your life in your home. Charles and I would simply continue the way we always have, these twenty-three years. Think it over, Miss Smith. You have everything to gain. Everything. Including any relationship you might desire outside the marriage as long as it did not interfere with the marriage. You would have all the benefits of being the wife of one of the most powerful businessmen in the world. What could possibly be more beneficial to a young woman like yourself than such an offer as this? Don't be naïve, Miss Smith. Most men have mistresses. The advantage to us would be that you accept this arrangement from the beginning. We would all be equals and share in the benefits it would provide for us. And, to set your mind at ease, all this could certainly be spelled out in a new prenuptial agreement."

Lauren stood there, momentarily dumbfounded. She struggled to get her mind around this preposterous situation. It was so obtuse; she had to suppress a sudden urge to laugh out loud. Perhaps Charles had assessed her properly. Perhaps her priorities had been focused on the wrong goals for the wrong reasons. Otherwise, he would not have described her thus to Sally Chong.

Lauren turned to Charles. Suddenly, he looked small and old, withering in the shadow of Sally Chong. Then Lauren looked at the tall beautiful woman sipping from her crystal glass. They certainly deserved each other, she thought. She said, without looking at him, "Charles, I will take that drink." There was always time to set oneself right, she thought, her mind clear at last.

Charles poured her a glass. Lauren took it and said with a dignity based in the honesty that had been sleeping at the core of her soul, "I do have something to say. Please sit down." She gestured to the couch. Sally Chong sat gracefully while Lauren took the chair opposite her. Charles wandered across the room, drink in hand, and stood with his back to the windows, facing her.

Lauren sipped her drink and then spoke. "You are cutting a business deal. It doesn't surprise me. I should have known it of you, Charles. It's just the way you see things. Your offer might be acceptable to another person, but I can tell you without reservation, it is totally unacceptable to me." Now her words came from a place within her she had forgotten existed. "It has nothing to do with sophistication. The time when women of our cultural background were forced to tolerate the infidelities of their husbands is over. I assume I am speaking about something that neither of you understand, but speak I will, just to bring closure for myself. Just to know no one can stop me from speaking. You see, I was raised to develop my ideals and stand up for them. One of my ideals, and the example I grew up with, is a loving marriage. I believe in love. Moreover, I believe in love at first sight and the most absurd notion, to you two, of true love. I will not abandon my ideals for anything. Not for penthouses or cars or careers or—" and here she looked at Sally Chong "—or diamonds and pearls. And when I choose to have children, I will raise them in the same way. Because *that* is power, Charles. You—both of you—have no power over me. Nothing you do or say can compromise my values and my ideals. I am a free person. My life will unfold before me in whatever way it will, but I will be free to make my own way, whatever that may be." Lauren set her glass down beside the ring on the coffee table. "I will never see you again, Charles."

There was nothing more to say. Neither Charles nor Sally Chong made a move or said anything. Lauren turned, picked up her carry-on bag, and walked out the door, shutting it quietly behind her. As though she was in perfect control, she made her way down to the concierge desk.

"Could you please call the car to take me to Heathrow? International flights."

"Certainly, miss." And the concierge picked up the telephone.

It was not until she was safely in the car and headed for the airport that the wave of nausea washed over her and she began to shake. She laid her head back against the seat and closed her eyes, gripping the door handle to steady herself.

The driver must have seen her in the rear-view mirror because he said, "Are you ill, ma'am?"

"Oh, no, thank you, I'll be fine. Just have to get on that plane and get home."

"Home's the place, ma'am."

Lauren felt her eyes burn with unshed tears and fought them back. He was right. Home was the place, but for Lauren, where was that?

The trip to the airport, then to the counter to secure her last minute ticket, moving through the line at the security checks, and finally boarding the plane was all a blur to her. She did it all automatically, feeling nothing. It wasn't until she was seated in the plane, seat belt tightened around her, that she suddenly felt like she had been mixed up in something very dirty and sordid. The sight of Charles in his dressing robe and that strange woman, so secure in her own dishabille, had made her physically ill. She asked the flight attendant for a ginger ale and sipped it slowly, crunching the ice and letting the cold shards slip down her throat.

She hardly noticed the take-off, but about halfway into the trip, she did manage to fall into a fitful sleep, waking some hours later under the gentle touch of the flight attendant who said quietly, "We'll be starting our descent into JFK now."

It was a repeat of her actions of a lifetime ago as she went back through customs and security, picked up her tote, put her shoes back on, and found herself standing alone in the terminal. She walked out to hail a cab, feeling as though she could barely put one foot after the other. She glanced up at a clock on the wall. It was twelve-thirty on Sunday, New York time. There was only one thing she could do now.

Walking out to the curb, she put out her arm. A yellow cab swept up and stopped, New York style, inches from her toes. She opened the back door, got in, and gave the driver Kelly's address in Tribeca. Hopefully her best friend would be home. She brought out her phone to call and make sure.

"Hello," answered her friend.

"Kelly?"

"Lauren, what is it? Where are you?"

"In New York. I'm on my way to your place. Are you home?"

"Yes, yes. Lauren, what happened?"

"I'll explain when I get there."

"I knew it!" said Kelly, through her teeth. "I just knew it! Brian and I have just finished brunch. Are you hungry?"

"I don't even know," Lauren said with a sigh. "It was awful, Kelly."

"Just come right here. Brian is leaving for a softball game. You can tell me everything when you get here. See you soon."

"Bye," Lauren said softly into the phone. Twenty minutes later, the cab pulled up in front of Kelly's building. Lauren paid him, exited the cab, and entered the lobby of the building. Kelly was there, waiting for her. She put both arms around Lauren in a big hug.

"Come right up," she said, leading Lauren by the hand to the elevator. Lauren followed numbly and soon found herself standing inside Kelly's loft.

"You look pale and exhausted," Kelly took Lauren's bag and tote from her. "Sit over there on the sofa, and I'll make some tea. Would you like something to eat?"

"I would throw up anything I tried to eat. I feel like throwing up now." Lauren sat down heavily on the sofa.

Kelly rummaged in a canister, brought out two tea bags, and popped them into two mugs. She opened a cabinet door and brought out a honey pot. Then she turned the gas on under the kettle.

Just then, Lauren's phone rang. She glanced at the screen. Her stomach clenched. Charles. At first, she refused to answer. Then, she reconsidered.

"Hello?" She tried to sound in control, but her hand was shaking so badly, she could hardly hold the phone.

"Lauren, I need to talk to you. Are you alone?"

"What difference does it make? Are *you* alone, Charles?"

"Please, I must explain."

"You already did."

"Are you alone?" he repeated.

Lauren glanced at Kelly. "Yes, I'm alone," she lied. Kelly raised an eyebrow.

"I want you to reconsider your decision concerning our relationship. I'll agree not to see Sally anymore."

"Really, Charles! Twenty-three years. I'm not stupid."

"Please, darling, we've made all the plans. We make a good couple. We make a good pair. We can have a life together."

"What kind of life? And for how long? Charles, this has tired me out. I thought you loved me."

"Oh, but I do, darling. You know I do. Sally is, well, a business associate of long standing. We can change our relationship. She's a reasonable woman."

"Charles, really, do you know how awful that sounds? Please, you're making me ill."

"Will you agree to one more chance? One more try? It's important to me. I'll make everything up to you. I'll make it worth your while."

I'll make it worth your while. That was how Charles thought of everything. As if he were talking about a business deal. Suddenly the image of Caleb was clear in her mind. His honest smile, his twinkling eyes, his simple and straightforward emotions. His touch and the soft urgency of his kisses.

Lauren sighed into the phone. "I'm sorry, Charles, I can't. I can't even talk about it with you now. We can't be together. Every time I'd look across the table at you, or see you each morning, I would see you standing there, in your dressing gown, with Sally Chong in her black negligee."

"I'm not a man to beg. You know that, but I'm asking you just to give it a second chance. You'll have the world by the tail when you're married to me. You won."

How odd, thought Lauren, to hear him talk like this. It was as though she was hearing him talk for the very first time, and she didn't like the conversation.

With resolution, Lauren spoke into the phone. "In the first place, Charles, I don't believe it. I don't think you broke it off with that woman. In the second place, what do you mean, *'I won'?* What did I win, Charles? *You?* Why did you want to marry me, Charles? Why didn't you just marry Sally Chong? Or is she already married?"

"Sally is a business woman. She wouldn't marry anyone. She doesn't relate to people like that. Can't you see that's why she was no threat to you?"

"What are you saying? What do you mean?"

"Sally and I are a power team," Charles answered. "We have been for years. We understand each other. Do you know how many takeovers and mergers we've orchestrated?"

Lauren said again, trying to keep all emotion out of her voice, "Why did you want to marry me, Charles?"

"Lauren, you're a young, contemporary career woman. Beautiful. Successful. You make me look young. I'm proud to bring you places and be seen with you. We complement each other. And you were always content with the life I lived. What changed you? What made you come to London?"

It was useless to talk any further to him. It was like trying to drown fish, as her mother would have said. Lauren was beginning to see things clearly, to put the pieces together. She had been as adept as Charles at avoiding the truth. Except she knew better.

She spoke clearly into the phone. "Charles, I came to London because I thought I should be with you, even on business trips. I think I'm kind of an old fashioned, small town girl after all. I believe in love. I believe in love at first sight, even. I think love makes up for everything, and maybe it won't happen for me, Charles, but at least I believe in it, and that's better than being stuck with you, no matter how many houses you own or how much money you have or how many mistresses you give up. I can't agree to what you're asking." She could feel tiny beads of sweat begin to form on her forehead, and her palms were clammy. She paused, thinking about what Caleb had said. "You don't have to give up anything for love. Love gives you everything. Goodbye, Charles." Lauren clicked off the phone.

Kelly jumped up and down, clasping her hands together. "Yay!" she cried. "Now tell me everything so I know what that conversation was all about."

Lauren told Kelly every detail. The events of the past twenty-four hours were seared into her brain, painful to recall, but so clear that she even remembered the graduated pearls Sally Chong had worn. While she talked, Kelly poured the boiling water into the mugs and set the tea and honey down before her friend. She scooched the overstuffed chair closer to the sofa and didn't speak until Lauren had finished. Finally, Lauren gave a shuddering sigh and sat, hands folded in her lap, staring at the floor.

"I can't even cry, Kelly," she said softly. "I'm just devoid of any feeling. I feel strange, odd, like I'm in a foreign country and nobody can understand me when I speak. It's like a nightmare. The whole thing is so surreal. Did I just make the biggest mistake of my life? I just don't think I could look at Charles's face again."

Kelly's brow furrowed as she dipped a honey-coated spoon into her mug of steaming tea. "That stinking, wretched worm! I am so furious right now, I'm finding it hard to speak intelligently. That disgusting, despicable *nasty* person! What a twisted son of a bitch!" Kelly slapped her knees in emphasis. She shook her head. She stood up and paced back and forth.

Lauren watched her with blank eyes, but she said nothing.

Kelly sat down beside Lauren and took Lauren's hands in her own. "Well," she said pragmatically, "every cloud has a silver lining. It's true. And I'm going to tell you the silver lining here."

This time, Lauren could not suppress a small smile. She knew her friend would bolster her spirits. "I knew you would," she said.

"The silver lining is that you discovered what a perverted, disgusting person Charles is *before* you married him. He *introduced* you to his *mistress*, or whatever she is. What did he think, you were going to have a three-way? I mean, really, Lauren, what if you had married him?"

"Then I probably would have never found out, and I could have lived on in perfect idiotic bliss," Lauren replied miserably.

"Oh, come on, you know that's not true. Your life would have been unbearable. Charles has issues, more issues than you think. Men like that always do! You don't think this is his only transgression, do you? I should say not! *And* I should say, we don't even *want* to know what else we'd discover if we started digging!"

Lauren straightened up and squared her shoulders. "Will you help me get my things out of Charles's penthouse?"

"Of course, honey!"

"And then, I have to really address the practical side of things," Lauren gave a sardonic little laugh. "I have no fiancé, no home, and no job."

Kelly impulsively gave her a big hug. "You have me!" she exclaimed. "We can figure this out." Then Kelly added quietly, "And I'm betting you still have Caleb."

At this, Lauren's eyes did tear up, and she shook her head slowly back and forth. "Caleb's not that kind. He's put me in his past. I know. He's gone." She gave another bone racking sigh and held her head in her hands. "I just want to cry and cry, and I can't. I can't even cry!"

"And do you know *why?*" asked her friend.

"Why?"

"You didn't love Charles." When Lauren attempted to interrupt, Kelly stopped her. "No, no! Don't start with me. Thou protests too much! Be honest with yourself, Lauren. You *didn't* love Charles. You loved the fact that a powerful man chose you and gave you a big ring and proposed. You loved all this magnificent wedding crap. You loved the Central Park West penthouse. You loved being asked to chair different charities. You loved going to exclusive parties and clubs on Charles's arm. You hardly knew the man! If you did, you would have never said yes. And it's a sure thing Charles didn't love you. *That's* been made painfully clear. A person like Charles is a sociopath. He can't love anyone. Really. He can go through the motions, but the real feelings, *normal* feelings, don't exist. And you're a normal person, Lauren, with normal needs and desires. You said so, just now to Charles on the phone. You said you were an old fashioned—what was it now?—small town girl. You need to address that. Don't forget, I've known you longer than anyone else in the city. You just got caught up in some nasty seduction. You didn't know Charles, but what's worse, you've lost touch with yourself. You don't know Lauren."

"What do I do about all the wedding plans?"

Kelly seethed with exasperation. "Have you heard a single word I've said? Walk away, Lauren. *Walk away.* It was all a sham! A ghastly sham. Wash your hands and your face and get that dirt off you. Start over. *Reclaim yourself.*" Kelly lowered her voice and spoke more gently. "Look, hon, I know it's been a shock, no matter what I say. We'll get your things this afternoon and this evening. You can stay here for as long as it takes to get on to the next step of your life. This is a good thing, Lauren, no matter how it feels right now."

Lauren nodded, and two big tears slid down her cheeks. Leave it to Kelly to lend the proper perspective to any situation.

Later in the afternoon, when Brian had returned from his softball game, the three friends went to the penthouse to begin to pack up. As they disembarked the cab, Lauren stopped on the sidewalk just outside the door of the building.

"You okay?" asked Kelly, her hand on Lauren's arm.

"I feel so weird," Lauren said. "Like I hardly recognize it. And it's just been a little over twenty-four hours since I left it."

"Well, let's get this over with," Kelly said grimly. "Brian, did you call the truck so we can load this stuff and take it somewhere?"

Brian nodded. "I'll wait here on the street until it comes. We can take it to the place where you stored your furniture from the Murray Hill place, Lauren."

"Thanks, Brian," said Lauren. Suddenly, Brian seemed even more like a golden retriever, infinitely good natured and completely dependable. She was beginning to feel truly grateful for having two such steadfast friends. "I don't have too much to take. Mostly just clothing, and some artwork and books." Lauren took a deep breath, and with Kelly close behind, she went into the building.

Albert, the doorman, greeted her. "Good afternoon, miss."

"Hi, Albert," Lauren answered. He pushed the elevator button for her.

The two friends rode up the elevator in silence. It came to a stop, and the door opened into the hallway of the penthouse. There were a number of boxes and some suitcases piled in the hallway. Dennis came out of the foyer.

"Oh, Dennis," began Lauren, "I'm so sorry, but—"

Dennis held up his hand. "A very unfortunate turn of events, Lauren," he said. "I've taken the liberty to pack as many of your things as I could identify. Charles called me shortly after noon."

"You packed my things?" said Lauren in disbelief. "Did Charles tell you to do that?"

"Yes, miss, he did."

"Well!" Kelly snorted with indignation.

Lauren looked at Dennis. "Did you know about Sally Chong?"

He coughed uncomfortably, but answered her nonetheless. "I did, yes."

"And you didn't tell me?"

Dennis looked her straight in the eye. "It's not my prerogative to comment on Charles's business. Frankly, I thought the matter would resolve itself."

Lauren laughed bitterly. "Oh, but it has. It has, Dennis. Why didn't you tell me? Why would you just stand back and let something like that go? I thought you were a different person."

"The man signs my paycheck," said Dennis flatly.

Lauren gave a sarcastic smile. So it came to this. All Dennis's fussing and caring, his attentiveness, these were a sham, too. She knew now that the minute she left the penthouse forever, Dennis and Tina would never think of her again. They were bought and paid for. They were owned.

"Ha!" said Kelly, not afraid of giving her opinion openly. "Like she said, she thought you were a different person! Well, this will be easier than we thought."

Dennis ignored Kelly's comment. "You may look through the rooms, Lauren, just to make sure I didn't forget anything."

"I will do that," Lauren said, and she walked by him into the foyer. Out of the corner of her eye, she saw Kelly curl her lip at him as she followed Lauren into the living room.

Instinctively, Lauren drifted through the rooms to the bedroom, and into her dressing room. They had been ruthlessly stripped of all sign of her. Dennis had been thorough.

"What a good employee he is," muttered Lauren cryptically. Then she paused. "Hey, I've just thought of something I have to do."

"What's that?" asked Kelly.

Lauren didn't answer her, but she dug around in her bag and brought out the wedding folder. She held it up triumphantly to Kelly. Kelly looked at her questioningly and watched while Lauren went to the French doors, opened them, and walked out onto the balcony. With a single motion, she threw the folder over the edge. The air currents caught it, and all the papers, clippings, photos, and contracts flew out in different directions like so many birds being released from a cage.

"Hey!" exclaimed Kelly. "Don't you have credit card numbers and stuff like that in there?"

"Only Charles's," said Lauren, and she actually smiled. "Let's get out of here."

Later on in the evening, Lauren sat at the dinner table with Kelly and Brian. She watched them carefully, enviously, even. For all her thinking of Brian as a golden retriever, she could see the real love her friends had for each other. She watched as they moved around the loft, each unconsciously aware of the other. She watched Brian's hand lightly touch the small of Kelly's back each time he passed her, even if just on his way to the refrigerator. Her heart nearly broke for herself when she saw them catch each other's eye, telegraphing something only the two of them understood. Something intimate. And then there were the smiles shared between them. Every time one of them came into the room. As acerbic as her personality might seem at times, Kelly always smiled at Brian when he entered the room.

This is what I want.

Brian poured red wine into crystal stemware.

"Let's toast," he said, picking up his glass and holding it high. "Let's toast to a new chapter of life for Lauren."

"A mystery though it is," said Lauren somewhat glumly.

"A mystery perhaps," Kelly replied, "but unfolding as we speak—or, ah, drink."

"I've been thinking…" Lauren paused to take a sip of the wine. "I've been thinking about what to do."

"And?" prompted Brian.

Lauren set the glass down and twirled it between her fingers. "I do have something left. I have my grandmother's house in Vermont. I know I've put it on the market, but it needs fixing up, and I need some place to be right now—and something to do. I've got a little stash, enough to finance me while I regroup. I'm going to pack up my things, go up to New England, and set up housekeeping there. It'll be temporary, but it's quiet and safe. And I can do a lot with the house. It needs painting and cleaning, and an occupied house always sells better than a deserted one."

"I like that idea," said Kelly. "I'll miss you dreadfully, but I like that idea."

"Doesn't Caleb live in that same town?" Brian asked, staring at the legs of wine as they slid down the inside of his glass.

"Yes, yes, he does," breathed Lauren, nodding her head slowly. "You know, I've been thinking about that, too. I'm no one to hold up as a paragon of morals. Look, I cheated on Charles."

"That's because you fell in love with Caleb," said Kelly. "If you had been in love with Charles, none of this would have happened."

"I did fall in love with Caleb. And I lost him. I lost him because I was afraid to give up what I had built, or what I thought I built. I only regret my total foolishness. I would give anything now just to have him back, but he's not that kind of guy. Once something's done, it's done for him." Lauren paused, sighed deeply, and took another sip of her wine. "I can live with it, though. At least I had that little interlude. That magic encounter. No matter what, I have my memory of that, and I can be pretty good at living with my memories, too."

Kelly reached over and put her hand over Lauren's. "You're seeing things more clearly than you have in months," she said. "Things are back on track. It will all come together now."

Lauren looked at her friend. She was not so sure, but right now, this was her only option.

Chapter Nine

A late summer day one week later found Lauren standing in the driveway of her grandmother's house, motioning to the driver of a midsized moving truck as it backed up to the door of the garage. "Okay, back a little more," she called, illustrating with her hands just how far he had to go before he should stop. "Okay, stop! Good."

The doors of the truck opened, and two men got out. "Where do you want this stuff?" the driver asked.

Lauren had already made a plan. The truck contained the contents of her Murray Hill apartment. She had sold most of the furniture, but she'd kept the sofa and two wing chairs, the dining table and chairs, drapes, some occasional tables, a small chest of drawers, and a few of the better table lamps. The boxes contained books and artwork.

"I'm going to store it here in the garage until I finish painting and redoing the inside, so it can all be unloaded here. I'll take things in as I need to."

The driver smiled at her. "That's easy enough. Usually we end up carrying pianos up three floors!" The two men began to unload the truck. Lauren looked up when she heard another vehicle pull into the yard. It was Joan Halloran, the Realtor. She stepped out of her car and smiled as Lauren went out to meet her.

"How lovely to see you up here, again!" said Joan. "What's this? Are you moving in? I came as soon as I got your call."

Lauren laughed. Joan was a good enough soul, after all, even though her demeanor could be somewhat irritating. "Oh, no, Joan," said Lauren, extending her hand. "It's good to see you again."

"Well, tell me, what's happening here?"

Lauren took a deep breath. "I'm taking a break from the city. I decided that I'd come up here, chill for a little while, and get the house in some kind of real order. You know, paint, paper, decent furniture. Thorough cleaning. New drapes. That kind of stuff. Don't you think that'll improve the chances of it selling before winter?"

As was her habit, Joan overreacted, clapping her hands and squealing. "This is wonderful! Yes, that will help us get a better price for it! And stir up some competition, too. And just in time for foliage season. The leaf-peepers come up here, and they're always looking for places to have as second homes. Summer places, winter escapes. This is wonderful news. My! And you're moving right along, I see."

"I have a specific block of time, and I'm going to get as much done as I can. I like the house a lot, and I want to see it restored. I've called a painting contractor already. They should be able to start tomorrow. At least that's what he said."

Joan shook her head slowly and tsked. "Don't you believe it! You've got to call them again tomorrow morning, or they won't show up until next week. Nobody's in a hurry around here, and you have to keep right on them. Why, where's your ring?"

Lauren started. Leave it to Joan! "Oh, well, um, I was scrubbing the upstairs bathroom, so I just took it off."

"And when is the wedding?"

"Oh, it was planned for October." Lauren wriggled out of a lie.

"Nice, nice," said Joan. "I'm glad things worked out."

Lauren pretended not to hear. She did not want to get into the details of her private travails with Joan Halloran. It would be all over town within a day, not that Lauren cared what these people might think. Joan, however, would not immediately drop the subject. Like all good salespeople, she could smell a weakness a mile away.

"I was hoping there might have been something developing between you and Caleb," she said pointedly. "Don't think I don't know why he went down to the city a couple of weeks ago."

"Oh!" laughed Lauren uncomfortably. "I did see him when he came to the city. It was a nice visit. Anyway, how's he doing?" She'd not meant to say it. She'd not meant to give Joan one iota of fuel for her fire.

"Caleb is Caleb," said Joan. "He goes around with a smile on his face, works all the time, and volunteers as a fireman every spare minute he has. Everybody in town loves him, and everybody wants him to find a nice girl and start a family." She smiled at Lauren and sighed. "I just thought it might be you. I was hoping when he went to the city, it meant something had happened between you."

Lauren turned away so Joan could not see her color rising in her face. "Well, it didn't," she quipped shortly. "Come on in, Joan, and I'll show you what I'm doing."

Lauren led the way into the house.

"Oh!" exclaimed Joan. "I'm impressed! You've been busy!"

It was true. In the three days she had been there, Lauren had ripped up the old linoleum floor. She had taken all the hardware off the cabinetry and stripped most of the old white paint off the woodwork.

"I've had to keep busy." Lauren laughed, recovering her good humor. "And actually, it's been fun. I'm going to restore the house to a 1930s farmhouse with arts and crafts and art deco touches. I know the house is actually older than that, built in the 1860s, but I like the twenties and thirties, style-wise, and I think it will fit the house."

"This is very exciting. Even in this state of restoration, we stand a better chance for a sale. People like to see work being done."

"I agree." Lauren nodded. "Now come out here in the yard. I think I discovered where the old milk house was, or something. There's a floor of flat stones in a corner of the yard. I'm going to clear away the weeds and make it into a patio."

Lauren led Joan out into the yard. Late as it was in the season, the Shasta daisies and phlox were still blooming, as well as the mints, oregano, and coreopsis. There was also a clump of deep red, late-blooming daylilies at the corner of the house. Joan paused and gently touched the blossoms. In a voice gentler than her customary gossipy tone, she said to Lauren, "I did know your grandmother, you know. She loved daylilies, and there are many on this property that she bred herself. One of her most successful varieties were these here. A lot of people in town would ask her for small rhizomes to plant, so they're all over town. She gave me some, too, and I love them. She used to enter them in the county fair. She always won."

"I remember that she really liked the garden and her flowers," said Lauren as she gazed at the large, purple-red bloom. "I remember going to the fair with her a couple of times, but if we were living far away at the time, I'd be in school and we wouldn't see her again until summer vacation."

Joan looked up at Lauren. "You should enter these in the fair. It's early in September. Starts Labor Day Weekend and goes for four days. The plants will still be blooming, and they're just as beautiful as they were when your grandmother was alive."

"Oh, I'm afraid I'm not much for county fairs."

"Now, that's just silly!" exclaimed the Realtor. "Everybody loves the fair! And we could use it as a selling point. 'Prize winning garden.' That would be different!"

Lauren knew it was futile to argue with Joan Halloran. Instead she said, "I'll do it if you help me enter them."

"Yes, I will! I'll pick you up an entry form today at the town office. You will have such a good time. Really, it's fun. The fair grounds are down on the main road between us and Windsor, right on the county line. It's one of the last real fairs in the state with livestock, vegetables, quilting, and a midway. It's the real deal. Fireworks. And entertainment. Last year, we had Keith Urban."

"Really! Why would Keith Urban come here?"

Joan looked at her seriously for a moment and said, "Sooner or later, everybody who is anybody at all comes here."

Chapter Ten

August gave way to September, and the weather cooled. Lauren began to truly enjoy her projects in the house. Each project required research, planning, the acquisition of materials, and lots of time. The rigorous schedule kept her grounded and seemed to sooth the anxiety and hurt that had occupied much of her thoughts since she'd terminated her engagement. She still thought about Caleb. After all, she was staying in the house where they had consummated their desire. When driving into town for groceries or materials, she couldn't help but look around for his truck, or try to catch sight of him perhaps coming or going from McTavish's. She had seen the fuel trucks on their rounds through town, and the plumbing vans, but he had not been behind the wheel. Her stomach knotted up when she remembered that, as the cool weather approached, she would have to call Cochran Plumbing and Heating for a fuel delivery. Well, she would cross that bridge when she came to it.

The painters were nearly done with the outside. Lauren bought new shutters—real wooden shutters—and painted them a deep, forest green. She also had the picket fence replaced and was appalled at the cost, but the fence showed the house and garden off to perfection, so it was well worth the expense. She did every project she could manage herself. For some of the heavy yard work, she found it necessary to hire a local landscaping company, but she kept the friendly boy with the lawn mower coming every week or so to keep everything looking neat and trimmed.

Inside, Lauren managed quite well. The table was stacked with do-it-yourself homeowner's books on tiling, woodworking, and retro-style design. She found a huge old high-backed double-porcelain sink in the woodshed, ripped out the old stainless steel sink, and had it installed in the kitchen. She splurged on the faucet and was satisfied with the results. She had kept the kitchen island from her Murray Hill apartment and found that it fit nicely into this kitchen as well. It gave extra work space and didn't interfere with the table. Lauren kept the old white enameled table, decorated with painted cherries. She remembered it from when she was a little girl, and it was really in very good condition. A varied collection of four chairs surrounded it, none of them matching. Lauren painted them all a deep red which tied them together and set off the table to perfection.

She was polishing the chrome on the old black wood-burning cookstove one afternoon when Joan knocked on the door.

"Come in," she called, drawing her head out of the oven to see who it was.

"Your grandmother used to bake the most wonderful beans and bread in that stove. And you wait until winter. You can fire up that stove, and it'll heat this whole downstairs. Do you have wood for winter yet? And don't forget, you need to have the chimneys cleaned. In these old houses, a crack in the flue can mean a house fire. Well, maybe we won't have to worry about the wood if we sell it by winter, but do get the chimneys cleaned and checked. Actually, I've got two parties to see it. One couple wants to come tomorrow. Is that all right with you?"

Lauren continued to polish the chrome, letting Joan babble on. "Oh, yes," she said. "Just make sure you let them know I'm working in here."

"I think that will just add to the appeal," Joan replied.

True to her word, Joan brought prospective buyers through over the next two days. The first couple was middle-aged and wandered around looking at the ceilings and muttering about which walls they would take out. Lauren didn't like them or the thought of them being in the house. The second showing was a young couple with two children who found the house in too much of a state of construction for their purposes.

"Don't despair, dear," said Joan after she had seen the young couple out the door. "We'll find someone."

Lauren was not despairing. She was enjoying her time in the house. She made occasional trips into town for groceries, but for the most part, she stuck to the business of restoration. Being trained as a museum curator, she was no stranger to hands-on work, and even the contractors were impressed with the results of her efforts. The constant work was therapeutic. During the day, there were always workmen of some kind on the premises, hammering and sawing or painting. They kept her from feeling too alone with their congenial conversations and their off-color jokes. It was the end of the day that was hardest for Lauren. When the workmen packed up and left each day at around four o'clock and she suddenly found herself alone, she always went through a period of worry and sadness. She talked to Kelly every day to bolster her confidence, but try as she might, she could not see what the future held.

Often, she sat on the top step of the old porch and sipped a beer, trying not to think of tomorrow, trying just to focus on the progress that had been made that day. Usually she was tired enough at the end of the day that she slept well, relatively uninterrupted by shadowy dreams of what might have been.

By the week of the fair, Lauren had finished tiling the kitchen floor. It had been a massive project. She cut black tile diamonds herself with a rented tile cutter and fit them between large, white squares. Even with rubber gloves, she had nearly taken the skin off her fingers, but the results were dramatic. Joan said so when she came to collect the daylilies for the competition of garden flowers at the fair.

"Why, Lauren! I am so amazed at you! You should go into the business! This is just beautiful. Black and white tile in this diamond pattern. How arresting, but subtle at the same time. Very, very well done."

Lauren smiled her thanks. She thought so, too. They went out to the garden to cut the blooms. The stems had to be eighteen inches long, in a sturdy vase, and the bloom ready to open the next morning. They cut three specimens. Joan was excited. "This is terrific! Wouldn't that be the best tribute to your grandmother? We'll call this lily the Kate Hamilton, after her. Is that all right with you?"

Lauren was surprised at her own enthusiasm. "Oh, yes," she exclaimed. "Joan, do you really think I might win a prize?"

"I do. I do indeed!"

That night when she called Kelly, Lauren told her about entering the daylilies. "Why don't you come up?" she said. "Wouldn't it be just a hoot to go to a real county fair? It would be like that old musical, *State Fair!* Honest, I'm not kidding. They have pigs and cows and everything. Tomorrow's Saturday. It's the day they judge the flowers. You can stay overnight and go back on Sunday after brunch. Wait till you see what I've done to the place!"

"Which," answered her friend, "will be difficult because we don't know what it looked like to begin with. However, you're right. A trip to a county fair would be fun. As long as they have cotton candy, we'll come."

"I'm sure they'll have cotton candy."

"Then we will see you tomorrow morning."

Lauren was excited to have her friends visiting. It grounded her, somehow. She made up the little room under the eaves where she and Caleb had spent that fantasy night together. There was a puffy duvet on the bed, a vase of fresh flowers on the bureau, as well as clean fluffy towels. The window was open, and the room smelled of sunshine. Kelly would adore it.

Since her arrival, Lauren had been sleeping in the bigger bedroom on the western side of the house. It had been her grandmother's room, and Lauren found this particularly comforting. She had made the bed up with a cream and peach duvet and matching shams. On a trip to a local furniture store, she had happened across a painted bureau with a matching mirror. It was pale green, with depictions of wheat sheaves and birds painted in ecru, brown, and white. Lauren bought the pieces on the spot. They fit the room exactly, lending it a certain sophistication. To round out the feel, Lauren painted the old maple four-poster a matching green and copied the bird motif on the head and foot boards. The peachy color of the bed linens and the white lace curtains blended with the green and made the whole room restful and serene. Lauren thought when she started on the bedrooms, she would paper this room and add a rug or two. She set her vanity up in front of one of the two big windows. Each morning when she put on her make-up, she could look out across the wide back lawn and the rise of the green mountains behind it.

Kelly and Brian turned into Lauren's driveway at about two in the afternoon. The sky was bright blue, and there was the first invigorating little nip of fall in the air. Lauren ran out and embraced them both. Her emotions at seeing her friends surprised her as her eyes welled with tears.

"I'm so happy to see you!" she admitted. "I've been so busy, I guess I really didn't realize how lonely I'd been. Come on in. I'll show you my plans for the house, and you can take your things up to your room."

Kelly looked around. "It is lovely, Lauren," she said honestly, dropping her usual sarcastic edge. "I'm surprised you haven't sold it yet."

"I'm expecting an offer from a couple next week," she responded. "I didn't really like them, though. They kept talking about taking out walls."

"What a classic old porch!" said Brian, going up the steps. "Where's the lemonade?"

Lauren laughed. "I've got some in the refrigerator!" she answered, opening the screen door and ushering them into the house.

Kelly stood in the center hall and looked around. "It's much bigger than I thought."

"Four bedrooms," said Lauren.

"Hmm, plenty big for a family."

"Come on, I'll show you around."

Lauren toured them around the house, explaining her plans for the renovation. The kitchen was the last stop. Kelly absently picked up one of the magazines while still taking in the room. "This is really beautiful, Lauren," she said. "You've done a wonderful job. You're really enjoying yourself, aren't you?"

"I am," admitted Lauren. "I almost don't want to sell it before I complete it. I want to see all my plans come to fruition."

"Don't we all," muttered Kelly.

"I know I've got to get back to the city," Lauren said with a sigh. "I've sent out a few resumes. Haven't heard back yet, though."

"It's a hard time to be trying to find a job," Brian said, "but with your qualifications, you should be able to find something before too long."

Kelly looked at Lauren. "You haven't seen Caleb, have you?"

Lauren gave a brave little smile. "No, Kelly. I'm afraid your Lauren-and-Caleb reunion plan is not going to happen. It's okay, though. I'm doing okay. I really am. I know I'll get a job offer soon, and then it's back to the city. Hopefully I can sell the house before that."

"I don't have any Lauren-and-Caleb reunion plan!" Kelly snorted indignantly.

Brian gave a little cough and changed the subject. "Let's go to the fair!" he said in a rousing voice. "I haven't been to any kind of fair since I was about twelve years old."

They piled into Brian's car and set off down the road.

The fair grounds were on a flat hilltop conveniently located where the three southern most counties in the state bordered one another. It was a traditional fair grounds, with a race track that was adaptable to either horses or cars, a grandstand, long rows of red painted livestock barns, a covered events building, a livestock show ring, and an exhibition barn. There was also a two-story round house where all the domestic competitions like cooking, gardening, preserving, quilting, sewing, and other handcrafting took place. The midway with its food vendors, games, and rides took up the wide center portion of the grounds.

Brian followed the directions of a scrawny, flag-waving little man with a cigarette hanging out of his mouth and parked the car.

"Where shall we start?" asked Kelly as she got out of the car.

"Let's get something to eat," said Brian eagerly. "I never get a chance to eat real fair food."

"That's probably a good thing," remarked Lauren, starting toward the midway. The three of them stopped at the American Legion tent, which looked relatively clean and smelled delicious. Brian ordered a huge sausage in a bun smothered in chili and sauerkraut. He proceeded to dump mustard on top of that, ordered a beer, and took a seat at one of the old picnic tables which sat under a forest of large sun umbrellas. He began to eat without waiting for Lauren and Kelly.

"Well, there's a gentleman for you!" Kelly scolded. She ordered her beer along with a large hotdog and some fried dough.

Lauren stepped up to the Plexiglas window and said to the little gray-haired woman behind the food counter, "I'll have a beer, please, and a small sausage grinder with onions and peppers."

"Coming right up," the older woman replied. Then she peered at Lauren from over the top of her glasses. "Are you that girl who's moved into Kate Hamilton's house?"

"Why, yes. Actually, I'm her granddaughter, and I'm getting it ready to sell."

"Well, welcome to town, honey. My son's one of the painters who's been working on your house. Michael Thurston."

"Oh, ah, yes," said Lauren. The truth was she didn't know any of them by name. "Thank you." She took her food and joined her friends at the table.

"Looks like everybody knows you already. And your business." Kelly laughed as she bit into her hotdog.

"That's a small town for you," said Lauren.

After they ate, they meandered along the midway. Brian took a couple of shots at a game but won nothing. They visited the poultry barn and the rabbits, went to see part of the horse show, and walked through the livestock barns where they saw children dressed in white shirts and jeans brushing and washing placid cows, pigs, goats, and sheep, getting ready for their various competitions.

"Well," said Brian, "how about your flowers? Where are they? When can we find out whether you've won or not?"

"I think they're in the round house," said Lauren. "Joan, my real estate agent, entered them for me. Let's go see what the judges thought."

They walked into the round house. There were exhibits of prize winning pies, cookies, and cakes as well as competitions for various vegetables. Preserves were next. The judges were sampling jars of blueberries when Lauren passed them. At last they came to the flowers. There were many different varieties, but Lauren managed to pick out her dark red daylilies at the back of the display. Lying on the counter top next to the vase was a blue ribbon. First place.

"Oh my! Look! Look, Kelly," she squealed happily. "I won! I actually won a ribbon at the county fair!"

"Ha! That's incredible!" laughed Kelly. "What a hoot! A blue ribbon!"

Lauren felt strangely happy as she picked up the blue ribbon and turned it in her hand. Why should it make her so pleased with herself, she wondered? Why should she care about an award from a county fair in rural New England? It was satisfying, however, and she looked over the array of other prize winners. Men and women had made these things, grown these things, and taken pride in their success. There had been a time when lives depended on one's ability to grow things, make things, preserve things, and this was a tribute to those times.

The three wandered out of the round house and looped around through the exhibit barn. There were a lot of information booths from the surrounding towns. The regional hospital had a booth; the animal shelters, farm equipment dealers, and car salesmen also had displays. There were some maverick salesmen selling food processors, vacuum cleaners, and other small household appliances. Lauren exited at the far end of the building and realized her hand was full of brochures. Kelly's was as well.

"And what are we supposed to do with these?" Kelly asked, holding them up.

"Make paper airplanes, I guess." Lauren laughed and turned to continue their tour. It was then that they saw the fire trucks.

"Oh, look!" breathed Brian excitedly. "I love fire trucks! I wanted to be a fireman when I grew up. Let's go look at them!"

"I'm sure there's still time," muttered Kelly.

About six trucks were parked in a line, each from a different town. A couple of them were antiques. They were all cherry red and so shiny it was hard to look at them in the sunlight. Three firefighters tended each truck, helping droves of little children climb aboard, sit in the cabs, and get their pictures taken. One 1930s hook and ladder antique was employed giving rides around the fair grounds.

Kelly gave Brian a good natured push forward. "Hey, get right in line. Maybe they'll let you take a ride with the rest of the kids!"

Lauren started to laugh, and that was when she saw him. His back was to her, but she knew it was Caleb. He was dressed in uniform blue slacks, black firefighter boots and a blue T-shirt with "FIRE DEPARTMENT" written across the back. Her stomach leaped. He turned toward her and bent to scoop up a little girl with curly blond hair in a yellow striped pinafore dress who looked to be about three years old. He held her in one arm, smiling down at the cluster of children clamoring at his knees. How was it that his clothes always seemed to fit him to perfection? No matter what he wore, that body underneath, with all its power and grace, was agonizingly evident. Lauren tried to turn away, but it was too late. He saw her.

Lauren was powerless, held by the tether of her emotion. Their eyes locked.

Lauren heard Kelly whisper, "Oh, no."

Still holding the little girl, Caleb waded through the sea of four- and five-year-olds to her.

"Lauren, it's nice to see you," he said congenially. He smiled his bright friendly smile. "Hi, Kelly. Nice to see you again, too." He held his hand out to Brian. "Caleb Cochran," he said.

Brian shook his hand. "Brian O'Hara," he said and then added pointedly, "I'm with Kelly."

Lauren found her voice. "Hi, Caleb," she said bravely. "Looks like you're busy today!"

He laughed. "Oh, yeah," he said. "We do this every year." The little girl sat easily in the curve of his strong arm and stared at Lauren critically. She was obviously not happy with this interruption of her plans to ride the fire engine. Caleb said, "I heard you were at the house, fixing it up. Just call the shop if you need any plumbing done. I'll send somebody up."

"Put me on the truck!" demanded the little girl suddenly. She grasped his chin with her tiny hands and turned his face to hers.

Caleb laughed. "Okay, pumpkin." Before turning back toward the fire truck, he looked at the trio and said, "Hey, why don't you guys stay for the fireworks? The fire departments put them on. They start about eight. We'll start setting them up as soon as we finish here. They're pretty cool."

"Oh, we'd love to," said Kelly urgently. "Wouldn't we, Lauren?"

"Yes, I would like to see them," Lauren heard herself say. "We'll do that."

"You'll enjoy it. Try to get a seat on that grassy bank over there," Caleb said. "Well, nice to see you. Good luck with your house." He turned his attention back to the child and walked away from them, the swarm of children bobbing after him like a school of little fish.

Kelly said, "What is it about a man with a baby that's so damn sexy!" Lauren was silent, still watching as he lifted the little girl up into the cab of the fire truck and climbed in after her. "Lauren, are you okay?"

Lauren nodded. "I don't think I want to stay for the fireworks."

Kelly was all over her. "Why ever not? He *asked* you to. He probably wants to see you afterward."

Lauren shook her head. "I doubt it. He spoke to me so impersonally. He might as well have been talking to his next-door neighbor, or — or his sister."

"Well, that's because we were with you," offered Brian, trying to be helpful. "A man doesn't just put his feelings out there for everybody to see. Besides, he was busy with the kids."

"Come on, Lauren, let's stay. You owe it to yourself. You know you're still in love with him."

Lauren sighed as they drifted back toward the food tent. "He said he knew I was in town," she said. "He knew, and he didn't call or stop by or anything."

"He thinks you're still marrying Charles," Kelly pointed out. "And he's trying to be a gentleman about it. You're lucky he even spoke to you."

"I think he spoke to me because he doesn't care anymore. He's over it. If he felt it to begin with. I think he just wanted to fool around." She felt as though all she wanted to do was go home, climb into bed, and sob.

Brian put a brotherly arm around her. "It's almost seven o'clock," he said. "You need a beer. Let's get some beers and something to eat, we'll watch the fireworks, and go back to the house. Come on. You're with us. We've got your back."

"That's right," persisted Kelly. "We're here to have fun. And we're your guests. This fair thing was your idea, after all. *And* you won a prize. Don't forget that!"

Lauren managed a wan smile. "Hmm," she said with a sigh.

The American Legion was putting on a chicken dinner. Hordes of burly men were turning half-chickens in wire mesh cookers over the huge fire pit and slopping on the barbeque sauce. Brian was in his element. A fan of almost any kind of food, Brian pushed Kelly and Lauren ahead of him. "Take a plate," he urged. "Let's get through this line. This looks fabulous!"

They took their paper plates and plastic utensils wrapped in paper napkins and went down the line, where a chubby jolly mustachioed man plunked half a juicy barbequed chicken onto each of their plates. They moved on to the next long table where several high school girls were dishing out more food. There was sweet corn, coleslaw, and potato salad, and for dessert there was apple pie with ice cream. Their plates were so full as they sat down at a nearby table, they had to support them with both hands. As they unfolded their paper napkins and armed themselves with their plastic knives and forks in preparation for their meal, Joan Halloran came by with a tray of pitchers filled with beer.

"Pitcher of beer, anyone?" she asked. She didn't wait for them to answer, but set the pitcher down and plunked large plastic cups in front of each of them. She gave Lauren a big smile. "On the house," she said. "Lauren, did you see? You won! I told you, didn't I?" Joan proffered her hand to Kelly and Brian, seemingly unaware of the precarious tilt of her beer tray. "I'm Joan Halloran," she announced to them. "I'm the listing agent for Lauren's house. Isn't she doing a magnificent job? And, we have more people who want to see it next week."

"Nice to meet you, Joan," said Brian, depositing a ten dollar bill on the tray. "Take this," he said. "My donation. This gig is worth every penny I'm spending here."

"He's easy to entertain," said Kelly, taking a bite out of her corn on the cob. "However, this food is excellent!"

"Glad you're having such a good time," said Joan. "And Lauren, don't forget to pick up your blue ribbon! Your grandmother would be so pleased."

Lauren forced a smile. "Yes, I think she would," she said.

"Well, I'll call you when I get the offer, and when the other couple tells me when they want to see it," said Joan, drifting away to other tables. "Bye-bye, now. Enjoy the fireworks!"

Lauren tried hard to keep her thoughts to the barbequed chicken dinner, her friends who thought enough of her to drive four and a half hours to visit her, and the fun time they were having at this county fair. She laughed at Kelly's sarcasms, discussed the plans she had for the house restoration, and giggled at Brian's remarks while they people-watched.

Her mind, however, was all about Caleb. Her stomach was churning, and her emotions had tied themselves in more knots than a ball of yarn abandoned by a kitten. Why had he been so distant? Why hadn't he called her? Was it as Kelly had pointed out — that he believed her to be marrying Charles, so he was staying away from her? When she had first come back into town and been in such close proximity to him, she had actually thought, actually entertained the idea, that he might try to win her back. He might call again, and then she would have the opportunity to tell him that she had broken it off with Charles, that they could be together, but Caleb was not a man to grovel. He had made his case. She had shot him down, and he had accepted the inevitable like the man he was. It was she who could not accept things as they were; it was she who still ached for him, desired him as she had no other man, ever. She squirmed internally as she faced the fact that it was her own greed, her own insecurity, her own blindness to her circumstances that had made her rebuff him. Well, she had been punished for placing value on valueless things. She was living that punishment now. Mentally, she squared her shoulders and held her head high. She deserved whatever she got, and she would take it.

Brian sat looking at his plate. It was scraped clean, with only the chicken bones left. He gulped down his last swallow of beer. "That was amazing!" he exclaimed. "I feel like a new man." Suddenly he pointed in the direction of the grassy field on the other side of the fair grounds. "Hey, look, people are starting to gather for the fireworks. Let's go over there and make sure we get a good place to sit."

They wandered across the midway and chose a place higher up on the bank. The sun was setting. Random little clouds floated across the sky, blushing pink in the sunset. The heat of the day was fading, replaced by a delicious crispness in the air. They settled themselves on the grass, still warm with captured sunshine, and watched as the crews prepared for the show.

Dusk had fallen, and the night was fast approaching. Lauren peered intently into the gloom. Even though the fireworks were located far away from the crowd on the opposite side of the field, she was sure she could pick out Caleb. There were six men, working in a line, setting the different explosives at various distances and patterns to get the most out of the pyrotechnic display. Caleb was near the end of the line. It appeared to Lauren that he was making a final inspection of the setup.

Kelly leaned over to her. "Is that Caleb?" she asked in a stage whisper.

"I think so," agreed Lauren.

"I think it's him, too," said Kelly. "You can't hide something that gorgeous. I think you should try to find him after the show. You two need to talk."

"I hope they're careful," was all Lauren would say. It was true. She longed to talk to Caleb. Just to unburden herself and let him know the truth. But could she? Did she even have the right to talk to him after what she had put him through? Perhaps it would be better for everyone to just let what was in the past stay in the past. After all, she didn't even know what she was going to do after the house sold.

The first stars were coming out, and the crowd around them was growing. People were spreading blankets on the ground. Couples were cuddling. Mothers and fathers were sitting together in family groups, holding small children on their laps. Then there were the groups of teens. Random groups of boys on the edge of the field, looking askance across the crowd at random groups of girls on the opposite perimeter. Lauren had to smile. You couldn't ignore the powers of attraction. It was what kept her staring at the man in the distance even though it was getting harder and harder to see him through the deepening shadows.

Suddenly the crowd seemed to hush. Brian leaned forward and whispered, "Here we go."

The display started with a series of pops and whistles and bangs that exploded into the air in reds, blues, yellows, and greens. Twinkling sparks fell to earth like so many stars. Then the show escalated. The fireworks grew louder and more spectacular; the crowd punctuating its satisfaction with gasps and applause. The whole show lasted about a half an hour, leading up to a sensational series of ear-splitting whistles, booms, and blasts, filling the sky directly overhead with sparkling patterns of multicolored lights and flashes. It seemed as though the cacophony would never end, but finally, a huge explosion sent a shower of brilliant sparks raining down on the whole area. Then, silence. The crowd erupted into applause, lasting almost as long as the final volley. At last, mothers began to gather up babies. Fathers carried little ones on their backs or pushed them in strollers along the bumpy ground. Couples strolled hand-in-hand back toward the parking lots. The clots of teens dispersed into the night.

"Terrific!" exclaimed Brian. "Terrific show! You couldn't see a better one in the city! And the food! This has been one of the more satisfying days of my whole life!"

"Brian's overstimulated," said Kelly, casting her eyes heavenward. "It was a good show, though."

"Pretty spectacular," agreed Lauren as she tried to identify which of the shadowy figures down by the fireworks stage was Caleb.

Kelly turned toward her friend. "Lauren, you march yourself right down there and find Caleb. You two are in love. You can't let it go."

Lauren did not take her eyes off the figures clearing away the debris from the fireworks display, but she answered Kelly. "We might have had the chance to be in love, Kelly. I really think we did, but I squandered it. I ruined it. And now I can't bring myself to tell Caleb the truth. What would he think of me? He might think I was making it up. He might think I was unpredictable and fickle in the worst way, that I might pull something like that on him—"

"Stop! Stop!" exclaimed Kelly angrily. "You don't know any of this. You're just speculating on assumptions. All this is groundless. You've got to talk to him, tell him the truth, and let what happens happen. Really. You can't move on—anywhere—until you do. It will erode your self-confidence."

Brian said simply, "Go try to talk to him, Lauren. Kelly and I will wait in the car."

Lauren stood for a moment. Then she made up her mind. She had caused her own misfortune. Her own dishonesty had led her into this awkward situation. At least she could set the record straight. At least she could tell him the truth.

"Thanks," she said to her friends, managing a small smile. "I'll go see him. I'll be right back." Squaring her shoulders, she set off across the field with determination.

It was difficult to see clearly. Smoke from the ignited fireworks still hung in the air. There was an acrid smell that burned the inside of her nose. The moon hadn't risen yet, and it was very dark. Lauren concentrated on the silhouettes of the men as they went about the business of packing up their gear. They were all dressed the same in their fireman's blue work pants and t-shirts. Which one was Caleb? Then she saw him. He was carrying a large metal box to a nearby truck. He didn't see her approach. She walked up behind him as he set the box in the back of the pickup.

"Caleb?"

He turned around. "Lauren!"

"I—I came to talk to you."

"I'm pretty busy right now," he said. "Cleaning up."

"Yes, yes, I see that. I'm sorry. Can we talk for just a bit when you finish?"

He looked around, then said, "Well, step over here a minute. I can take a break. What can I do for you?"

What can I do for you? His impersonal tone made Lauren's heart sink, but she steeled herself and spoke. "Caleb," she said, trying to hide the desperation in her voice, "I just came to say how nice it is to see you again."

"It was nice to see you again, too."

"And I wanted to tell you something," she went on, feeling as though she must be babbling like an idiot. "I'm not going to marry Charles. I broke it off. I'm staying here for a while to—"

"Lauren, I—"

"No, please, hear me out. I realize I was wrong, Caleb." She was talking fast now.

"Lauren, listen, before you go any further—" Caleb started to say.

"I just want you to know that I'll be here, working on the house. I thought maybe you could come by and…and we could talk. Just talk, that's all," she finished lamely.

"Caleb?" A female voice came out of the darkness.

"Right here, Amy," he called back. "I'm just finishing up. I'll be there in a minute. Just wait for me over by the gates."

Amy? The flame of hope that had flickered in Lauren's heart was snuffed out as surely as if one of the fire hoses had been turned on it. *Amy.* The name clattered against her eardrums. Suddenly she was hot with embarrassment, sick to her stomach with an all-consuming feeling of foolishness.

"Oh, oh my," she stuttered frantically, "I'm sorry. I'm so sorry. Just forget what I said. I didn't mean to—I'm sorry, Caleb. I didn't mean to—I have to go now." She turned to leave, then thought she might faint. She stumbled and felt his hand close around her arm. He turned her around to face him. The shadows played on his face, hiding his emotion, but the green lights in his eyes flared.

"Our timing sucks," he said. She thought she heard a tremor in his voice. Lauren could not make herself speak. Her breath caught in her throat, and she swayed a little in his grip. "I appreciate you telling me the truth," he said. "I really do. And I meant everything I ever said to you, but I'm seeing someone now, and I'm trying to put my life on a solid path. I took two hits. I can't afford another."

Lauren took a deep breath. All her emotion seemed to drain from her, and she felt desolate and hollow, like the empty casings of the fireworks that littered the ground. "It's all right," she whispered, looking up at him, gazing into those burning green-lit eyes. His eyes never left her face. She could feel his fingers trembling on her arm. So this was to be it. This was the situation she would have to live with. "It's all right," she spoke again. "I wish you the best of everything, Caleb. Goodbye now." He let go of her gently. His fingers slipped down her arm, searing her skin with his touch. Lauren turned away from him and started to walk back toward the parking lot. She looked back once over her shoulder and saw him disappear into the night.

Haltingly, she told Kelly and Brian what had transpired, and they rode the rest of the way home in silence. She dragged herself up to her room, undressed, and crawled into bed. The duvet settled around her like a soft, protective shield.

Then she began to cry. She cried most of the night. She cried at her own foolishness. She cried for the abandonment and loneliness. She cried for lost love.

In the morning, she rose and steeled herself for the future. If this was where she was, then she would accept it. She would not seek anything more, but she would go on with her life in one capacity or another. She would make a plan.

Lauren went downstairs to the big kitchen where Brian was standing over the stove. The seductive smell of bacon whetted her appetite in spite of her mood. Kelly was standing beside the table, a mug of coffee in her hand.

"Sit down, honey," she said to Lauren. "I've poured your coffee."

"And I've made the most delectable breakfast you'll ever have. Sit down, girls, and prepare yourselves for real food!"

Kelly and Lauren sat down. Lauren sipped her coffee, letting the smooth warmth of it slide comfortingly down her throat. Brian set plates of food in front of them and then joined them at the table with his own plate.

"Oh, Brian!" exclaimed Lauren. "This is too much!" The plates were piled high with sugar-dusted French toast, bacon, and fried eggs. A pitcher of cold orange juice was on the table, the condensing water droplets glistening in the sunshine flooding in the window and sliding in liquid rainbows down its side.

"I was inspired by the fair food yesterday," Brian said proudly. "I made a real country breakfast."

"And it is just magnificent!" said Lauren, holding a maple syrup soaked piece of French toast on the end of her fork.

They ate in silence for a while. It was Kelly who spoke first. "Brian and I have been talking," she said. "We think you should wrap things up here and come back to the city. You can get a job. You can't just hide out."

Lauren chewed pensively on her French toast and then swallowed. "I don't intend to hide out," she said. "I think I have a plan."

"And that would be?" asked Kelly.

"I think I'm going to stay here until I finish restoring the house or it sells. All the outside work is done, and at the most, it'll only take the winter to finish the inside. I can do a lot of it by myself, and I enjoy doing it. It's therapeutic, and about now, I need some therapy! In the meantime, I'll send resumes out everywhere. I thought I might even go to San Francisco or Los Angeles. There are plenty of museums out there. I might even opt for a career change and try to get into academia or publishing."

"Okay," Brian said, "you just have to make sure that you go where you really want to be. The geographic cure never works. I personally think you should come back to New York. You know New York. New York knows you. The whole Charles thing is already down the drain like yesterday's bath water."

"Would you be able to stay here through the winter?" asked Kelly.

"Why, of course. The house is heated. I'd be fine."

"That's not what I meant," said Kelly pointedly. "I meant would you be able to live here knowing you could run into Caleb and this new girl at any moment?"

"That's the way things are," said Lauren with finality. "There's nothing I can do about it. I'm not saying it wouldn't bother me. I'm just saying I have to get on with things. And I have to follow a plan. It will keep me on course."

"We could come up and help on the weekends too, couldn't we, Brian?" offered Kelly.

"I'm a pragmatist and a realist," said Brian. "I think your idea of a plan is healthy. And, for what it's worth, you'll be fine. You will extricate yourself from this heartbreak, heal, and move on. We're here to help you."

"Brian is not a pragmatist or a realist," remarked Kelly. "He's a total romantic. However, he's right. We're here for you."

Kelly and Brian left a couple of hours later. Lauren stood on the porch and waved goodbye as they drove down the road. Then she turned and went back inside. On the kitchen table was the little blue rosette that she had won for her flowers. She picked it up carefully, almost tenderly, and stroked it thoughtfully.

Chapter Eleven

The days began to blur together for Lauren. She had put in a call to her parents, explaining that the wedding was being postponed due to Charles's business responsibilities. She did not want to get into the whole story just yet with her mother and father who would have more opinions about it than Lauren would want to listen to. She hardly reflected on it herself. Instead, she worked hard at her restoration project, finding comfort in the satisfaction of seeing the house blossom. Outside, September was unusually warm, even as it passed its midway point. Lauren cut back the gardens and gave the flower beds a last weeding. Joan came up once and helped her divide some of the perennials, helping herself to some of each variety along the way.

Inside, the house was taking shape nicely. Brian and Kelly visited twice, helping wherever they could. The kitchen was painted a cool celadon green. The cabinets were white with the original porcelain knobs. The new gas stove and refrigerator were reproductions in the style of the thirties. The dishwasher was cleverly hidden behind a wooden panel. Lauren kept the old black wood-burning stove more for its beauty than anything, although she was eager to try to bake some beans in it. She had the old Formica removed and replaced it with solid cherry wooden countertops. She stubbornly refused to change her mind when warned by the contractor that "they would stain" and she would have to "oil and polish them" and "never forget to use cutting boards" or "they would scar." For accent, she picked up the red of the painted cherries on the tabletop. She found a beautiful set of vintage canisters at a local antique shop, cream colored with red rooster decals and red lettering that indicated their contents:

"Flour," "Sugar," "Coffee," and "Salt." She hung airy white curtains with a bright red border.

The living room was next. Using the fireplace as the anchor piece, she built the room around it. She ripped up the old carpeting to reveal a beautiful wide spruce board floor. She rented equipment, sanding and polishing it herself until it shone with a deep blond glow. Then she found her good oriental rug rolled up in the garage and laid it across the floor. The rug was authentic, hand woven of wool. She had to get Lawn Mower Boy to help her drag it into the house; it weighed as much or more than a full grown sheep.

She decided to splurge on the furniture and bought a good sofa upholstered in soft, flowery chintz with a matching upholstered club chair. For accent, the dark blue ticking-covered wing chair from her old apartment blended beautifully. Lauren left the large gold-framed mirror hanging over the mantel and hung some of her own art on the walls. Cream colored, floor length velvet drapes pulled it all together, lending the whole room an air of comfort, grace, and country sophistication. It was such an inviting room, it became Lauren's habit to curl up on the couch in the evenings and read there before going to bed.

September flew by. Mornings were very cool now. When Lauren looked out the window every morning before she dressed, she could see the trees beginning to change. The deep greens were slowly replaced by the scarlet, yellows, and oranges of the approaching foliage season. Soon Lauren's view would be awash with brilliant colors, a last hurrah before the world around her was hushed and cloaked under winter snows. Joan Halloran stopped in one afternoon just as October was settling in. Lauren was waving goodbye to Lawn Mower Boy, who had just delivered a load of winter firewood and stacked it neatly beside the garage. Joan struggled with three beautiful bright orange pumpkins.

"Goodness, you've kept busy," said Joan, who did not wait for an invitation but walked right through the garden gate, depositing the pumpkins on the porch steps. "Something for Halloween," she explained, looking around. "The place looks wonderful, and a good thing, too, because I think that retired couple is really interested. They want a place in the country where their grandchildren can come and visit and the family can use it as a ski lodge. This place will accommodate a lot of people. I'm sure I can talk them into it. Are you willing to negotiate a price?"

For the first time since she had the house up for sale, Lauren felt a pull, the gentlest pull at her heartstrings. Quickly, she repressed the feeling before it could mature into a fully blown thought. "Oh, well," she said, "that would depend. I've put a lot of effort into this place and people are just going to have to be willing to pay to get it. That's just good business. Thanks for the pumpkins, Joan. You didn't have to do that, but they're very nice."

"Don't mention it," said Joan cheerily. "I've got them all over the garden. Oh, and there's another thing. My nephew is visiting. He's just about your age. He's not married —"

"Oh, Joan, I can't go out with anyone."

"Hmm, really?" said Joan quietly. Then in her customary voice, she said, "Relax. I'm not trying to fix you up or anything. I just wanted to round out the table. And I thought Josh would appreciate the company of a woman his own age. My husband and I want to take him out to the pub tonight."

Lauren stared at the ground and blinked, thinking the matter over. She couldn't shut people out. That wasn't healthy. She couldn't continue to hide out of fear of seeing Caleb again. Would she be able to stand a whole evening with Joan and her husband? What the hell! It might be downright comical. She looked up and met Joan's gaze with a smile. "Sure, I'll go. It'll be fun. I'd like to meet your husband…and…and your nephew."

Joan stepped forward and gave her a little hug. "Oh, thank you," she said earnestly to Lauren's surprise. "We'll have fun. I'm going back to the office now. I expect we might get that offer today, and I'll ask for it in writing so there's as little tomfoolery as necessary. Sometimes these deals can swing back and forth for weeks." As she turned to leave, Joan looked at Lauren. "One more thing," she said and this time her voice held none of the real estate agent glib. "One more thing," Joan repeated, "there's another reason I got Realtor of the Year. I notice things. Now, I don't know your business, but I do know that your wedding has been postponed, that you have a post office box in town, and that you're not wearing your engagement ring."

Reddening, Lauren started to protest. "I, well, that's because —"

Joan held up her hand. "I don't need you to talk about it. I don't care, but I wanted you to know that I noticed." She flashed Lauren her usual smile. "It will probably be easiest and least awkward to meet you at the pub about seven-thirty. See you tonight, dear." She was out the door and heading back to her car before Lauren could speak.

Lauren became agitated as the afternoon wore on. She had been starting on the dining room, peeling the old wallpaper, when Joan arrived. Now, when she tried to go back to her project, she found herself unable to concentrate. Random thoughts crowded her brain, swinging like a pendulum. One minute she would think it was the most foolish thing she had ever agreed to. Why on earth would she want to go to dinner with Joan and her probably boring husband and her most assuredly idiot nephew? The next minute she would say, out loud to herself, "You've got to get out and do something. Anything."

Later in the afternoon, Lauren put in a call to Kelly and told her the plan. "Your assessment is probably right," Kelly replied. "The husband probably drives the snowplow for the town, and the kid is probably unemployed and got kicked out of his mother's house, hence his staying with Joan. However, it's Friday night, and you're stuck up there in no-man's-land, so you might as well put your heart on the shelf for this evening, go out, and meet the Hallorans. You should get at least a couple of funny stories to tell me tomorrow morning. Not too early, though. Brian and I are sleeping in. We don't have anything to do, so we're not doing anything. It's kind of nice."

"You're right," Lauren said with a sigh. "And anyway, who am I to judge the Hallorans or anybody else up here? Everybody seems happy, that's for sure. They have their husbands and wives, their children and jobs. They have friends. They have lives. It's alive here. Me, I'm from the big city. I'm the only one without a life."

"Go get 'em, girl!" exclaimed Kelly. "Go get yourself a life."

Sad as she was, Lauren laughed. "I'm trying, Kell," she said. "I'm trying."

The dilemma was what to wear. Lauren stood in front of the closet in the bedroom, wrapped in a towel. She stared into the chaos. It was not the closet she'd had at Charles's penthouse, she observed ironically. All her clothes were crammed into the small space, some hanging, some folded on the single shelf. Her shoes were a veritable tower of disarray. It was hard to see what she had, let alone choose something. She did want to look nice, even pretty. She had that much self-respect. And, in a strange way, she was fond of Joan. The woman was a broker, and brokers after all did the jobs the rest of society deemed unsavory, but she did it to the best of her ability and was successful at it. And it did seem that she was honestly trying to be nice to Lauren, drawing her out. So, Lauren wanted to appear respectful of Joan's thoughtfulness.

While she tried to decide on the outfit, she dried her hair, this time putting hot rollers in it. While they worked, she put on her make-up, shadowing her eyes a little deeper, glossing her lips with a bit more shine. She took out the rollers, flipped her hair over her head, and fluffed the soft curls with her fingers. She threw her head back and looked in the mirror to observe the effect. A couple more pushes and prods with the brush and fingers, a little spray, and Lauren looked at herself with satisfaction. *Not so bad for serving so much time out here in the nether regions of civilization*, she thought with a grin.

Finally, she chose her skinny leg jeans and slipped a red, black, and white plaid flannel top over her head. It was gathered under the bust and detailed with little vertical ruffles across the bodice. It was scooped just low enough to show an occasional glimpse of cleavage. Gold hoop earrings and a gold cuff for jewelry. She topped it off with a black velvet blazer. Heels gave it a fun evening look. She grabbed her black Tory Burch bag and was ready to go.

It was dark when she got to the pub. The windows shone with a friendly glow, and she could hear the rise and fall of happy voices as she went up the steps and through the door. It was quite crowded. The little candles on the tables were all lit. Lauren peered through the throng of people and the dim light. There was Joan. Lauren caught her smile.

"Over here," Joan called, waving her arm. They were at a table close to the bar. As she approached, the two men stood up. Secretly chagrined, Lauren extended her hand.

"My husband, Roger Halloran," said Joan, doing the introductions. Roger took Lauren's hand in a warm grasp. He was a tall, handsome man with thinning gray hair and invisible-rim glasses. He wore a white shirt, open at the collar, with a gray tweed sport coat and gray slacks.

"Lauren Smith," said Joan.

"And this is my nephew, Joshua LaPlante. Josh, this is Lauren Smith."

The nephew smiled broadly and took her hand. He was also quite good-looking, with a long, amiable face, and high cheek bones. He had lots of brown hair that fell attractively over his forehead, and friendly dark blue eyes. He, too, was dressed in shirt and sport coat, although he wore jeans.

"Please, join us," said Roger, gesturing to the empty chair.

Lauren thought ruefully to herself as she sat down, *I seem to be wrong about just about everything lately.*

"I hope you haven't been waiting too long," she said.

"Oh, no," said Joan, "we just arrived. And not a minute too soon. All of a sudden, everybody decided to come to the pub."

"Well, we're in no hurry," said Roger. "We'll have a drink and order. I know what I want already."

Joan sputtered good-naturedly. "Oh, Roger! You always have the burger and fries! Branch out, will you? Take chances."

"I'm an accountant," he retorted, smiling at Lauren. "Accountants never branch out. And we never take chances. That's why I married you, dear."

"Really, Roger! You've kissed the Blarney Stone tonight!"

There must be something to Joan after all, Lauren thought as she laughed along with everyone else.

The waitress came by and took their orders for drinks. Lauren ordered the Long Trail Ale and everyone followed suit.

"It's a good evening for beer," offered Josh. "It's chilly out there."

"It's the middle of October," Lauren pointed out, taking a sip of foam off the top of her glass. Then, to keep the conversation flowing, she said, "What do you do for a living, Josh?"

"I'm a lawyer in Boston," he said. "I'm up here helping my aunt and uncle with their estate planning."

"Not that we plan on dying anytime soon." Joan laughed.

Lauren was beginning to relax. She liked Joan's husband, and she liked Josh. He was easygoing and didn't talk too much. By the time their food order had arrived, Lauren had finished her beer, as had Josh, so they ordered another round. Lauren was shocked to find herself actually laughing, and laughing because she thought something was funny, not out of sarcasm or bitterness at circumstance. She smiled at Josh and took a big bite out of her hamburger.

Things were going so smoothly, but the stars were not aligned just yet. The evening was not what it appeared to be. The front door creaked, as it had all night long, as people came and went. Lauren, seemingly the only one to hear it this time, instinctively looked up. The little bubble of happiness within which she had found herself suddenly quivered and burst. Caleb Cochran walked in.

Lauren felt her surroundings falling away from her in all directions with the speed of light. The second she saw him, she was alone in a vortex. Voices seemed far away. She could concentrate only on Caleb's back as he made his way to the bar. With the greatest effort, she pulled herself back into the fold. *He hasn't seen me. Thank goodness for that.* She could tell Josh was speaking to her, but she hadn't heard a single word of it. *Get a grip.*

Lauren leaned forward and said, "I'm sorry, Josh, what did you say? I didn't hear. Some woman laughed out loud right in my ear just as you were speaking."

Josh pulled his chair closer to her, also leaning in. "I said, what are your plans when the house sells?"

Lauren shook her head. "I don't really know. I need to find a job. I was thinking of relocating from New York, at least temporarily."

"Your background would qualify you for a few things," said Josh. The noise in the pub had escalated, so he moved in closer, his face inches from hers. "You should come to Boston. I could help you get your resume distributed to the right people."

"How kind!" said Lauren. Still gathering her wits, she concentrated her focus directly at Josh, listening intently to him. Perhaps Caleb would fade into the woodwork or leave, and she wouldn't get caught staring at him.

"I'm serious," Josh continued. "Just let me know when you can come. I'll line some people up for you to talk to."

All at once, Lauren couldn't hold the temptation any longer. She took a quick look up at the bar. Caleb was standing, leaning on the corner of the bar, eating a sandwich. He set the sandwich down and looked around the room. Lauren, bent close to Josh, saw him move, but she couldn't avert her gaze fast enough. Caleb saw her. Their eyes locked. It must have only been a couple of seconds, but it seemed as though they stared at each other for minutes. Time for them stopped. Then Caleb looked away. Lauren saw him leave money on the bar. He said something to a man on the bar stool next to him and then walked right past her. Lauren was ready to say something, even "hi," but Caleb said nothing as he disappeared back out into the night.

Unconsciously, Lauren watched him go. She felt Joan's hand on her arm. "Are you all right, dear?" she asked.

Lauren's heart was fluttering. She thought it might stop altogether, but she smiled at Joan and said, "I'm fine. Probably just a little tired. I was sanding floors all day. I'm sorry, but I think I'll excuse myself now. It's been so nice to meet you, Roger, and you, Josh. Thank you so much for asking me."

They exchanged pleasantries. Josh gave her one of his business cards. As she smiled her goodbyes for the final time, she saw Joan looking at her intently.

The outside air hit Lauren like cold water on her face. She took a deep breath of it and felt a little better, although her hands were still shaking. So much for trying to move on. Well, it wouldn't be tonight, that's for sure. Lauren pressed the "unlock" button on her key fob and climbed into her car. The sight of Caleb had rattled her confidence, as it always did. How could she overcome such an attraction? How could she leave such a love behind? And was it a love? Her resolve to deny it was destroyed by the sight of him. She sighed as she started the car. Yes, she admitted, it was love. Real love. Tonight, she wouldn't fight it. She would concede. She would take her broken heart, go home, and crawl into bed—alone.

Chapter Twelve

The house was chilly. Lauren thought about going directly to bed, but she was still too flustered at having seen Caleb to settle down. And why hadn't he spoken to her? Why had he left in such a hurry when he saw her? If only he had just said *something*. Lauren tried to think of anything to distract her mind as thoughts of Caleb and their time together whirled in her brain like a hamster on a wheel. She went to the Welsh cupboard in the dining room, opened the bottom door, and took out the bottle of Jack Daniel's. A little whiskey might help.

Carefully, she took one of the crystal whiskey glasses down from the top shelf of the cupboard. Its weight felt good in her hand. She needed something solid. She poured a shot into the glass and held it up, absentmindedly swirling the amber liquid around the inside of the curved crystal. She took a sip. The warm liquid burned her lips, burned her mouth and throat in a most pleasing manner. She turned, and when she did, she saw the fireplace. She would light a fire.

Lauren hadn't lit a fire in the fireplace yet, and this would be the perfect night to do so. It would take the chill off and comfort her at the same time. She placed the glass of whiskey on the low table in front of the sofa and went outside to the woodpile. Shivering, she gathered as much wood and kindling in her arms as she could and struggled back inside. She knelt on the brick hearth, crumpling up newspaper and arranging the wood over it. Lauren was no stranger to starting fires. Often, as she was growing up, it was the only heat her parents allowed in their various homes.

As Lauren struck the match and held it to the newspaper, a pang of nostalgia pierced her heart. The comfort of the fire would feel good, warming both bones and spirit. The fire caught immediately on the dry kindling, and the flames leaped and danced. Lauren sat back on the sofa, cupping her whiskey glass in her hands. She was surprised how much heat the fire threw. This could turn out to be her favorite spot if the house didn't sell by winter.

The fire calmed her, the whiskey relieved the tenseness in her, and she felt her shoulders relax. She read a few pages in her book and then began to feel tired. She glanced at the old clock on the mantel. It was eleven. Yawning, Lauren stood up and put the screen in front of the fire, checking to see that no sparks could escape. Then she climbed the stairs, washed her face, and brushed her teeth. In her bedroom, she undressed and slipped into her long white nightgown. Although made of gauzy see-through material, its long sleeves would keep her warmer than the black silk shift. She crawled beneath the covers. This time, instead of trying not to think of Caleb, she gave her thoughts over to her memories of the time they'd had together. It was oddly comforting to recall his touch on her body, awakening myriad feelings and emotions that she had previously only dreamed of. She remembered his lips on hers, his warm mouth seeking her capitulation. She drifted off to sleep imagining again the weight of his body on hers.

How long she slept, Lauren had no idea, but she was suddenly aware of a heaviness in her chest, as though she could not take a deep breath. Slowly, she willed her mind out of the sleep that dulled and confused her senses. Her eyes burned as she opened them. The room seemed to be filled with fog. She took a gasping breath for air and felt a searing pain in her nose and throat. The realization exploded in her brain. Fire!

It was not fog. It was smoke! Trying to control her panic, Lauren slipped out of bed, bending close to the floor. Her eyes watered so much she could hardly keep them open. Struggling for breath, she crawled along the floor, trying to reach the window or where she thought the window was. The swirling smoke obliterated all sense of direction. Lauren frantically felt around until her fingers closed around the flannel top she had worn the night before, discarded carelessly over the chair of her vanity. She clapped it to her face. Now she couldn't open her eyes at all. The smoke was suffocating. Blindly, she fought her way to the window. Holding the shirt to her face, she clutched at the windowsill with her other hand, exerting every ounce of effort she could muster to pull herself up. She must open the window. She must get air. Lauren hauled herself to her knees, but then she began to cough uncontrollably. The room was spinning around her. She clenched her teeth. The pain in her throat and chest was unbearable. Suddenly, all her strength left her. She fell to the floor, unable to move. Lauren felt her arms and legs tingling with a strange sensation. She fought to stay conscious, but she could not make her body move. Then a strange peace settled over her. Thoughts flitted in and out of her mind. She was dying, here in the old house. Should she struggle against death, or melt into the trap of the smoke, waiting for the relief death would bring? She could not move. Just before she lost consciousness, she thought she heard voices. She imagined someone was calling to her. Calling her name, over and over. She felt herself sinking into darkness.

The next thing Lauren was aware of was that voice in her ear, calling her name.

"Lauren! Lauren!"

She could not answer. She could not react physically. She could only listen to the voices. Hands were on her now. Strong hands. Strong arms were lifting her. The voices were frantic in the background.

"Did you find her? Is she in there? Caleb, get out of there. The whole top floor is full of smoke!"

Caleb. Her mind fixed on his name.

"I've got her!" Lauren heard the familiar voice. That dear, familiar voice. "I found her. I'm coming out! Get that medical oxygen ready now! I gotta breathe through the mask." Lauren heard him cough once. She was aware of being carried, and just before she lost consciousness again, she felt the exquisite sting of the cool night air.

When she opened her eyes, she was lying on a blanket on the lawn. People were moving around her, and there were flashing lights everywhere. Something was over her face. She struggled up, up through the blackness, and pulled at it. A gentle hand closed over hers. A man's hand. Caleb's hand.

He bent close and whispered to her, "Shh, don't struggle. It's the oxygen. You're going to need fifteen liters before we even get you to the hospital. Breathe, Lauren, breathe for me."

She could see him now. She tried to focus her eyes on his face. Caleb had removed his helmet. His face was close to hers. He was smiling, but there was fear in his eyes. He still wore his firefighter's jacket. The Scott Pack, that life-saving supply of oxygen that enabled the men to search through smoke and fire-filled buildings, was still strapped to his back. He was kneeling beside her, his soul in his eyes.

She reached up and touched his cheek. Two tears ran down the sides of her face. Caleb bent and kissed her forehead.

"It was a chimney fire," he said. "The creosote build-up in the chimney caught fire. Must be a crack in the flue because the smoke got into all the upstairs rooms. You were lucky one of your neighbors was coming home late because he saw the flames coming out the top of the chimney and called nine-one-one." Caleb's voice caught just then, and he brought his hand to his eyes. When he lifted his head, he said, "You had a close call, Lauren. I don't know what I would have done if anything had happened to you. Lauren, I love you. Breathe for me. I have to go up on the roof now. The fire's out. We've got to drop chains down the chimney and shake the rest of the creosote loose. We have to assess the damage. You go with these guys. They'll take good care of you. I'll see you as soon as I can."

She could hear his voice, talking about the roof or something, but her mind was stuck on the words "Lauren, I love you." It was all she could focus on. It was all she wanted to hear.

It must have been several hours later when a nurse pulled back the curtain that cordoned off her bed in the emergency room at the regional hospital. Lauren had been sleeping, and the nurse's voice woke her.

"I'm sorry, Miss Smith. There's someone here to see you."

"It's me, Lauren," said Caleb, stepping past the nurse.

"Oh, Caleb!"

"I'll leave you two alone," said the nurse, closing the curtain.

"Don't talk if it hurts," said Caleb. He sat on the edge of the bed. Lauren could tell he had come directly from the firehouse. He was unshaven and his hazel eyes were tired, but he was the most wonderful sight Lauren could imagine.

"I'm all right," she said, smiling at him. She pushed herself up on her pillows. "I was sleeping, I guess. What time is it?"

"It's nine o'clock in the morning. How does your throat feel?" He spoke a little awkwardly, as if unsure of her reaction.

"I feel pretty good, actually," she said. "I'm glad you came, Caleb. Thank you for saving my life."

"Lauren, I — I…" He stumbled on his words and was silent for a moment.

Lauren looked into his eyes, searching his face. Then, unexpectedly, he cupped her face in his hands and kissed her on the mouth. It was that same, warm sensual kiss that had burned its way into Lauren's memory, firing her desire. Her own lips softened and pressed into his. She felt the moist warmth of his mouth. The tip of his tongue touched her lips, and she parted them, letting him in to explore her. Too soon, though, she felt him draw back. She gazed up and saw his brow slightly furrowed. He enfolded her then, in his arms, cradling her against his chest, her face under his chin, against the soft cotton of his t-shirt. Lauren felt him sigh, a deep, shuddering sigh.

"I was so scared," he whispered. "So terrified. When I went into the house and it was full of smoke…I could only think — "

Lauren pulled gently back from his embrace and put a finger on his lips. "I'm fine," she said softly. "You came in time. Here I am."

He smiled. "We got everything under control at the house. The damage isn't as bad as I thought it would be, considering the amount of smoke. No flames broke through, so it'll only be some cleaning and repainting. Drapes will have to be cleaned. Get rid of the smoky smell. The downstairs is pretty much untouched. The fire started up high, or, at least, that's where the crack was."

"I can't believe I forgot to have the chimneys cleaned. Joan told me to do that, too!"

"Did someone say my name? Is someone talking about me?" The curtain was whipped back, and there was Joan. "Oh, you poor girl! You could have died!" she exclaimed, sitting down in the chair next to the bed.

"That's what everyone keeps telling me," said Lauren, ruefully. She leaned against Caleb, loath to pull away from that warm, muscular safety.

Joan held up a canvas tote. "I brought you some clothing," she said. "I went to the house and rifled through and found some jeans, underwear, and this shirt. You can't be going home in your nightie!"

"Oh, thank you," said Lauren, truly touched. "How thoughtful of you."

"Do you have a ride home?" asked Joan.

"Yes, she has a ride home." Caleb answered the question.

"I see," said Joan, smiling. "Do you know when they'll release you?"

"I can remember the nurse saying after I woke up from my nap," said Lauren. "So I guess any time."

Joan stood up. "You take care of yourself. Don't worry about a thing. We'll see to the damage in the house, and I'll keep those buyers interested until everything is cleaned up. I didn't get Realtor of the Year for nothing!" She bent forward and kissed the top of Lauren's head. "See you both later." Then she left them.

Lauren and Caleb walked out of the hospital hand-in-hand. They crossed the parking lot and climbed into the big white pickup truck. Lauren pulled the seat belt around her and settled back, closing her eyes for a second.

"Are you okay?" asked Caleb.

"Yes," Lauren assured him. "Will you go into the house with me when we get there? I'm kind of freaked out to see it alone."

"Of course," said Caleb, turning onto the main road. "I don't plan on being very far away from you ever again."

Lauren said nothing. She did not want to break the magic.

They swung into the driveway of the old house. The lawn was trampled, as were some of the shrubs and lilacs that grew close to the house. Shingles littered the grass. Caleb followed Lauren as she went through the gate and into the house.

She was thankful that the kitchen and the rest of the downstairs, where the bulk of her work had been done, were largely spared. There was a slight acrid smell of smoke in the air, but a good airing out would take care of that, she reasoned. She went into the hallway and looked up. Smoke stains smeared the ceiling and sooty patches blackened the corners of the walls. She took a deep breath and started up the stairs. She went into the bedroom where she had slept. Where she had almost died. Where Caleb had found her. The smell of smoke was strong here, and the soot was thick on the ceiling. Lauren threw open each of the windows. A breeze wafted in, doing its best to clear the odor.

Caleb stood in the doorway. Finally, he said, "It won't take as long as you think to clean this up. We can get ahead of it in no time."

Lauren caught the "we," but she was afraid to acknowledge it, afraid to have her dreams dashed yet again. "I can see I have a lot of work cut out for me. Well, I planned on repainting and papering this room anyway. I guess it'll postpone the sale, though."

Caleb coughed. "The first thing to do is to get those chimneys cleaned and relined. These days, they drop a metal liner down them and, with proper care, they're safe for a long, long time. Let's go back downstairs. I'll give you the number of a guy I know who works on chimneys. I work with him a lot when we install heating systems. He'll come right away. Come on, you're looking a little depressed."

She gave him a grateful smile. He seemed to know everything about her. She followed him downstairs into the kitchen. Caleb wrote the name and number on her notepad. Then he turned and took her hands in his.

"I'm going to check in at work, but the day's almost over. We need to have a serious talk, Lauren. We really do. You gave me a real fright. I'll check in at the shop, and then I'll pick up some Chinese food and come back this evening. We'll talk then. Okay?" He dropped her hands and backed toward the door.

She yearned for another kiss, but she stood where she was.

"I'd love that," she said. He winked at her and went out the door. Lauren thought of something and ran, calling after him, "Don't forget the beer!" She could hear him laughing as he drove out onto the road. She couldn't shake her uneasy feeling, that feeling of seeing him go away from her. Would he ever return?

He did return, at dusk. The evening chill had fallen, and the first stars were twinkling between the pale blue and the purple velvet of the darkening sky. After a long shower and putting on some clean clothes and make-up, Lauren was still upstairs, stripping the smoky smelling sheets off the bed and collecting all the clothes that would likewise have to be professionally laundered. She went into the little bedroom, where there was very little evidence that there had even been a fire. She made up the bed with fresh sheets. She would sleep there until she could fully restore the rest of the upstairs.

"Lauren?" It was Caleb, calling to her from the kitchen. Her heart soared.

"Here I am," she answered, skipping down the stairs.

He was at the table, taking white cardboard containers of Chinese food out of a large brown paper bag. "Grab some dishes," he said. "I'll open the beer."

They sat at the enameled table, eating take-out with wooden chopsticks, sipping their beer out of the bottle, and each enjoying the other's company.

"Why did you walk right by me, last night, at the pub?" asked Lauren.

"I didn't see you when I walked in," Caleb answered. "It was crowded, so I just made for the corner of the bar and ordered myself a sandwich. I was just getting some supper before I had to go to the firehouse. When I saw you with Josh LaPlante, I was so angry and jealous I had to get out of there."

"You know Joan's nephew?"

"He grew up here. He was a year behind me in high school. Then he went off to college and law school, but he still comes around."

"You were jealous?"

"Well, yes. He's single, a good looking guy. A lawyer with a big firm in Boston. I figured I was screwed. I just got out of there."

"Hmm," mused Lauren. "When I saw you, I just wanted to touch you. I just wanted to leave that table and be with you."

They ate in silence for a minute, each thinking about the close call they had experienced. Finally Lauren poked at her shrimp and Chinese vegetables with her chopsticks and made her decision. She might as well bring it out in the open. This was it. There were no holds barred.

"What about Amy?" she asked quietly. "Are you still seeing her?"

Caleb put his chopsticks down. He leaned forward over the table and took Lauren's hands in his. "After I saw you at the fireworks, I was wiped out. I knew then what the deal was. I knew then I was still in love with you. I just didn't know how to make it happen. I hung around with Amy for a while. I guess you could say I was in denial. I was trying to hide the truth from myself, because I knew you weren't staying. I knew you were going back to the city. So I made a real effort with Amy, telling myself this was security, this would keep my heart intact, but I couldn't do it. I couldn't. I had to break it off with her. I just told her I wasn't ready for commitment. And I guess that was the truth. I wasn't ready for commitment to her. You're the one I love, Lauren."

It was as though a great weight had been lifted from Lauren's shoulders and that dark tunnel that so often haunted her dreams was suddenly lit with bright, warm light. *He loves me*, she thought, *and I love him*. The thought flitted through her brain, as it had the first time he embraced her. *This is what I want.* The memory was overwhelming, and her eyes blurred with sudden tears. She looked down at his strong hands holding hers, and the tears splashed on them.

"Why are you crying?" he asked, frightened.

"I am so happy," she whispered. "I love you too, Caleb."

Caleb stood up, not letting go of her hands, and pulled her gently up to face him. "I'm not hungry anymore," he said huskily. "Not for food." He wrapped his arms around her and clasped her to his chest. She felt those familiar, hard muscles, those powerful arms holding her. She could face the world with this man. She lifted her face to his and kissed his mouth, felt his tongue probing between her lips, wet and warm.

"Let's go upstairs," she whispered in his ear. "Please."

They climbed the stairs together. Lauren went up first, with Caleb following close behind. He ran his hand down the curve of her hip and over her buttock. The thrill shot through her like electricity. She had almost forgotten she could feel like this. She thought she might never feel this intoxicating exhilaration again.

In the little bedroom upstairs, Lauren turned to face Caleb. The look of desire in his eyes was unmistakable, and her heart leaped at the sight of it. He said nothing, but began to slowly unbutton her chambray work shirt until it fell open, revealing her red lace bra. She heard him utter a little gasp as he cupped each of her breasts in his hands. She tipped her head back and leaned into him. His thumbs and forefingers found her nipples and softly squeezed them through the lace. They grew erect at his touch, and she groaned audibly. Now he reached up and unclipped her luxuriant hair, letting it cascade down her back in a soft, fragrant wave. He took her face in his hands, and, tipping her head back, kissed the hollow of her throat. With his lips, he blazed a trail of kisses down her cleavage, lingering over her taut nipples through the bra. Lauren could feel them straining against their lacy prison. "Please, please," she whispered. He laughed softly and slipped her open shirt off her shoulders. Then, with one adept motion of his fingers on her back, he unclasped the offending article of clothing and freed her round, firm breasts. Her nipples tingled as he took them, one by one, in his teeth in tender little love bites.

"Ohh," she breathed. Her hips gyrated against him, instinctively sending him her invitation to placate her passion. In wordless answer, he knelt down, unbuttoned and unzipped her jeans, and slipped them down to the floor. She stood before him in the lacy red panties, her body shivering with expectation, her thighs hot with desire.

"You are so beautiful," he whispered. "So beautiful. I can't get enough of you. I want to explore you until I know every inch of you." He bent his head to her navel and tickled it with his tongue. The effect was startling. There was a rush of heat through her body. She thought her heart stopped beating for a second. She moaned, hardly able to stand. He hooked his thumbs into her lace panties and peeled them over her curves to her thighs.

"Every inch of you," he repeated hoarsely, nuzzling the outer softness of her most private self. She could feel his breath, hot and sweet, at the very core of her femaleness. Then his tongue touched her. Lauren felt she might faint from sheer pent up passion. She could feel herself swell with yearning for him. She struggled to let him in closer, but the red lace bound her. She moaned with delicious agonizing anticipation.

"Please," she gasped. He began to kiss her with his full, warm lips, paying tribute to the silken skin of her soft inner thighs. He gently kissed all around her mound of pleasure, teasing, taunting, titillating until she thought she would burst with the fever of it. Then his tongue probed her secret hidden recess of passion so gently, but oh, so firmly, sending shock waves through her until she shuddered with the suspense of it. She cried out, throwing her head back and gripping his shoulders, pulling him in closer, closer. She strained against the binding lace.

Lauren felt Caleb rise under her hold. Suddenly his arms were around her, lifting her right off the ground. He laid her on the bed and stripped the panties off. She was completely naked. She held up her arms to him. He pulled his shirt off over his head and stepped out of his jeans. For just a second, he stood, in all his masculine glory. Then, he leaned over her.

Lauren reached out and ran her hand over his belly, feeling the muscles quiver at her touch. With a newfound wantonness she could barely contain, she slid her hand along the length of his silken shaft. Propping herself up on her elbow, she bent toward him as he stood beside the bed, and covered the length of his manhood with hot kisses. Her passion was ignited now, and she used her tongue to transfer her fire to him. He groaned with the sensation, then knelt on the bed beside her. She lay on her back and closed her eyes as he ran his hand up the inside of her thigh and, with the slightest pull, urged them apart. She was beyond resistance. She gave him full access, eager for what was to come. Caleb tenderly caressed her secret sweetness. He exposed the satiny center of her physical hunger, pressing with his fingers, stroking her until she cried out. He explored her deepest recesses. She moaned, thrusting up to meet him. She was throbbing with the suspense of impending satisfaction. Tiny beads of perspiration formed between her breasts. She gripped the sheets and twisted her hips. She cried out, begging him to satisfy that physical excitement surging through all her nerve endings.

Caleb put a hand on each of her hips as he knelt at the altar of her desire. She lifted her legs to receive him. He entered her all at once, burying that manifestation of his passion deep into her sweetest niche. She met his penetration, melting into him.

At first his thrusts were almost frantic, as if he needed to be sure she was really there, really his. She met him just as desperately, heaving herself against him, enfolding him with her legs. Then, suddenly, he slowed. They breathed as one. His thrusts became more tender. She moaned, almost cried, with wonder and delight as the sensation washed over her in a flood of ecstasy.

"Oh, Lauren," he whispered, "I love you. I want all of you." Again and again he moved in her, stronger and stronger, until she felt transported by the motion. A mounting heat surrounded her, spreading out over her entire body. Her nipples tingled with anticipation. And then, a wave of such incredible intensity flooded her soul, crashing through her, setting off millions of tiny explosions of pure pleasure as she reached the height of her desire and spun off into the dizzying delight of her climax.

She gasped as she felt Caleb join her in that indescribable place of ecstasy, felt him shudder with the attainment of his desire, filling her with the power of his own sweet pinnacle of passion. They clasped each other, their bodies tightly entwined, keeping that feeling between the two of them for as long as they could.

When their breathing had slowed, when the frenzied flames of their desire had waned to a warm glow, they pulled the crisp sheet over themselves. The moon was just rising over the eastern hills. A silver shimmer slid into the room through the gauzy lace curtains, casting playful shadows on the walls. Lauren snuggled into the curve of Caleb's arm, resting her cheek against his chest. She could feel those muscles, now at rest. She could hear his heart thumping the rhythm of their love.

"I can't be away from you any longer, Lauren," he said. "When that call came through to the firehouse, all I could think of was how much I love you. I can live anywhere, Lauren. I can sell the business. I'd find something to do in the city, as long as I can be with you."

His honest, almost schoolboy adulation shattered her last reservation.

"I'm not going back to the city," she said, almost before she knew it herself.

There was a note of urgency in his voice as he asked, "Where are you going, then?"

"I'm not going anywhere, my love," she whispered. "I'm not going to sell this house. I've put too much into it. The fire made me realize how much this place means to me."

"Then you're—you're staying? Here?" He spoke as if he did not believe his ears.

"Yes. I need to be near you, too. I love you, Caleb." She felt him take a deep breath. He wrapped his arms around her and held her close.

"We can't let anything else come between us ever again," he said. "Are you sure you can be happy here? What will you do?"

"I'll be happy wherever you are," she said plainly, and she meant it.

"It gets pretty quiet up here in the winter." She could hear the smile in his voice.

"Not for us, it won't." She laughed, pulling herself up on the pillows and planting a big kiss on his mouth. His arms tightened around her, then his hands traveled down her sleek sides, entrapping her waist.

"I can't take my hands off you," he said, smiling up into her eyes.

"No one is asking you to," she replied with a laugh.

He pushed her playfully back onto the pillows and straddled her. "Roll over on your stomach," he said. "I'm going to give you a massage."

"Oh, yes," she exclaimed, doing as he directed. She relaxed into the bed, stretching her arms over her head. Caleb began to knead the muscles in her shoulders. He made broad strokes down her back over her ribcage.

"Will you miss your job?" He talked softly, almost cautiously, as though not to break the spell of their union.

"I don't think so. These past few weeks, I've been so involved in the house, I haven't thought about much else—except you. I thought about you a lot. I thought, what was I going to do now that I'd lost you?"

"Ah, but you didn't lose me." Caleb bent down and placed a kiss between her shoulder blades.

"There must be some way for me to make a living up here," she mused. "I just can't go away from you again."

"If you did, I'd follow."

He massaged down her long waist, kneading her lower back with his warm, strong hands. A sense of total contentment rippled through Lauren. For the first time in longer than she could recall, she felt at peace. Her thoughts floated into a place between dreaming and waking. Caleb lay down beside her, cradling her in his arms. They drifted off to sleep.

Chapter Thirteen

Could the sun be any more brilliant? Could the sky be any bluer? Could the New England fall foliage be any more spectacular? Lauren was in the garden, planting narcissus and daffodil bulbs for next spring. She looked around. Suddenly, she raised her arms in tribute to the elements and took a deep breath of the pristine air. In doing so, she noticed that the sun was just over the western hills and the shadows in the yard had elongated. *It must be almost six o'clock*, she thought. Caleb had said he was coming by this afternoon. She clapped her hands together to loosen the garden dirt and then wiped them on her jeans. As she made her way across the wide lawn, she saw Caleb's big white truck pull into the drive. She gave him a lighthearted wave and ran to meet him.

Caleb came through the gate. In his right hand he carried a six-pack of Long Trail Ale. As Lauren reached for him to give him a hug, he wrapped his left arm around her, and picking her right off the ground, he swung her around.

"Oh my!" she exclaimed. "You make me dizzy!"

"I'm happy today," he said. "Here, open us a beer. Let's sit on the steps." He sat down and patted the step beside him.

Lauren plunked down happily. "Okay, I guess cocktail hour has arrived."

The bottles clinked as he took them out of the pack. He handed one to Lauren and took one himself. It wasn't until she went to hold it by the neck in order to apply the opener that she noticed a fine, white ribbon around the bottle.

"What's this?" she asked, holding the bottle up for scrutiny. There was something suspended on the ribbon.

"Hmm, I wonder," said Caleb. Lauren looked at him. His eyes were dancing, the green lights in them fairly flashing. She had a momentary feeling she could not quite identify, and her stomach leaped. She slipped the ribbon off the bottle and held it up.

It was looped through the gold band of a large diamond solitaire. Lauren's eyes filled with tears, and she clapped her free hand to her mouth, covering the squeal of delight that escaped involuntarily. Caleb wrapped her in his arms and held her against him.

"Lauren Smith, will you marry me?" he asked.

She answered before he had even finished, "Yes, yes. Yes, I will marry you, Caleb Cochran!" She was laughing and crying at the same time. With shaking hands, she untied the knot in the ribbon and slipped the ring off, holding it in her palm. Caleb picked it out of her hand and, taking her left hand in his, he slipped it on to her third finger.

"Oh, it's a perfect fit!" she exclaimed.

"Of course," he laughed, and then he kissed her. "Of course it's a perfect fit."

"Caleb, it's beautiful!" She held her hand out in front of her. The last rays of the sun caught in the stone and flashed like a lighthouse.

"I figured the beer on the porch steps was important to us," he explained shyly. "Remember, it was the first time we really discovered each other."

"I remember," she giggled significantly. Suddenly, she heard something. "What's that sound?" she said. "Did you hear that?"

Caleb lifted his head to listen. "Nope. Didn't hear a thing."

She held up her finger and listened carefully again. He sat there in silence, a smile playing on his lips.

"I do hear something!" Lauren insisted, standing up. "It sounds like, like a squeak or—or some kind of bird or something."

Caleb got to his feet. "Maybe it's your engagement present," he said.

Lauren stared at him. "What are you talking about?" She held up her hand, flashing her ring at him. "What's this?"

Caleb planted a kiss on the back of her hand, like an old-fashioned knight in shining armor might have done. "That, my lovely, is my desire of you, and you wearing it is your pledge to me. Now for the engagement present. Wait right here on the lawn."

He strode through the gate and opened the back door of the cab of his pickup. When he turned around, he held a large cardboard box in his arms. Lauren heard scuffling and whining. Caleb set the box down in the grass, and a blond ball of fluff scrabbled over the side and rolled out onto the lawn.

It was a puppy. "Oh! Oh, Caleb!" Lauren cried, utterly charmed. "That's the cutest thing I've ever seen!" She bent down and picked up the puppy, who grunted contentedly as she cradled his little pot belly. He was soft as silk. She held him up to her face, and he covered her cheeks with eager puppy kisses.

"He's a golden retriever," explained Caleb proudly. "Do you like him?"

"Oh, I love him!" she said with a sigh, holding the puppy close. "I haven't had a puppy since I was a little child. With my lifestyle, I just couldn't have a dog."

"Well, you're lifestyle is different now. You've just signed on. And I didn't want you to be up here all alone. You need a dog."

"Does he have a name?"

"His name is Brady."

"Ooo, that's a wonderful name," said Lauren, setting the puppy down in the grass. He immediately pounced on her foot and began to chew her sneaker.

They walked around the yard, hand in hand. The puppy muddled around after them, digging and chewing and making them nearly choke on their beers with laughter.

Caleb said, "I called Joan today and had her list my house."

Lauren stopped mid-stride. Brady pulled at her sneaker, but she was unaware. "Caleb, is this really what you want to do?"

He looked at her, his soul shining in his eyes. "Yes," he said. "I thought we would live here. It's bigger, and you've done so much work on it. And it's your house, Lauren. I want to live here with you, in your house."

She was silent, letting his words sink in. He squeezed her hand, brought it to his lips, and kissed her fingertips.

"There's no competition between you," he said, knowing what she was thinking. "I loved Julie very dearly, but we were children together. Lauren, to you, I pledge my love as a man."

"Oh, Caleb!" she whispered. She clasped her arms around his neck and kissed him. "I love you so much!"

Then she did something she hadn't done for too long a time. She brought her cell phone out of her pocket and punched in her mother's number. She smiled at Caleb as she heard her mother's voice.

"Mother! It's me," she said. "How are you?"

"Well, I'm just fine, baby, and so is your father. How are you?"

"Mother, I am better than I have ever been in my life!"

"Really! Are the wedding plans proceeding nicely, then?"

"That's why I called, Mother. The wedding plans are proceeding wonderfully! I want to tell you about them."

The evening was warm for early June in New England. The sky was deep purple velvet studded with the first twinkling stars. A crescent moon hung in the sky like a chandelier, and the errant petals of the last apple blossoms floated fragrantly at the slightest puff of the crystalline air. Throughout the large lawn and flower gardens, white clothed tables, alight with candles, had been set amongst the thickets of young birches, lilac bushes, and old maples trees. Small groups of candles and torches were glowing in the small orchard and lit the aisle between rows of white folding chairs where the guests sat, patiently waiting. The night was fragrant with the perfume of the June roses.

At the head of the garden, underneath a backdrop of old lilacs, two massive arrangements of white flowers cascaded from stone urns. Kelly, dressed in a long, midnight blue gown, stood beside one of the urns. All day she had been shouting orders and moving tables, directing caterers, and pruning the occasional rebellious lilac branch, making sure this day would be unparalleled. Now, she stood quietly smiling, holding a large bouquet of white and yellow roses, freesia, and lilies, and looking as fresh and sweet as a dew-bejeweled flower. Bob Cochran stood beside the other urn, dressed in a blue blazer, red striped tie, and gray slacks. He was smiling from ear to ear. Between them was a young man in a white collar and black robe, peering into the deepening evening.

A single, invisible musician began to play a violin from somewhere in the garden. Caleb, also dressed in a blue blazer, gray slacks, and red striped tie, with a rose boutonniere, walked up and stood beside his father. The guests turned as one in their seats and looked down into the orchard.

Lauren pierced the evening darkness with radiant bridal splendor. She walked up the grassy path between the apple trees, dressed in an elegant satin dress with tiny spaghetti straps that set off her figure to perfection and trailed out, sweeping the ground behind her for six feet. Her hair was swept up in a simple twist and held with a large rhinestone barrette. She wore diamond studs in her ears. Her bouquet, of the same roses, lilies, and freesias as Kelly's, was larger as befitted the bride and filled out with variegated ivy, cascading down to her knees. Lauren walked to meet her love on the arm of her father, a tall, thin man. His long hair was gathered back in a neat pony tail, and although he was unaccustomed to the jacket, tie, and gray flannel slacks he wore, his big white teeth showed in a wide grin from beneath his handlebar mustache. Brady, nearly grown and decked out in a large white bow, padded alongside his mistress, looking up at her with a newfound dignity.

Lauren's blood pounded in her ears. Through the gathering darkness and candlelight, her eyes met Caleb's. They reached out and caught each other's fingertips. Lauren's father released her arm from his, and she stood, clasping hands with Caleb. The young man in the white collar began to speak. Lauren could barely hear him, but her eyes never left Caleb's as she repeated her vows, and he, his.

Caleb slipped the circle of diamonds that was her wedding ring onto her finger. Lauren took the gold band from Kelly and put it on Caleb's finger, smiling all the while.

"Lauren Smith, do you take this man to be your lawfully wedded husband?"

"I do."

"And Caleb Cochran, do you take this woman to be your lawfully wedded wife?"

"I do."

"Then I pronounce you man and wife. You may kiss the bride."

Their kiss was warm, full, romantic. Then they turned and faced the laughing, applauding guests, and Brady began to bark. All the noise faded into the background, though, as Lauren felt Caleb turn her around to face him. Once again their lips met, but this time it was that passionate kiss they had always shared.

This is what I want, she thought contentedly.

The End

CORPORATE AFFAIR

Will opening the door for business close the door to love?

A Small Town Girl novel by Linda Cunningham

Aiden Stewart stood with his head bent, letting the pulsating hot water of the shower beat down on the back of his neck. He remained there, motionless, for a minute or two before he reluctantly turned the water off and stepped out onto the soft, white bath mat. He grabbed one of the fluffy towels and began to dry himself.

Aiden was just vain enough to catch his own reflection in the mirrored wall surrounding the free-standing bathtub opposite the shower. He took pride in the tall, lean body he saw reflected there. His muscles were not bulky, like a man who spent too much time trying to outdo his last bench press. Instead, they were the long, supple muscles of a true athlete, the muscles of a healthy, thirty-two-year-old man who was comfortable in his own skin, who was used to doing anything physical with ease and grace. He was pleased with how his dark brown hair, even damp and tousled after his shower, dipped attractively over his forehead. He liked how his slightly bushy brows accented his black-lashed, clear brown eyes. He smiled at his own image and saw how his long nose and high cheekbones were softened by the curve of his full lips and the flash of white teeth.

Aiden was just vain enough to take pleasure in his own physical attributes and, whenever he had the opportunity, use them to get what he wanted. Especially from women. He thought about this as he picked up his toothbrush. He was juggling four girls at the moment, and it seemed like overload, even for him.

A bold knock on the bedroom door jolted him out of his self-serving reverie.

"Yes?" Aiden called out, wrapping the towel around his waist and going to the door.

"You in there, son?" It was his father. Aiden loved visiting his parents' gracious home outside of Portland, Maine. The house was welcoming, soothing, and beautiful, much like his mother herself, and a visit always made Aiden feel secure and comforted.

"I'm here."

"Well, open the door and let me in!" A visit with his mother, however, also meant a visit with his father. The cantankerous old Yankee had built his life from the ground up and was careful not to let anybody forget it. Aiden rolled his eyes, sighed, and opened the door.

"You're not dressed yet!"

"It'll take me two seconds," said Aiden calmly as he began to pull on his clothes. "What's the big hurry?"

"Are you all prepared for this meeting?"

"Ah, yes, I guess so."

"Now, Aiden, you've got to be prepared. I need to acquire this company to keep us on top. Trade Winds is still the biggest communications company in northern New England, and I want to keep it that way! Acquiring Chat Dot Com will give us a greater range and a jump on where the growth will take place over the next twenty years. I want Trade Winds customers to know our company offers more choices than our competitors."

"Dad, I know all this. We talked about it last night."

"You've got a three-hour drive ahead of you. Why did you stay out so late last night? Was it that Webb girl?"

"I was out with Jennifer Webb, yes."

"Well, you stayed out too late."

"Dad, I'm thirty-two."

"Is it serious between you? You've been seeing her off and on since high school."

"That's just it, Dad, off and on."

"Well, I'm not that impressed with her. Never was. She thinks she's entitled, like so many kids your age. She thinks because her father is head of the finance committee and she went to Harvard she's better than everybody. I'm not that impressed with her father, either, if you ask me."

"I didn't ask, Dad," Aiden muttered as he threaded his belt through the loops of his gray slacks. He picked up a blue and yellow striped tie and turned toward the mirror over the dresser.

"When are you going to find yourself a real woman and grow up?"

"Dad—"

But his father was not listening. The older man sputtered as he changed the subject back to business. "Now this Fenton creep is going to make a move. He's going to make a move to undercut us and try to snatch Chat Dot Com. He knows we don't have a lot of cash right now and we're expanding."

"Now, Dad, you don't know that."

"Trust me, I know the type. Fenton is smooth and cagey. Just a little older than you. Clawing his way up. And he's not a spoiled rich kid, either. That makes a difference. Aiden, you're a grown man now. It's your job to make sure Trade Winds acquires Chat before Fenton gets wind of it. If he found out we were going after it, he'd try to steamroll us right under. And believe me, that guy will stop at nothing!" Aiden glanced at his father as he straightened the knot of his tie. The old man's eyes bored into his. "Trust me," he repeated, "I know the type."

Aiden sighed. It was pointless to argue with his father. It was like trying to drown fish. Instead, he slipped on his sport coat, a dark blue linen and silk blend appropriate for the warm spring day. He said, "Hey, Dad, what do you know about this Fitzgerald guy? Is it mandatory that he come with company? What if we don't want him?"

Aiden's father shook his head vigorously. "I don't know anything about him," he said, "except that Gene Palmer, who owns Chat, won't consider a sale unless we take Fitzgerald too, and in full capacity as CEO, and for five years."

"So that means he's in control of Chat Dot Com for the next five years, even as part of Trade Winds?"

"Yes, unless we find a loophole. Now, if the guy's doing his job, then we leave him right where he is. It's your job to find out what's going on."

A female voice called up the winding staircase. "Gordon, are you up there bothering your son?"

It was Aiden's mother, Eleanor. Immediately, Aiden saw the old man soften. "We'll be right down, Nellie. Hurry up, Aiden, your mother's waiting breakfast on us."

Aiden followed his father down the stairs and into the large kitchen at the back of the house. They sat down at the big antique farm table in front of steaming mugs of coffee, and Nell Stewart set their breakfasts of sausage, scrambled eggs, and English muffins in front of them as she had been doing since Aiden could remember. Then she took her own seat opposite her son.

Nell Stewart was seventy-six years old, still lithe and active. Her few gray hairs softened the color of her thick wavy hair from its original dark brown to a lighter, tan color. She wore it caught back in an elastic at the back of her neck. Her face bore the wrinkles of her age, but it was easy to see the beauty she had been. Gordon Stewart reached over and squeezed his wife's hand. It was a gesture of affection familiar to Aiden. He watched them in silence for a minute as they all started to eat, and his mind wandered.

Aiden was the youngest child. His two older sisters were nearly grown when he was born. They had been raised during the lean times. He had heard the stories of how his father's business dealings had nearly failed several times, threatening the family with bankruptcy. His sisters had told him how they'd had to move into this beautiful, gracious home when it had been an old, decrepit, and neglected house with a leaky roof and no insulation against the Maine winters. It sat on a spit of cliff, so close to the Atlantic's waters that the salt spray coated the windows during the autumn storms. The family had lived downstairs in the house for the first ten years, heating it with wood stoves, but both Gordon and Nell knew the value of ocean view land and the potential of the house itself. They just had to stay afloat until that became a reality.

Aiden's sisters had lived through the lean times, but Aiden was the child of his parents' success. Born right after his father's first real profitable business coup, Aiden had been raised in the lap of luxury. He had foggy memories of the house being renovated and his mother's careful planning and execution of those renovations. He also remembered his father asking her repeatedly if she might want to move and build a new house. Aiden was glad his mother had wanted to stay where they were. It always impressed people, especially the women he brought home, to see the place with its magnificent views of Casco Bay. Aiden liked to bring them down the steep path that ran across the face of the cliff to the small pristine and private beach. He enjoyed watching how obviously impressed they were when he opened the boathouse door and revealed the sleek and shining Eleanor, his father's prized sailing yacht.

"What are you thinking about, Aiden?" asked his mother. "You're staring into space."

"Oh, oh, I was just looking out the window. It looks like spring is finally here. The lilacs are blooming. They weren't even budded the last time I was here."

"Yes! And about time. It's been a long winter. I'll open the windows today and let the smell of lilacs fill the house. Are you coming back tonight, Aiden, or going back to Boston?"

"I think I'll just go back to Boston. I have a date."

Gordon snorted. "You had a date last night."

Aiden laughed. "Well, I have another date tonight."

"You should date less and tend to business more."

Aiden cut the conversation short. "I better get going," he said, rising from his chair. His parents stood and, hand in hand, followed him to the door. Aiden kissed his mother on the cheek. "Love you, Mom," he said.

Gordon caught him in a great bear hug. "Do your best, Aiden! Get this thing in the bag!"

An hour later, Aiden found himself driving through New Hampshire on the old Route 4, headed for central Vermont. His mind wandered. He thought about his date the previous night with

Jennifer Webb. They had gone to Grace, one of Portland's finest restaurants in a city of fine restaurants. He didn't know why he couldn't work up any enthusiasm for Jennifer. He genuinely liked her. They had known each other a long time and had dated on and off, sometimes seriously, sometimes not, throughout the last five years. Jennifer was a tall, attractive girl, Harvard educated in economics, a broker for the upper echelon clientele at Greater Bank of Maine in Portland. Her family, although not close friends with his, was a familiar entity. She had an abundance of energy, and they shared similar interests in sailing, skiing, and hiking, but the relationship would not progress beyond a certain point. Last night they'd had sex, which Aiden could only remember as being rather clinical, on the sofa of her condo. She had not invited him to stay the night, and he had been relieved because he had not wanted to stay.

Then there was Alexis, the cool blonde with whom he would sleep tonight. They had only been on two dates, but Aiden knew she was ready. She had a body most men would salivate over, and he tried to entertain himself thinking about the physical pleasures he was looking forward to. He had even called his cleaning lady to ask her to be sure to put fresh flowers on the dining room table and in the bedroom and to make the bed up crisp and fresh. He was that sure of himself.

Aiden's thoughts drifted to his parents. Perhaps they were part of the reason he went from woman to woman, or juggled two or three at once. Where, he thought somewhat sardonically, would he ever find a woman who made him feel the way his mother obviously made his father feel? Where could he possibly find a woman who loved him as completely as his mother loved his father? It was hard, especially these days, to live up to such an example. Every time Aiden thought of marriage, he thought of his parents. That was what marriage was. It was love, respect, sticking together through all the ups and downs of everyday life. It was someone who squeezed your hand at breakfast. It was being kissed on the top of head as you sat brooding over your books.

Aiden stared at the ribbon of road stretching out ahead of him. He heaved a deep sigh and dismissed his idea of marriage like the one shared by his parents as unattainable.

Aiden pulled into Clark's Corner, Vermont, exactly three and a half hours after leaving Portland. The BMW's GPS system instructed him to turn left and follow the road along the river for 2.4 miles. He slowed to the posted speed limit of forty miles an hour.

"Destination on right in point-zero-one miles," said the metallic voice of the GPS.

Aiden saw the sign on the front of an old brick factory building along the edge of a canal that came off the river. CHAT.COM *Communications For Today and Tomorrow.* He turned as instructed and crossed a narrow bridge to a newly paved parking lot. He pulled into the spot marked "Visitors" and shut the engine off, opened the door, stepped out into the sunny spring day, and stretched. It was ten-thirty in the morning.

Aiden looked up at the building. It had obviously been an old paper mill or perhaps a tool company, built along the rushing river during the hay days of the New England industrial boom. The building had been skillfully renovated, and the artistic details imparted by bricklayers of long ago were again visible. It was quite a grand building. Whoever had overseen the renovations had done so with an eye to not spoiling its original character, and the many windows winked once again in the morning sun. Aiden had always liked old things, and he felt oddly comfortable as he walked through the door into the spacious lobby.

There was a circular, marble-topped desk in the lobby behind which sat a pretty young receptionist.

"Can I help you?" she asked politely.

"I'm Aiden Stewart," he replied. "I'm here for a meeting with M. Jordan Fitzgerald."

"Oh. Oh my," said the receptionist, slightly flustered. "You're from Trade Winds. The company that wants to buy us. I'm sorry I didn't recognize you, Mr. Stewart. I'll announce you right away. Just wait here. Can I get you coffee or anything?"

The girl's agitated manner amused him. *My reputation must have preceded me*, he thought.

"It's okay," he said. "Take your time. I'll wait. And I prefer to call it a merger, rather than 'buy.'"

The girl hurried away, through two big glass doors behind her desk, muttering, "Merger, yes, merger. That's the word."

Aiden put his hands in his pockets and looked around. He wondered if CEO M. Jordan Fitzgerald was as excitable as his receptionist. He gazed around. How odd it was that one of the most successful small Internet providers should be cloistered away in the backwoods of Vermont. *Well, the Internet could flourish anywhere,* he thought, *and that's why we want to own them. We have to own them.* As much as he tried to dismiss his father's irritating lecture before he left Portland this morning, Aiden could not. He knew in his heart that even at his advanced age, his father was still a consummate businessman. Aiden squared his shoulders as the receptionist came back through the big glass doors.

"Follow me," she said tersely.

Aiden walked after her down a wide hallway. On either side of him were glass walls through which he could see people working in their cubicles or gathered together around conference tables. At the end of the hallway was a solid wooden door with gold lettering that said M. JORDAN FITZGERALD on it. The receptionist opened the door, slipped through, and shut it again, leaving Aiden standing in the hall. Soon she reappeared, slipping back through in the same manner, closing the door behind her again.

"You may go in now," she said formally, stepping aside to allow him access to the door. "You're actually early. Your appointment is for eleven."

Altogether weird, thought Aiden as he reached for the handle of the door. *I wonder what Fitzgerald is like.*

He pushed the handle down, opened the door, and stepped into the room. Aiden felt the shock hit him. A young woman, in her late twenties or early thirties, stood behind a large desk. Her feminine, floral spring dress might have been too casual for office wear, except for the blue linen blazer she wore over it.

"He" was a "she." Fitzgerald was a woman. And a beautiful one at that. Aiden grappled visibly with his surprise. He had assumed something entirely different.

ABOUT THE AUTHOR

photo by James Peterson

Linda Cunningham grew up a small town country girl, and it is here where she's still most comfortable. She has written steadily throughout the years, although usually other people's speeches, articles, and grants, primarily for medical and agricultural trade journals. Now that her three children are grown, Linda is writing full time and writing the stuff she loves—Romance!

Linda lives in a romantic stone house in the Green Mountain State of Vermont, surrounded by her gardens and animals which include horses, dogs, cats, chickens, sheep, a parakeet, goldfish and the wild visitors who tiptoe through on a regular basis. When time permits, she also enjoys cooking, sketching, and painting.

Young Adult

Shades of Atlantis and *Ember* by Carol Oates
Breaking Point by Jess Bowen
Life, Liberty, and Pursuit by Susan Kaye Quinn

Anthologies

A Valentine Anthology including short stories by Alice Clayton, Jennifer DeLucy, Nicki Elson, Jessica McQuinn, Victoria Michaels, and Alison Oburia

Summer Lovin' Anthology: Summer Breeze including short stories by Hannah Downing, Nicki Elson, Sarah M. Glover, Jennifer Lane, Killian McRae, Carol Oates, and Susan Kaye Quinn

Summer Lovin' Anthology: Heat Wave including short stories by Kasi Alexander, Debra Anastasia, Robin DeJarnett, Jessica McQuinn, Lisa Sanchez, and BJ Thornton

Alternative Romance

Becoming sage by Kasi Alexander

coming soon from
OMNIFIC PUBLISHING

Grave Refrain by Sarah M. Glover
Poughkeepsie by Debra Anastasia
Destiny's Fire by Trisha Wolfe
Embrace by Cherie Colyer

And more from Sylvain Reynard, Jennifer DeLucy, Alice Clayton, and Hannah Fielding

Nancy

CPSIA information can be obtained at www.ICGtesting.com
Printed in the USA
BVOW031132011111

275031BV00001B/2/P